# Heart of Deceit

# Heart of Deceit

*Book 4 of The Ripple Affair Series*

Erin Cruey

To God, who is faithful and true.

To Stefanee, Karen, Kim, Rachel, and Megan – you are not only my friends, but my sisters. I am so thankful for your encouragement and support!

A Cast of Main Characters

# From the Kingdom of Audlin...

**Maria Engel, the Queen Mother:**
Mother to Edward and the former queen of Audlin, Maria advises her son in putting the country first to keep the peace both at home and abroad.

**Edward Engel, the Leader:**
The king of Audlin, Edward struggles to balance his duties and family life, hoping to save his cousin and former fiancée from a treacherous prince and maddened queen.

**Calimus Engel, the Heir:**
The infant son of King Edward and Queen Malina, Calimus is the heir to the throne of Audlin and his father's greatest treasure.

**Malina Engel, the Queen:**
The queen of Audlin, Malina continues to plot her husband's demise under the watchful eye of the Velori, Malum, while trying to keep her lover, Vacius, from messing up their plans.

**Marcus Peterson, the Guard:**
The leader of the royal guard and best friend of the king, Marcus is entrusted with the most important duty of protecting the king and his family.

**Samuel Rikert, the Advisor:**
The head advisor to King Edward, Sir Rikert is known for his wisdom and experience in the royal guard, willing to serve his country in any way necessary.

**Jacob Ichabod, the Knight:**
A member of the royal guard feeling betrayed by the king, Sir Ichabod now serves Queen Malina as the personal bodyguard to her son, Prince Calimus.

# From the Kingdom of Edeland...

## Susanna van Echt, the Mother:
The queen of Edeland, Susanna continues in her disdain for Emmerich van Ketten, despite his loyalty to her daughter.

## Antoinette van Echt, the Wife:
The eldest daughter of Queen Susanna and King John, Antoinette seeks to balance a fake marriage to Prince Arnold while being secretly married to her childhood best friend, Emmerich.

## Bernette van Echt, the Princess:
The younger sister of Antoinette, Bernie is fun, playful, and hiding an insecurity about her appearance.

# From the Kingdom of Hugellia...

## Aldaric van Ketten, the Ambassador:
The father of Emmerich and husband to Anna, Aldaric is the head ambassador to Hugellia, caught in a war between family and foreign affairs.

## Emmerich van Ketten, the Husband:
Married in secret to his childhood best friend, Antoinette, Emmerich is banished from his homeland, desperate to find a safe place for him and his wife to be together.

## Erick van Ketten, the King:
The aging king of Hugellia, Erick refuses to listen to his stepson, Aldaric, in allowing Emmerich back into the country.

# From the Kingdom of Liegen...

## Arnold von Liegen, the Charmer:
Going along with a fake public marriage to Princess Antoinette, Arnold toys with the secret he keeps, putting Antoinette and Emmerich on edge.

# From the Kingdom of Verloris...

**Vacius, the Assassin**:
A member of the Velori and lover to Queen Malina, Vacius grows tired of being in the shadows while Edward stays on the throne of Audlin.

**Malum, the Planner:**
The mysterious head of the Velori, Malum carefully plans the downfall of the nations around him, preparing to step in if those under him do not obey orders.

# From the Lands of the Recu...

**Bohden, the Chief**:
The young and mysterious chieftain of the Recu, Bohden's visions and dreams guide him in the days ahead, causing him to seek out Aldaric and Emmerich.

# Chapter Index

Chapter 1: The Challenge          17

Chapter 2: Left Behind          38

Chapter 3: The Wrong Road          46

Chapter 4: The First Test          58

Chapter 5: The Truth About Love          67

Chapter 6: Love or Loss          72

Chapter 7: A New Problem          85

Chapter 8: Of Bears and Bernie          92

Chapter 9: Lost          104

Chapter 10: The Jealous Lover          114

Chapter 11: Wandering          124

Chapter 12: By the River          136

Chapter 13: Return to Staalberg          146

Chapter 14: A Night Under the Stars          161

Chapter 15: The Princess and the Guard          177

Chapter 16: A Dire Message          194

Chapter 17: A Growing Sprout          202

Chapter 18: Uncaged          210

Chapter 19: The Assassin Strikes          217

Chapter 20: Entering the Game          226

Chapter 21: A Common Life          237

Chapter 22: Aftermath          255

Chapter 23: The Ambassador          265

Chapter 24: The Repentant Heart          280

Chapter 25: The Search          285

Chapter 26: The Queen's Saudade          296

Chapter 27: The First Move          305

Chapter 28: Archery and Frost       313

Chapter 29: Lost and Found       329

Chapter 30: The Husband       341

Chapter 31: Vengeance       352

# Heart of Deceit

*"In love, there is trust."*

.

*The story continues...*

# Chapter 1: The Challenge

Bernie was never one to quit while she was ahead.

The memories of dinner earlier replayed in her mind, enough to inspire an encore of such a wonderful show. She snuck into the gardens, gathering more bugs (or performers, as she liked to call them), and took them back into the kitchen to their stages atop the morning pastries that had been set out to cool after a late baking.

She was careful to be quiet while everyone slept, and she giggled to herself as the last centipede was lowered onto the food, completing the mission for the night.

"There," she said with a rub of her hands. "Now remember to be on your best behavior and dig in real deep through the crust. You don't want to be caught before being served!"

She was about to do one last check until a voice from behind made her freeze. "Served to whom, exactly?"

The sound made her cringe, for she knew who it was that stood waiting for her, though how he was able to see so clearly in nothing but moonlight and lantern flame was beyond her. Mr. Grumpy Guard, also known as Sir Marcus Peterson, waited patiently for an answer and said nothing as she turned to face him.

She had to play it cool before saying a word. He was by no means dull-witted or slow – no, his paranoia proved his intelligence – so getting away would be a challenge. Luckily for her, she enjoyed stretching her abilities, and the knight would be perfect practice for just how creative she could be in getting out of a bind.

"Serving me, of course," she replied cheerily, meeting his sour look with a grin. "Sorry. Since dinner was a little too lively, I got hungry and wanted to get a snack. Can't blame a girl for getting food."

He lit another lantern so they'd have more light. "Why didn't you ask one of the servants for assistance?"

"Didn't want to bother them. It's pretty late."

"It would be no inconvenience. Many remain on duty through the night."

"Yeah, but just because you don't sleep doesn't mean other people stay awake."

He frowned further. "Then you should've asked one of the guards stationed in the halls. They remain awake every night and rest during the day."

"Alright; you got me." She lifted her hands in surrender, seeing as the man clearly had an excuse for the palace staff. Audlin he could account for, but there was one thing he missed. "I didn't want my mother to know I was snacking. She's so picky about what I eat, and I didn't want her to find out I was sneaking a pastry."

His look softened until he noticed her hand trying to slip behind her back. "So the jar is for holding your snack, I take it?"

Her eyes widened for a second before she calmed herself. Bless it, if the man wasn't so observant, she'd have been out of the room in no time! She fumbled the jar forward, shrugging as if it was commonplace to bring a jar when getting a pastry. "Yeah, uh…it's an Edelandian thing. We mush them in the jars and eat it with a spoon." Far from the truth, but she hoped his lack of experience with foreigners kept him ignorant.

"And the grasshopper in it is supposed to add flavor?"

She looked at the jar, acting quickly to hide her frustration. Apparently she forgot one. She made a grimace as she held the jar forward, ushering it towards the knight. If her words couldn't fool him, maybe her actions could. "Ew! Take it away! I don't like bugs!" She forced the jar into his hands, jumping and shaking her arms in feigned fright.

"So you didn't notice the giant grasshopper in the jar when you picked it up?" he asked.

"It's nighttime. I didn't see it."

"But you have a lantern."

"I was looking for the pastries with it."

"Well, then," Marcus replied, finally showing a grin. "Normally protocol requires me to fetch a servant for you so that the bakers know their pastries were taken with permission, but seeing as you and I are both already here, I can take their place. Here." He picked up a pastry from beside her and held it in front for her to take. She gave a gulp, remembering it to be the same pastry not one, but *two* earthworms squiggled into. "One pastry snack for a hungry princess."

He put the pastry on her palm, and she looked up, faking a smile. "Thanks. I'll…uh…just take this up to my room now. Best to not disturb anyone else."

"Oh, no," Marcus said. "At least try it here. If you don't like it, you'll be close enough to the other pastries to see if you like them."

"Well...this is a plain jelly pastry," Bernie said. "I prefer mine with fruit. I think the ones over here have some berries..."

"I'm sorry, Princess. Those are reserved for the king and queen. As much as I'd like to share those with you, I'm afraid I can't." He smiled further, leaning forward with crossed arms. "At least *try* the jelly one. You never know - you may find it's quite appetizing. The baker is known for putting in the best secret ingredients."

His look never left hers, as if he were challenging her to try him. Of course, that made her want to accept the challenge all the more, and she met his gaze with her own defiance. She took the pastry firmly in her hand and planted it to her lips. Mr. Grumpy Guard could never make her admit to defeat!

"You know what? I think you're right. Might as well try it. After all, I sure am hungry!" Then she took half of the pastry, stuffing it into her mouth, making the knight's face grimace in shock.

She stood there proudly at first, but after feeling a squirm of one of the worms near her tongue, she suddenly realized eating bugs wasn't as pleasant as she thought it would be.

She held it together, refusing to give the man the satisfaction of proving her guilty in ruining dinner. She swallowed the worm whole, along with the pastry bits, holding the other half of the food proudly in her hand. "That was tasty! Want a bite?"

He shook his head, still looking at her in shock. "There's a worm coming out of that pastry..."

She looked down at it, seeing worm number two peeking its head (or tail? She really couldn't tell which end was which) out of the jelly, and that was all it took to put her in a panic.

She just ate a worm. A living, squirming, dirt-loving worm, all just to prove a man wrong.

It didn't take long for the gagging to start, and she rushed forward to the nearest bowl, vomiting what she ate only seconds before into the bin. Marcus rushed forward, now panicked, and as Bernie looked into what she threw up, seeing the worm she ate alive and squiggling still, she suddenly felt a new sickness come upon her, and whatever she ate for dinner suddenly came up, too.

Victory never felt so terrible.

---

Marcus didn't know how long they had been in the kitchen, but it felt like hours.

Princess Bernette had been throwing up ever since she ate the worm-infested pastry, and he had never left her side, partially out of guilt for goading her into eating it and partially because he feared trouble was ahead for making a guest of the king sick.

Of course, he never planned on her illness. He was actually heading home after too long of a night and only stopped near the kitchen because he heard noises coming from the dark. When he heard the princess' voice, he knew he had to intervene, either in preventing another bug attack or seeing why a princess was wandering about the palace unescorted.

What was supposed to happen was quite the opposite of reality. He was supposed to catch her in the act of planting insects in the food, getting her to admit the crime and telling her parents of what she had done. When getting her to confess was proving difficult, he thought for sure challenging her to eat the pastry would put enough fear in her to admit pulling the prank, but he never expected her to stuff the thing into her mouth and eat it!

Now he was being punished for being so foolish, having to care for a princess he *clearly* did not like and who *clearly* did not like him. He tried to put his arm on her shoulder, holding her hair back so she wouldn't get vomit on it, but she smacked his hand away, clutching the bin and giving him a dirty look.

"I'm fine," she muttered, swallowing hard to stifle another gag. "I don't...need your help..."

"I apologize, Your Majesty. I just wanted to make sure you're alright." He paused, seeing her sorry state and feeling guiltier. "I didn't think you'd eat the pastry..."

"So why did you offer it to me?"

"You said you were hungry." He wasn't foolish enough to admit he was trying to get a confession about the insects. If she wouldn't admit to it then, she certainly wouldn't admit to it now. The girl was more stubborn than a tired mule.

"So you gave me a pastry with worms in it?"

"Pastries typically don't have worms in them, Your Majesty. Eating them like that risks illness! How they got in there is anyone's guess. I'm sure you know just as much as me as to how this is."

"I know nothing."

He muttered his disapproval quietly so she wouldn't hear. "At least let me call for your mother. I'm sure she'd want to know if you are ill."

She gave him a look that made him shudder, and she held the bowl in her hands, putting it in front of him. "I have puke and I know how to use it, buddy. You get my mother and I'm sure you can guess what happens next."

"Your Majesty, be reasonable." He gently pushed the bowl away from his nose and softened his response. "At least allow me to call for a physician."

"All I did was barf up a worm. Not like it's anything major," she said, setting the bowl down beside her. "I'm feeling better, anyways. I don't need a doctor."

He shook his head. Even if she did, she'd probably never go to one. "Then what can I do?"

"Enter a truce."

"A truce?"

"Yeah." She turned to him, wiping her mouth with her sleeve to make sure she looked clean. "You keep quiet about me being here getting my late-night snack, and I'll keep quiet about you feeding me a rotten pastry."

"But..."

"Truce or not? If you squeal on me, I'll squeal on you."

"But I was doing my duty."

"Feeding a princess bugs?"

He scoffed. "Trying to figure out who put the bugs here in the first place. We've never had a problem until this evening."

She lowered her brow, looking insulted. Surely she was only pretending, though her acting was near perfect. "Are you accusing me of putting bugs in the food?"

"I'm not accusing you of anything," Marcus replied. "I'm just trying to figure out where they're coming from."

"Well, they're not from me."

"I never said they were."

She was about to offer another retort, but after a quick gag, she decided to stay quiet. Marcus frowned, scooting closer after seeing her sickness try to return, and sighed. "Your Majesty, let me escort you out of the kitchen and to the parlor where you can lie down and rest."

At first she looked as if wanting to refuse his request, but after a moment of thinking, she agreed. "Fine," she mumbled, taking his hand as he helped her to her feet. He put his right hand on her back and held her left hand with his own, helping her out of the kitchen and towards the parlor next door. She walked slowly, moaning if they went too fast, and Marcus held her carefully as they went into the room, setting her on the couch and kneeling at her side.

"What can I do for you?" The least he could be was a gentleman. He never made a girl sick before, and he felt bad enough doing it once, even if it was to his worst enemy.

"I'd be so appreciative for a cold, wet rag to put on my forehead." She gave a pout as she put her hand to her stomach.

How could he say no? "I'll get it for you. I'll also send for a physician."

Bernette widened her eyes, sitting up. "No, you don't have to do that."

"I insist, Princess. It's the least I can do. I want to make sure you are well."

"But..."

"No. Now stay here. I'll be outside the door getting a guard and will be back soon."

"But you don't have to get someone..."

"Don't worry, Your Majesty. I'll take care of you." And with that, he hurried outside the door, waving down one of the guards.

The young man scuttled forward, giving a salute as he approached Marcus. "Yes, Sir Peterson?"

"I need you to fetch a physician. Princess Bernette is ill."

"How ill?"

"Nothing serious, but I'd like to be sure just the same."

"Yes, sir."

Off the guard went to find a physician, and Marcus turned to go back into the room. He promised her he wouldn't be gone long, and not a minute had passed before he would be back in her presence.

But when he entered the parlor again, he found the princess gone, the window wide open.

He wasn't one to curse, but he let one slip as he rushed towards the window to find her.

---

Bernie hated to climb, but desperate times were calling.

She thought pretending to be ill longer than what she really was would get the knight off her back and make him leave her alone, but unlike all the other men she had dealt with, that one was proving stubborn. Instead of pawning her off on someone else or leaving her to fend for herself, the man wouldn't leave her side! She didn't know whether to be flattered by his insistence or annoyed by it, but the end results stayed the same. If he called the physician, Mother would be notified, and she wasn't about to be scolded for sneaking off to the kitchen in the middle of the night.

So that left only one option: while the knight went to fetch the doctor, she would have to make a run for it.

Of course, the only way out was the window, and without a rope to hang on to, she had to make do with the small patches of brick that were sticking out for her to grab. Never mind that it was dark out and a cloud just so happened to cover up the moon when she needed it most. Also never mind the fact that heights scared her and made her *really* want to be sick again. But she wasn't about to be defeated. Oh no, she had a perfect record of being the smart one, and she wasn't going to give that grumpy, stick-in-the-mud knight the satisfaction of getting her in trouble!

But after putting her foot out to step on a piece of brick and finding nothing but air, she realized trouble had found her anyways!

She looked down, feeling her heart start to beat fast as she noticed the nearest brick was too far for her to reach. Unable to climb further down, she looked around to see what her options were, and found that only two were doable. She could climb back up, face Marcus and (eventually) her mother, or jump down the seven feet towards the grassy plain underneath and hope she didn't break anything. She took a deep breath, swallowing hard as the cold night air hitting her face gave her a chill, and made a decision.  She hoped and prayed that grass was soft as a pillow…

As she was about to let go, however, she heard a shout from above.

"Your Majesty, *what are you doing?*"

She glanced up to see Sir Peterson standing above her, looking frantic now as he probably never saw a princess trying to climb out a window before, and she shrugged, knowing she was caught.

"Oh, you know…I thought the fresh air would do me good."

"But you're hanging out the window…"

"I was being sarcastic," she muttered, shaking her head. "Dumb-dumb."

He leaned forward, reaching out his hand.  "I'll pull you up."

Oh no he wouldn't.  He wasn't about to get her in trouble for climbing out a window, too.  "Thanks for the offer, but I'll take my chances here."

He blinked in surprise.  "Are you serious?"

"When it comes to facing my mother, I am."

"Your Majesty, you could get hurt."

"The ground would be nicer to me than Mother."

"It's too far a jump!  Here."  He leaned forward further, offering his hand.  "Try to climb back up and take my hand.  I'll pull you up."

"I don't need any help."  She wasn't about to admit that even if she did climb up, he wouldn't be able to lift her.  Mother reminded her daily on how big she was, and though the knight had his share of muscles, even he wasn't strong enough to pull her up. She'd rather break her bum on cold, hard ground than break his back.

"Your Majesty, this is ridiculous. I'm trying to help you! Why won't you let me?"

"Because I don't need it."

"You're hanging out a window. Is it really worth risking your life just to keep your pride?"

She gave him a nasty glare. "I'm not prideful!"

"Then why won't you let me help you up?"

She looked away, embarrassment flushing her face. She refused to admit it was her weight that worried her. She wouldn't give him an excuse to tease her like he clearly did behind her back.

Regardless, her silence didn't stop him from trying. He leaned even further, reaching out, almost able to touch her fingers. "Take my hand, Your Majesty. Please."

She shook her head. She wouldn't be embarrassed like that.

"I can lift you up if you'll let me!"

"I don't think you can..." she muttered under her breath.

"Your Majesty, if I can pull out a horse that's stuck in the mud, I can pull you up! Now take my hand!"

She grumbled at his persistence, knowing he would never give up until she made his choice for him. She wasn't about to face the humiliation, so she did the only thing she could think of.

She let go, falling down and landing painfully on the ground.

The knight gave a gasp as he reached out to grab her before falling forward himself, and pretty soon Bernie and the knight were both groaning side by side on the grass, their arms and legs so sore they could barely move.

"Why...did you jump?" Marcus asked, rubbing his lower back as he sat up.

"Didn't want you to break your spine," Bernie answered as she caught her breath. "Although by the looks of it, I think you already did..."

"So breaking your leg was a better option?"

"I didn't break my leg," she sneered as she wobbled, trying to stand to her feet. After a sharp pain came from her ankle, however, she realized walking was now out of the question, and she immediately cringed, falling back to the ground. "I think I broke something, though."

Marcus crawled over to her, putting his hand towards the injured foot. "Let me look at it."

She kicked his hand away with her free foot. "Not a chance, buddy! You've caused enough trouble for me tonight!"

"Me? What did I do?"

"You gave me a rotten pastry!"

"Have you forgotten what you've done to me tonight?" he asked, finally sounding perturbed. "You've vomited in the royal kitchen, ran away, and then jumped out a window! Even my dog doesn't give me this much trouble!"

"Well if you'd just leave me alone like everyone else, we wouldn't have this problem!"

"Why would I leave you alone if you were ill or about to get hurt? Do you really think I'm such a monster that I'd just let you suffer?"

"Well everyone else would!"

"But I'm not everyone else," he answered, his voice a little harsh. "I know you're not fond of me, Your Majesty, but at least allow me to care for you. Now I'd like to make sure your ankle isn't broken. Will you let me check it?"

She looked at him, curious as to why he was so insistent on making sure she was alright. What sort of madness was it that out of all the men she ever knew and met, the one she found the most annoying was the one who insisted on sticking around and taking care of her? It was insufferable, God bless it!

"Fine," she said, looking away and sticking her foot out. She refused to watch him as he worked, crossing her arms in a huff and wanting to pout like she used to as a child when being denied her way. But after feeling gentle hands barely touch her foot, caressing her ankle so lightly that any pain she felt was minimal, she looked back at him in curiosity. Was he actually being careful in how he handled her injury?

"Does this hurt?" he asked, pressing against her ankle.

"A bit."

"How about here?"

"Not as much."

He paused, looking at it some more. "I don't think it's broken...maybe just a sprain...but we should have the physician look at it just in case."

"But..."

"If you don't wish your mother to find out, we don't have to tell her. I can get your sister instead."

Bernie pursed her lips, thinking back to what Antoinette was probably doing at the moment. Assuming all went well with Emmerich, then she'd probably be busy...

"I'm sure she doesn't want to be disturbed," Bernie replied.

"I'll send a messenger, anyways."

"Why can't you tell her yourself?"

"And leave you alone to run away again? Not a chance. I'd rather not chase you across the roof." He gave her a playful smirk, and she couldn't help but roll her eyes. "Now here. I'll help you stand." He got up, wincing in pain but trying his best to hide it, and helped her to her feet.

She fell back down as soon as she stood. "I'm sorry. Let me try again..."

"I can carry you." He moved to lift her, and she gave a protest.

"But I'm too heavy..."

"You're not heavy," he replied as he put his arm around her. "But if you'd rather me help you walk than carry you, I can do that."

She tried standing once more, the pain shooting up both legs as her other ankle gave way. "I...confound it, I can't...I..."

"I'll carry you, then."

"But..."

Before she could object, she felt him lift her off her feet, and to her surprise, his back remained intact. Her eyes widened in disbelief at seeing him carry her, though she could tell it was a struggle for the poor man as he was clearly still in pain from his fall.

"I'm sorry..." she said. "I know I'm too heavy and..."

"You're no bigger than Queen Maria, Your Majesty. If I'm expected to carry her when she needs rescuing, then I should be able to carry you."

She pressed her lips together, nodding, rather enjoying the fact that he wasn't screaming and being crushed by her weight. Mother always said that would happen if a man ever had to carry her. At least now she could prove that thought wrong.

"Thank you," she said quietly.

"Of course," he replied, carrying her into the palace through the back door.

---

Princess Bernette had calmed once she had been seen by the physician. Just like Marcus observed, the ankle was only sprained, though it had come close to being broken if she had fallen a different way. As the physician was finishing wrapping her ankle, Marcus stood at the doorway, waiting for the messenger he'd sent to come back. It wasn't long until the man returned.

"Did you tell Princess Antoinette of her sister?" Marcus asked.

"She was busy speaking with her mother. Apparently the family was discussing something important. Everyone was up."

Marcus lowered his brow. "Why were they all awake at this hour?"

"I don't know," the servant replied. "Though I think it had something to do with a disagreement with King Edward."

Marcus sighed, rubbing his tired eyes. Though he was supposed to be off-duty at the moment, he was sure he'd have a story to hear once Antoinette arrived to take over in caring for her sister. "I see I'll have to speak with the king, then. Was it anything serious?"

"Not to my knowledge. Prince Arnold said everything was fine and under control."

"Prince Arnold?"

"Yes, the husband to Princess Antoinette. He was the only one who would speak to me. I told him to tell his wife of Princess Bernette's injury."

"What else did he say?"

"That he would send his wife to her when able."

"And when would that be?"

"Soon, I suppose. Though Prince Arnold looked rather ill himself. I think the dinner caused everyone to become sick."

Marcus sighed, nodding in thanks to the servant and sending him back to his duties.

That had been an hour ago, and now, as both Marcus and Bernie rested quietly in the parlor waiting for Antoinette, the knight began to wonder if something worse was going on. It wasn't like Antoinette to not rush to her sister's side, especially at word of an injury, and he began to wonder what was really happening.

"Ugh! Can I go back to my room now? I'm tired and want to go to sleep."

Bernette's complaints were well-warranted, as the couch was very uncomfortable, but he didn't want to leave her alone lest she tried to escape and nearly hurt herself again. "I sent a message to your sister. She should have been here by now."

"Then go and get her."

"With all due respect, Your Majesty, I'm afraid of leaving you alone." He paused as she gave him a frown. "Past experience and all."

"If you sent a message to Antoinette, shouldn't she have gotten it by now?"

"I thought she would have."

"It's just not like her to be late. Something's wrong." The princess sat up and tried to stand on her own feet, clutching the edge of the couch. Marcus rushed to her side, urging her back down.

"No, Your Majesty. The physician said to stay off your feet."

"But I want to make sure my sister is alright."

"I can send another messenger," Marcus replied. "Prince Arnold may have forgotten to give her the message."

"Wait..." Bernette's eyes widened and she grabbed his arm. "Arnold got the message?"

"According to the man I sent."

"No wonder she's not here, then! That monkey wouldn't tell her even if the world was ending!" Bernie stood up, hopping on her free foot that pained her as well, holding on to whatever she could grab. "I'm going. That stupid piece of smelly garbage Arnold is such a jerk!"

"At least let me help you." Marcus scrambled to her side, putting her arm around his shoulders, nearly carrying her as she hopped out of the parlor.

They made their way out of the room and into the hallway, and they were both surprised to see the palace so alive at such a late hour.

"You people don't sleep here at all, do you?" she asked as they looked around.

Marcus lowered his brow. "We usually don't have this many out right now."

"What does that mean?"

"I'm not sure."

They hurried forward towards a servant who was just coming down the stairs from the guest rooms, carrying a pile of linens in her arms. "Noble maid," Marcus called out, making the girl turn and face them.

She approached, giving a quick curtsey as she faced Marcus, but as soon as she saw the princess, her mouth fell agape and she dropped the linens to the floor.

"Oh my!" she gasped, covering her mouth with her hands. "The...the princess! She's here?"

"Of course," Bernette replied. "Where else would I be?"

"With your family, Your Majesty! They left just minutes ago!"

Bernette's face paled. "Wait – *WHAT?*"

"What do you mean they left?" Marcus asked, trying to keep the ladies calm.

"After the fight between King Edward and Prince Arnold..."

"THERE WAS A FIGHT AND I MISSED IT?" Bernette groaned as she stomped her free foot in anger, mumbling a curse.

But Marcus didn't have time to be interrupted by the princess' hysterics. "What do you mean there was a fight? Is the king alright?"

"The king is well, sir. Prince Arnold was beaten pretty badly, though."

Bernette's face changed to joy as she nodded in approval. "Well at least something good happened tonight. Please tell me Eddie smashed his face in."

"Where are they now?" Marcus hated to interrupt, but he didn't have time to gossip.

"They returned to Edeland. Queen Susanna would not wait 'til the morning as she was greatly insulted."

"But they wouldn't leave without me," Bernette replied. "I mean, I know I can be annoying, but it's not that bad..."

"I'm sorry, Princess," the servant replied. "Your mother, father, and brothers left first. They and I were told by Prince Arnold that you would be in the second carriage with your sister."

"Wait a moment..." Marcus turned to find another servant rushing from down the hall, a look of confusion on his face at seeing the princess, too. "I just came back from the stables. When I inquired about Princess Bernette, Prince Arnold told me that she had went in the carriage with her mother!"

Marcus looked to Bernette, only to be met with a glare. "And *you* told him that I was in the parlor with an injured ankle! That snobby-nosed, stuck-up pig snout lied to everyone to leave me here!" She paused, her voice seething. "Oh, this is war. I am so getting revenge on him…"

Marcus felt like panicking, but he kept his cool as he turned back to the first servant. "Get the king. Tell him about the situation. And you…" He turned to the second servant. "Gather a horse and ride after them! If you hurry, you should at least be able to catch up to Princess Antoinette's carriage to have them turn around. Now go!"

The man nodded, rushing back towards the stables as the first servant fetched the king.

# Chapter 2: Left Behind

Edward had never run so fast in his life.

Emmerich couldn't have gone far in his following of Antoinette and Arnold. Traveling through darkness was always a slow business, and with a lack of rest during the night, the king's former guests would have to stop soon for a break to relieve themselves and stretch their legs. Earlier departures meant earlier stops, so if he mustered the knights quickly, Emmerich could be back by sunrise.

As he hurried through the palace, however, he was suddenly stopped by his mother.

"Edward! Whatever is the matter? You look frantic!"

She had just ordered the servants to begin cleaning out the guest rooms since everyone was already up after the great fight. Edward stopped, knowing she would want to know of her missing nephew, and approached.

"Emmerich is gone."

"Gone?" she asked with raised brow. "Whatever do you mean?"

"He's left to follow Antoinette. To get her back, to save her, to make sure she's alright...I don't know. All I know is he is gone, as is his horse!"

Maria put her hands on his arms in an attempt at comfort. It barely worked. "Son, calm yourself. This isn't the first runaway guest we've dealt with. Need I remind you of that one nobleman from the Bear Lands with the thieving problem?"

"I know, but..."

"And besides," Maria reminded, "if he has left on his own accord, we cannot stop him."

"But Susanna may find out and..."

"Edward, what did I tell you earlier?" Her look was so similar to when he was a child, being scolded for disobeying. "Let it go. He is not your responsibility, either. Unless he has been taken against his will, there is nothing you can - or *should* - do. If he asks for help, provide it, but if he remains silent, keep your distance."

"But Aldaric and Anna are coming here soon."

"Then we will tell them of the situation and they can decide what to do with their son."

Edward sighed, knowing he would get nowhere with his mother. Distance was something he used to be so good at, but after seeing it only hurt the people he wanted to protect, he realized closeness...loyalty...would be a better approach. Had he stayed closer to Antoinette, she might not have been given to Arnold. Had he stayed closer to Emmerich, his cousin may not have been hurt.

He nodded, feigning agreement with his mother as he backed away. She wouldn't understand his need to make things right. After all, what wrong had she done?

He was about to sneak off to the stable and get on his own horse to catch his cousin, but a quick interruption from a servant changed his plans.

"Your Majesty, we have a problem."

Edward turned to the servant, perturbed. What else could go wrong that hadn't already? "What is it?"

"It's Princess Bernette," the servant replied. "She's still here."

Edward's face showed the surprise, and joy, growing in his heart. If Bernie was still there, that gave him an excuse to go after Antoinette and Emmerich. Finally, a problem he was allowed to fix! "Where is she?"

"With Sir Peterson, Your Majesty. Apparently the princess was accidentally left behind."

Edward knew better. Antoinette would never allow such an event, but Arnold was an exception. He saw the way Arnold glared at Bernie during dinner, muttering under his breath about how he wanted nothing more than to send the girl away to "learn her place".

"Take me to her."

The servant nodded, leading Edward down the hall to where the knight and the princess were at.

He was led to a parlor; as he entered, he saw Marcus standing beside Bernie as she sat on the couch, her wrapped foot resting atop a stool. Edward cocked his brow at the sight, turning to his friend. "What happened?"

"She jumped out a window," Marcus replied, his arms crossed and eyes too heavy for a man who supposedly didn't need rest.

Edward faced Bernie, snickering. "You jumped out a window?"

"It was either that or face Mother for getting a snack. Which would you choose?" she scoffed.

"Good point."

Marcus shook his head in disbelief. "Am I the only one surprised by this?"

The man never had to deal with Bernie much. Jumping out of a window was mild compared to what he had to put up with. But Edward had no time for stories or reminiscence. He looked to Bernie, ignoring his friend's words. "So you were left behind?"

"Disappointed?" Bernie asked, her eyes beading. Edward bit his lip in frustration. The girl was never one to forget the past, and he was not in the mood for a beating.

"On the contrary," Edward said, making both the knight and princess raise their brows. "I'm rather glad you're here. I could use the help."

"Are you kidding?" Bernie asked.

"I'm not," Edward answered. "But first let me ask you this. Why were you left behind?"

"Three words," Bernie said. "Prince Snob Man."

"She means Prince Arnold," Marcus added.

Edward smirked. "I figured."

"I know, I know. What a shocker that he hates me," Bernie continued as she leaned back on the couch, propping her other foot up and wincing before bringing it back down. "Look, Eddie, don't even bother trying to be all nice with me because frankly, I think you're an idiot who deserves a good kick in the rear." She paused, scratching her chin. "Although I have to add that you kicking Arnold in the rear does give you more credibility in my book. Okay...maybe you just deserve to be slapped in the face. Less painful, but still proving a point."

Marcus approached the king, whispering quietly. "Is she always this violent?"

"She's more bark than bite," Edward replied. "Sometimes..."

"Anyways, my point is this," Bernie continued, ignoring their comments. "You want my help? Tough luck. Antoinette doesn't want you back and I don't want you to have her, either. She's already got herself a good guy and doesn't need to be bothered with a snot like you."

Marcus opened his mouth to defend the king, but Edward clasped his shoulder, holding him back. He no longer cared about his honor or his name. He only cared about Antoinette. "For you having such a low opinion of the man who left you here, you're certainly quick to defend him."

Bernie lowered her brow. "What?"

"You say Antoinette already has a good man. Frankly, I don't think Arnold fits that description, and I don't think you believe he does, either."

Bernie let out a snarl, lowering herself in the seat and pouting. She was caught, and Edward couldn't help but be proud of himself. There was a first time for everything, apparently. "I'm just repeating what Mother says. Arnold knows I don't like him."

"I'm tired of being pushed around, Bernie. I want answers. Emmerich's gone."

Bernie's eyes became bigger and she sat up straight. "Gone? Where to?"

"I believe he's following Antoinette."

"And you're sure about this?"

"I found enough proof in my observations, Bernie. No one's telling me a thing, so I'm hoping you'll be honest and let me help!"

"No offense, but your past 'help' wasn't very helpful," Bernie replied. "Look. I'll be frank with you because no one else will. You want to help us? Don't. You want to chase after Antoinette and get her back? Don't. You want to go back and pretend that you can have both the cow and milk for free after buying a dog? Don't. Now either help me get back home so I can beat up Arnold myself or step aside so I can borrow one of your horses and go on my own."

Edward pressed his lips together in a frown, cursing his rotten luck. Even Bernie would be no help to him, (not that he was surprised). In her mind, he was still the enemy, and why wouldn't he be? She didn't know the guilt he felt or the sorrow he lived with after losing her sister.

But that didn't mean he had no more chances in finding out the truth. He'd just have to be smart about it. "Very well," he replied casually, pretending to not care. He turned to Marcus. "I assume you've already sent a messenger to find them?"

"I have," Marcus replied.

"Well if Antoinette and Arnold turn around and come back, then it's settled," Edward said, going back to Bernie. "But if the messenger fails to catch them in time, I shall have a carriage waiting to escort you back to Edeland."

Bernie nodded. "Thanks," she said, though her tone was less than grateful.

"For now, get some rest. I'll have the physician check your ankle again after sunrise." Edward gave a slight bow, tapping Marcus' arm as he raised back up. It was a signal he hoped the knight would catch, and after a quick glance from his friend, he realized it worked. "I'll let you know when the messenger returns."

"Fine by me," Bernie said, resting back on the couch.

Edward turned to leave, Marcus quickly following. As they entered the hallway, the knight stopped and faced the king. "Should we really leave her there? What if she runs off?"

"She won't," Edward replied. "Not if she thinks Antoinette may come back. And now that she knows Emmerich has gone, my guess is she's going to wait and know what's happening first before she makes a move."

Marcus nodded, putting his hands on his hips. "What if the messenger finds them?"

"Then she can go back as planned."

"And Emmerich?"

"He'll be where Antoinette is. If they both return, then I want to see them in private. Emery and Bernie may remain silent, but Antoinette will speak to me. I know it."

"The servants said you attacked Prince Arnold," Marcus said quietly. "May I ask why?"

Edward's voice lowered to a growl. "I caught him with another woman."

Marcus' eyes widened in surprise. "Your adventure may have been even more exciting than mine, then."

Edward took in a deep breath, recounting the tale.

# Chapter 3: The Wrong Road

"Oh what pain I am in!" Antoinette wanted to cover her ears to drown out Arnold's whines. Ever since they'd left Reigal, it had been one complaint after another. Whether it was a sincere reaction to pain or just the man having a flair for the dramatic, she didn't know, but she was about to shove him out the carriage regardless if the racket continued.

"The physician looked at you before we left," Antoinette replied as she sat across from him, watching him wince at every jolt from the wheels. "Aside from bruises and a broken nose, you're fine."

"I think I've lost some feeling, though." Arnold made a moan as he pointed his hand to his face. "That blasted king may have damaged the most important part of me!"

"What? Your pride?"

"You know very well what I speak of, Antoinette. This handsome work of the Almighty is all red and bruised and swollen!" Arnold replied, and she couldn't help but roll her eyes over it. "I think you should come over here and test it, at any rate. Maybe a little kiss to help get the feeling back?"

She'd rather kick him. "You're arrogant," she muttered, looking away.

"But you could make me feel better."

"I'd rather make you feel worse!"

Arnold gave a shrug as he leaned back, resting his head. "Don't tell me you're still angry over that little charade with your mother."

"I'm not angry," Antoinette replied. "I'm furious!"

"Why? Because you can't be rid of me so easily?"

Antoinette kept her eyes to the window, watching as the sunrise started washing over the southern hills that led to the sea. Circh was far in the distance, and she couldn't help but long for it. Memories of the night with Emery tugged at her heart, his suggestion of running away to the great port city feeling more desirable than her homeland. Had she left, she would be with him instead of the man who wouldn't let her go. She'd be in Emery's arms, lying in a bed with the warmth of his skin as her only covering. She longed for his embrace more than anything else.

Arnold's voice broke her reminiscence. "You're angry you're not with your lover, aren't you?"

"That lover is my husband."

"And yet it was another who defended your honor. You must feel special."

"I don't feel special in the least," Antoinette replied, thinking back to Edward's beating of Arnold. She couldn't deny it made her proud, in a small sort of way, that Edward came so quickly to her aid. But Edward was no longer hers, and if anything, he was probably beating Arnold for his flirtations with Malina. "I am embarrassed, however. I had to lie to everyone thanks to you."

"Me? Whatever did I do?" His voice showed shock, but she knew him better than to know he was serious.

"You ruined my night with Emery, made me a liar in front of everyone I care about, blackmailed me into going back to Edeland and leaving my husband..."

Arnold pursed his lips, looking away. "You put it all so negatively..."

*"How else am I supposed to react?"* She didn't care that her voice rose and the carriage drivers could possibly hear. She was livid, angry, hurt. To be denied a wedding, a honeymoon, time with her husband and an honest life? She had no choice but to be infuriated!

Arnold threw his nose high, crossing his arms. "Really, Antoinette. I'm surprised you'd be this way. When you came to me with that deal of yours, you were adamant you knew what you were getting into. You had no proof you'd ever see your husband again, yet you were willing to go along with your plan because 'you loved him, you trusted him'...blah, blah blah. But you forget that there are two people in this deal. You can't just push me away and expect to double cross me and take it all back. You promised me money, freedom with the ladies, and the chance to keep my position of power in King John's government, all in exchange for you to keep your silly ambassador's son. Forgive me if I can't help but want to keep my end of the bargain longer than a few months!"

Antoinette gave him a glare but knew there was nothing she could do to counteract his argument. He wasn't willing to part with his money and power just like she wasn't willing to part with Emmerich. And he was right – she knew the sacrifices that would have to be made in staying with Emery.

She just hoped that she was wrong.

She turned back to the window and looked out into the rising dawn, and to her surprise, the road looked different to what she typically took back to Staalberg. There were more trees and narrower paths, the terrain so uneven that getting home would take twice as long.

"Did Mother say to take another road home?" she asked.

"Ah…no," Arnold replied after a pause. "I suggested we take a more scenic route. I thought it'd be more romantic."

She pressed her lips together to prevent a snarl. When would he learn that she would never share his bed? Or was he up to something else? "I don't want to take this road. It's much longer."

"Oh Antoinette, where's your sense of adventure?"

"Wherever it is, it's not with you," she replied. "At the next town, I want us to stop and ask for directions to get back on the right road."

Arnold gave a scoff, rolling his eyes in disgust. "You're no fun at all, dearest. Enjoy the scenery, at least."

She didn't care to be fun. As far as he was concerned, since he made her life miserable, she'd have no problem making his the same way.

---

It was late in the morning when the messenger returned to Reigal palace. Edward was in the throne room, his eyes tired and heavy from not sleeping since the middle of the night, but he stood at attention when the young man came in, waving him forward to approach past the noblewoman who was next to speak.

"Did you catch them?" the king asked, ignoring the noblewoman's objections as she gave a huff.

The messenger shook his head. "I'm sorry, Your Majesty. The road was clear of Princess Antoinette and her husband. I stopped at a farm just outside of the city and talked with the owner. He said that Queen Susanna's caravan had already passed. Apparently she was complaining to the king and it woke the cows. But aside from that, he saw no royal caravan pass by on the road." He paused, frowning. "I'm afraid the prince and the princess may have taken a different route."

Edward rubbed his eyes closed, falling back into the seat. He was hoping for good news that morning, but like his luck in the evening, it promised only to be bad. "Thank you," he muttered to the servant as he faced him. "This changes our plans, then. Make sure you inform Princess Bernette of what has happened. Before you go to her, however, I'd like you to send for Sir Peterson and Sir Rikert. I need to convey with them on this matter."

"Yes, Your Majesty. I shall go right away."

Edward thanked him again as the servant rushed off towards the door. Edward motioned for the other guards to dismiss the nobles waiting on him, saying that he would meet with them in an hour after what was to be an emergency meeting with his counselors. The nobles left the room in a grumble, but Edward didn't care. If he could wait an age to get his cousin back, then they could wait an hour with their complaints.

It wasn't long before Sir Rikert and Sir Peterson had entered the throne room, the former looking well-rested and refreshed and the latter looking as if he had seen better days. The poor lad hadn't slept at all during the night dealing with Bernie, and he walked with a small limp after falling out a window.

But that didn't stop him from serving, and though Edward hated to ask it of him, he needed his friend's loyalty now more than ever.

"I'm sorry to call you on such late notice," Edward began as Marcus and Samuel approached.

"It's fine, Your Majesty," Samuel replied. "What can we do to help?"

"I trust you've been updated on the situation?" Edward asked.

Samuel looked to Marcus, stifling a laugh. "I have. Apparently a princess fell out a window and was subsequently left behind while your cousin ran away. You also beat up a guest so well that the entire city is astir with gossip. Have I missed anything?"

Edward sighed. "That's the gist of it."

"I see."

Edward leaned forward, clasping his hands together and resting his chin atop them. He always imagined his first counselor meeting to be over a great incident of security and involving every member of his guard. Instead, he called upon the two that he trusted the most to bring back his cousin and to check on his ex-fiancée. He couldn't help but think that his father would be cringing from above at such a "wasteful use of the most honorable men in the kingdom", but he was on the throne now, and he couldn't lead a country unless his mind was at peace first.

"What this meeting is about stays with us," Edward said quietly as the two knights nodded in agreement. "I only tell you these things because I trust you and your judgment. The queen mother and the queen both wish for me to attend to matters here with the nobles, but my mind is worried over my kin. Though I have no proof, it is my belief that my cousin has left because he feels Antoinette has been threatened by Prince Arnold."

"Did Arnold give reason to threaten?" Samuel asked.

"He mentioned exposing a secret of hers," Edward replied. "I believe Emery to be a part of it, though he has not admitted to anything and he left right after we spoke."

"Could he be going to Braiden? You said he mentioned it before," Marcus said.

Edward shook his head. "He was watching Antoinette leave with Arnold and was clearly distraught over what happened with her."

"And what of Princess Bernette? It is hard to believe she would be forgotten by her own family."

"I believe that to be Prince Arnold's dealing, Marcus," Edward replied. He turned to Samuel, a desperate look in his eyes. "Which is why I need your advice. If Antoinette is in danger and my cousin is involved, I don't want to stay idle and let them suffer. How do I save them?"

"Have you spoken of this with others?" Samuel asked.

"The queen mother," Edward answered. "She said to let it go."

"Then I would have to agree with her."

Edward frowned, the advice far from what he wanted to hear. It wasn't surprising that Samuel would disagree with him, though he hoped for once they'd be on the same side. "Should I not let it concern me?"

"Your concern is both your kin and country," Samuel continued. "However, I would urge caution in dealing with

Emmerich. His meddling with Edelandian affairs could cause repercussions that spill to us."

"How so?"

"Emmerich is your kin and has stayed here since his banishment from Hugellia. If he involves himself with an Edelandian princess, for whatever reason (be it noble or not), Queen Susanna may suspect your support. If he offends and his actions displease her in any way, the queen may turn to us in blame."

"So what do you suggest?"

Samuel pressed his lips together in a frown, shaking his head. "Both options require a sacrifice. If you support your kin, you risk making Edeland angry to the point of war, depending on the actions your cousin takes. However, you could also distance yourself from Emmerich. Cut ties, relations, and support, so that if he offends the queen, you will not be involved."

Edward cocked his brow. "Surely such a trivial thing would not cause that much chaos! He is merely protecting the woman he loves."

"Wars often begin over trivial matters, Your Majesty," Samuel replied. "Especially when those in charge are easily offended. Susanna has never been a woman of reason, and John has never been a man dedicated to his position."

"But it's only Emery and Antoinette we are speaking of. As much as I care for my cousin, even he would be willing to admit he is no one of consequence."

"Your grandfather banished Emmerich because he knew his actions could lead to war, Your Majesty," Samuel said. "Rumors have stated that Emmerich was already bound for imprisonment and possible execution when he attempted to elope with the princess. If he is caught a second time, would you risk saving his life at the expense of your country's safety? Or would you be willing to war with a maniacal queen who cares for nothing but her pride?"

Edward paused, looking at the knight with worry. He had never thought of Emery's actions having such a great ripple effect, but after hearing Samuel's explanation, everything made sense. No wonder Erick banished his grandson in such harshness. He wanted to protect his nation.

But he couldn't leave his cousin to rot. Emery was a good man with a noble heart. Why should he be punished simply for loving a woman and wanting to keep her safe? And if Emery really was imprisoned by Susanna, could he just sit idly on the throne and let his cousin die just to keep the queen happy?

His heart burned at the thought. Folly or not, he refused to let both Antoinette and Emmerich suffer for mistakes they never made.

"The choice is yours, Your Majesty," Samuel continued. "Though there is a way we can help both kin and country. We would have to be discreet, but we can bring Emmerich back to Audlin to see if he can shed more light on the situation. Perhaps since Aldaric and Anna van Ketten will be arriving, they will have better chances in getting him to talk. That will buy us time to figure out a new plan (should the need arise) as well as learn the truth behind Antoinette and Emmerich's strange behavior."

"I appreciate the advice, Samuel. I will heed your wisdom," he said. "I will not abandon my kin. By appearances, I shall distance myself from him and his actions, but in reality, there will be no abandonment. I've lost too much family in my lifetime to push who is left away, and Emery shouldn't have to pay for Susanna's madness or Antoinette's desire for protection."

Samuel nodded solemnly, saying nothing as the king turned to Marcus. "My friend, step forward. I have a mission for you."

"What can I do, Your Majesty?" Marcus asked.

"As head guard, you are in charge of the safety for myself and my family. I ask you, now, that you bring my cousin home. Protect him as if you would protect me or my son."

Marcus nodded, though doubt shone in his eyes. "What of you and the prince, though? I'd rather not risk leaving you both abandoned."

"I am of no consequence, Marcus, and Sir Ichabod is guarding my son. My cousin, however, has no one, and I don't wish harm to befall him."

"Forgive me, Your Majesty," Marcus stammered, "but surely you must realize your life is just as important as his, if not more. You...you are our leader, and if anything should happen..."

Edward frowned, making Marcus sigh as he bowed his head. "I'm sorry. I will do as you say and bring Emmerich back to Reigal."

"It won't be for long," Edward said, trying to be consoling. He couldn't blame his friend for wanting to do his job, yet Marcus couldn't blame him for wanting only the best to bring Emmerich home. "I will have you escort Princess Bernette back to Staalberg. Fate has been fortunate to allow her here. You could not ask for a better cover in finding Emmerich."

Marcus widened his eyes, his face paling. "Wait, I'm doing what?"

"You'll need to escort the princess to her home and find Emmerich after you drop her off."

"Lord help me, you've asked for much," Marcus muttered, rubbing his brow as Samuel let out a laugh.

"Should I lend you my plate armor in case she attacks?" he teased.

Marcus looked to the knight in hope. "Could you?"

"You won't need any armor," Edward said with a smirk. "Though it wouldn't hurt to take some extra herbs and bandages in case you need them."

Marcus exhaled slowly as he ran his fingers through his hair. "I suppose now is not the best time to ask for a raise in my pay, is it?"

"I never said being the head guard would be easy."

"You also never said I'd have to deal with *her*. Enemies and attackers I can handle, but Princess Bernette is a completely different category!"

"Worry not, my friend," Edward replied. "For now, focus on returning Emmerich to Reigal."

"And what if he does not wish to return?" Samuel asked.

Edward blinked as Marcus turned to him in curiosity, waiting for an answer. What if Emmerich refused to come back?

His words from the evening prior repeated in his mind. *LEAVE ME ALONE! I DON'T NEED YOUR HELP.*

"If he gives you any trouble…" Edward paused, finding it hard to believe he was about to speak such harsh words, "subdue him, though try not to harm him if you can."

"You're forcing him back?" Samuel asked.

"If he will not care for himself, then I will care for him," Edward replied. "I can't lose anyone else, nor can we put our country at risk."

"Yes, Your Majesty," Marcus said quietly, bowing his head.

"Now go," Edward said after a moment of awkward silence. "Samuel, have the carriage for the princess prepared. We can spare a few guards to go with her. Marcus, pack your things and be ready to leave by this afternoon. I shall send some servants to Bernette to assist her in getting ready."

"I'll head home right away to get my things," Marcus replied, giving another quick bow before exiting the room.

"And I'll have the carriage ready," Samuel replied. "Let me know if there is anything else you need."

"There is, actually," Edward said as Marcus left the room and Samuel was about to follow. The knight stopped, facing the king expectantly. "While Marcus is gone, I trust you will keep myself and my family safe?"

Samuel nodded, a warm smile coming upon his face. "I will protect you and your family as if it were my own," he said.

"Thank you," Edward replied. Samuel nodded and bowed before leaving, the king motioning for a guard to allow the nobles back in.

## Chapter 4: The First Test

Emmerich ignored the exhaustion overwhelming his body as he rode on through the early morning hours, trailing Antoinette's carriage at a safe distance lest he be discovered and caught. The chilly winds of spring's bloom cut through his face and hands, but he paid it no heed as he snapped the reins faster, urging Waffles to go on.

He had to get to his wife. Had to make sure she was safe, had to get her away from that scoundrel of a man named Arnold who *dared* to threaten her. Emmerich feared this would happen, trusting the prince with their greatest secret, and after seeing Antoinette bow to his wishes and be blackmailed into submission, Emmerich knew he had only one choice.

Antoinette had to leave, and they would have to go on the run.

He didn't know how they'd escape or where they would run to, and he worried over going into the rescue unprepared. He prayed fervently for guidance, hoping the Almighty would somehow hear him and help, but in the back of his mind, Bohden's dire words came haunting back.

The clouds. The rain. The hurricane. Drowning in a current and struggling to survive. Was fighting for his wife the event that would lead to his undoing? The bane of his existence that would consume him if he wasn't careful?

*The sun shines through the clouds. You must remember that!* Bohden's words of comfort whispered in his mind, and he tried his best to make sense of them. Was it that good would still be at work though evil surrounded him? Did it mean he should hold on to the memories that gave him strength as the clouds overtook him?

The memories of just hours before came flooding back, and he held on to them as hard as he held on to the reins of his horse.

*He remembered lying in bed, her head resting in the crook of his neck and her hand gently caressing his chest. He was starting to doze as his fingers slowly traced the curvature of her back, and all he could think of was how much he loved her.*

And he would never forget that moment.

He would follow them through the unfamiliar trail they took, going to wherever it would lead, and as soon as they would stop to rest, he would make his move, helping his wife to escape.

---

Antoinette didn't know how long they'd been traveling, but it felt like it had been days. Her bones and muscles ached from sitting too long, and when the carriage finally pulled to a stop at Arnold's suggestion, she rushed out, telling the guards she wanted privacy as she had to relieve herself. They nodded, agreeing to give her a moment as Arnold remained behind to check his bruises.

She walked down the small slope into a grove that was nice and secluded yet still close enough to the guards where she could call for help. She let out a heavy sigh, plopping onto the ground and burying her face with her palms, stifling a sob. How could she have been so blind to think...to hope...that exposing Arnold would somehow free her, that somehow Mother would see the error of her ways and allow her daughter to remain married to the man she truly loved? Antoinette felt like a fool to ever believe in fairy tales, that somehow, beyond reason, she and Emmerich could live happily ever after.

No. Instead, they were both doomed to secrecy...probably for the rest of their days. And when she would see her husband again was anyone's guess.

She wiped the tears from her eyes, refusing to cry anymore. She was so sick of her emotions and the whirlwind they put her through. She had to be strong, had to find a way to fix things.

But the sound of approaching footsteps put her thoughts to a halt as she turned to the side, seeing what was undoubtedly Arnold wanting more attention.

"You know, you left without saying good-bye."

Antoinette jumped to her feet and ran to the man before her, nearly crashing into his open arms as he swept her off her feet. "Emery? How did you...?"

"I followed you," he answered after giving her a quick kiss. He held her close, staying hidden behind the trees, and spoke quietly. "Don't worry. Waffles is tied to a tree down the road. I only want to make sure you're alright. What did Arnold say? Is it true that he threatened you?"

"Didn't threaten me directly," Antoinette clarified as she kept her arms around him. "But he did threaten to expose us. I'm sorry, sweetheart. I hoped his infidelities could be exposed, but Mother wouldn't listen. Her anger is so strong and I was afraid she would hurt you and..."

"It's okay," he interrupted as he caressed her cheek. "Arnold only wants to look after himself, so none of this surprises me."

"What can we do?"

"We can run away."

Antoinette lowered her head, frowning. "Emery, you know how that will turn out."

"I'm willing to risk it."

"But I'm not." She looked back at him, her face firm. "If I leave now, then Arnold will go back to Mother and say you kidnapped me. Then we'll have an entire army searching for us."

"But – "

"Besides, we can't leave without Bernie," Antoinette continued. "She's with Mother in the other carriage. I won't leave without her."

She watched as Emmerich's face scrunched in disappointment, but after a long pause, he nodded. "Fine. I'll follow you back to Staalberg so we can get her. But after that, we should leave."

"Emery, we can't."

"Why can't we?"

"You know, for someone in a discreet relationship, you both certainly are loud." Antoinette and Emmerich turned to see Arnold approach with a wobbled limp, his arms crossed and grin smug. She was about to scold the man for eavesdropping, but after a second of silence, she suddenly felt Emmerich leave her embrace and rush towards the man.

"*You!*" It didn't take long for Emmerich to tackle Arnold to the ground, his hands grasping the collar of the man's shirt and pinning him down. "How *dare* you try to blackmail my wife and treat her with such disrespect!"

"A...little help here...my dove?" Arnold stuttered as he glanced quickly to Antoinette.

Emmerich gave a hit across Arnold's mouth, silencing him as he sneered, "*Call her your dove one more time and I promise Edward's beating of you will be just a warm-up compared to what I can do.*"

"Emery, stop. He's not worth it." Antoinette put her hand on Emmerich's shoulder, and instantly his tense muscles released. He gave one final shove to Arnold as he let go, standing back to his feet and putting a protective hand around his wife's waist.

"My, what short tempers you van Kettens all have!" Arnold muttered as he picked himself back up, dusting his dirty shirt and pants. "All because I'm the only one wanting to be honest in my deal!"

"You've never been an honest man, Arnold," Emmerich said. "You only care for yourself."

"Very astute of you, my good sir," Arnold replied. "But as noble as you wish to be, you can't deny that your lady over there has made a deal not easily backed out of. She promised me power and riches and I promised her you."

"You would still be able to keep my dowry, Arnold," Antoinette said. "Even if you returned to Liegen, you would still have my money."

"Yes, but that's only a tiny thing compared to what I have now," Arnold said with a pout. "I'm an advisor to the king and have access to every coin he owns, not to mention I've bedded more noblewomen in the last few months than I could ever have done back in Liegen." He turned to Emmerich as if they were two friends catching up. "I mean, I don't know about the women in Hugellia, but the women in Liegen are far from able to meet a man's needs, if you get my drift. Too many old housewives and too little adventurous maidens. In Edeland, however, I have so many to pick from, I can barely decide who to have first!"

Antoinette and Emmerich met him with silence as the man expected agreement, and after a clear of his throat, he shrugged, turning back to Antoinette. "My point, Princess, is that you are foolish to think that I'd be willing to give up everything you gave me. You knew going into this deal that your marriage would be secret."

Antoinette exhaled slowly, looking away. As much as she hated to admit it, Arnold was right. At the time she made the deal, she was only thinking of Emery and how much she wanted to save him. Now, however, she could only think of the struggles they were about to face.

"Disappointed?" Arnold asked with an exaggerated pout. "Or were you hoping fate would somehow reward you for lying?"

"You are a sick man, Arnold, to prey on a woman who wished to save a life," Emmerich snarled.

"And you are an idiot, Emmerich, to think making a deal with the devil would go unpunished by the Almighty," Arnold replied. "But fear not! I am much more an angel than I appear. I shall help you in your endeavors."

"How so?" Emmerich asked in feigned excitement.

"By helping you keep your secret, of course!"

Antoinette cocked her brow. "You said that before and we were nearly exposed," she said angrily. "And need I remind you that you were the one about to expose us?"

"That is in the past now," Arnold continued, "and I will apologize for it. I only was trying to help you keep quiet about our deal so both you and I would be protected. Really, if the truth *did* come out, I would've calmed the queen for you."

"Oh, I'm sure you would've," Emmerich replied with a roll of his eyes, "because you're such a good, honest friend."

"I am," Arnold gleamed. "But now I have a proposition for you. Allow me to keep my position with the king, and I will help you hide your marriage."

"And how would you do that?"

"By keeping you hidden, of course!" Arnold replied. "It's rather simple, really. I will request that Antoinette and I get our own home outside of the palace where we can have privacy. Meanwhile, you (dear, kind Emmerich) can live there in secret and be with your wife every little moment you both desire. I will keep everyone preoccupied and away from your little love nest." He paused, grinning widely. "And...for an added bonus because I'm a romantic at heart...I'll even speak to Susanna about what a good man you are! She may hate you now, but in time, I'm sure she'll come around."

"She'll never agree to me being there, Arnold," Emmerich said, his voice low.

"Fine. Be a downer for all I care. Wait until the woman's dead, then, and her son takes over for the king. Then Antoinette and I can 'divorce' and you can be openly married to her while I take my well-earned money back to Liegen. But..." He leaned forward, squinting his expressions. "I must remind you that until Susanna goes, you are left with few options. Either stay apart and hope the lady trips and breaks her neck soon, or stay together in secret. Really, Emmerich, I'm giving you the deal of a lifetime. Free rent and an opportunity to live with your wife? What a chance!"

"I'd like to earn my own living, Arnold."

"Fine, fine. I can pay you for cleaning the house. But only a copper coin a week!"

"You're kidding me, right?" Emmerich scoffed as he shook his head. "Here you are, already making another deal when the first one clearly was a bad idea!"

"It did save your life, Emery," Antoinette replied quietly. "And it allowed us to be together."

Emmerich turned to Antoinette, his face showing hurt. "And look at all the heartache it's caused, my love. Separation, lies, deceit…this isn't us…"

"I know, but what other choice do we have?" She leaned in closer, hating to admit the truth of Arnold's reasoning. "I don't want to be separated from you, Emery. Not again. Not ever again." She wrapped her arms around his waist and he gathered her close, kissing the top of her head.

"We won't be separated, but we can find another way."

"How?"

"I don't know, but I'm sure we can think of something."

A call from one of the guards in the distance made them silent, and Antoinette strained to hear what they said. After another call, she heard both her and Arnold's names, and she quickly turned to Emmerich. "I've been gone too long. The guards will come looking for me if I don't go back to the carriage."

Emmerich looked disappointed, and his hand didn't leave her waist. Despite his not wanting to leave, however, she pushed herself away, urging him to go back. "I'm sorry, Emery. I don't want you to get caught. Now go!"

"I'm not leaving you, Antoinette."

She both hated and loved his stubbornness, but she knew it would only get him hurt.

"Fret not! How about a sneak peek into my proposal?" Arnold approached and leaned close to both of them. "This evening, when we stop to rest, I will have a room ready for you. I'll lie to the guards and then sneak you into Antoinette's room where you two can have a private evening all to yourselves. Think about it! An entire night alone. I don't think you've ever had that, have you?"

"We haven't..." Emmerich muttered.

"It's settled then! Follow us until tonight and go to the tavern while we settle in. I'll come and fetch you."

Emmerich lowered his brow. "I don't think..."

"We'll do it," Antoinette interrupted as she heard the guards' voices once more. "Now go, Emery. I'll see you tonight."

Before he could say anything in objection, she hurried up the hill with Arnold, leaving Emmerich alone in the woods.

# Chapter 5: The Truth About Love

"So why are you escorting me, again?"

It had only been a few hours since they left Reigal, but already Marcus wished he was in Staalberg so he could be rid of Bernette. Heavens, the woman was insufferable! Constantly asking questions and constantly showing her displeasure at his being there…

"I already told you," he replied in an attempt to be polite. "King Edward wanted you to have the best security for your trip home. He still cares very deeply for Princess Antoinette and would not wish any harm to come to her sister."

Bernie scoffed, shaking her head as she set her gaze out the window. "He only cares about himself."

"If that were true, then I would be in Reigal and he would've sent another guard."

"I'm not dense, you know," Bernie continued as she rested her chin on her palm. Already the girl looked bored, and Marcus could tell it was going to be a long journey. "Edward isn't going to send the head of his personal guard away from his family for so long without a reason. He wants you to bring back Emmerich, doesn't he?"

Marcus blinked in surprise. How could the girl have possibly figured that out?

"I don't know what you mean."

"Please. Emery leaves to chase after Antoinette and Edward just lets it slide like no big deal? I've known him since I was a kid, Sir Peterson. Once Edward has something in his head, he'll do anything to accomplish it."

"The king is only concerned for the safety of his cousin, Your Majesty. Surely if your kin went missing, you would do anything to get them back."

"Of course. But there's a difference between me and Edward. I actually care for my kin. Edward doesn't."

"Then why would he send a knight of the guard after Emmerich?"

"Because he wants to make sure Emery doesn't get Antoinette."

Marcus frowned, Bernette's constant judgments getting under his skin. "With respect, Your Majesty, I don't think it's fair to judge the king in that way. He cares very deeply for his family and friends."

"Oh, I'm sure," Bernie replied as she looked back at him. "I mean, he really showed how much he loved my sister, huh?"

"If you are referring to what happened last summer, I assure you, the king was very hurt by it."

"Of course," Bernie mocked. "He was just *so* distraught when he told Antoinette that he loved Malina instead and practically kicked her out!"

"Your Majesty, as difficult as this may be for you to believe, the king was acting in your sister's best interest."

"By breaking her heart?"

"By saving it from being broken further."

"How could it have been broken further?" Bernie seethed. "My sister cried every day for *weeks* after he left!"

"And you think he didn't?"

Bernie scoffed as she turned back to the window. She looked as if she didn't believe him, but Marcus didn't expect her to. She was not a girl to listen to reason, that was for certain. "Why do you try to make him out to be this hero?" she asked quietly.

"Who?"

"Edward," Bernie replied. "You always defend him no matter what. Even when he came back from Verloris, you stood by him. Why?"

"Because he is a good man and my dearest friend," Marcus answered.

"A good man?" Bernie laughed bitterly. "How can he be a good man after doing what he did?"

"There is much more to this story than you will ever know, Princess Bernette," Marcus said with a sigh. "Though I am not permitted to tell everything on the king's behalf, I can tell you the months after Princess Antoinette left were the most difficult of his life. He was ridiculed by the people and his own father threatened to take away the throne."

"Not like the bum didn't deserve it," Bernie muttered.

"Perhaps," Marcus continued. "But what you, and others, did not see was what I did. The king loathed himself so much that he barely left the palace. When he was being pelted with insults, he embraced them. When King Arden threatened to take the throne, Edward gladly gave it up and suggested Emmerich have the kingship."

Bernie rose a brow, her face showing confusion.

"Were it not for the king refusing to sign the decree changing Edward's inheritance, Emmerich van Ketten would be on the throne." Marcus paused, seeing Bernie's suddenly changing demeanor. Was she actually believing him? It was hard to tell, but the look in her eyes showed doubt in what she thought before. "The king was terribly depressed after Antoinette left, becoming so ill that the queen mother feared for his sanity. Had it not been for the birth of Prince Calimus, I doubt Edward would have ever come out of it, but guilt still plagues his heart."

"Then why did he marry Malina if he loved Antoinette so much? Why did he send her away?"

"Because he thought he was preventing further hurt," Marcus replied. "My lady, I was there in Verloris with the king. He had never met Malina until our arrival, and he admitted to making a mistake when he got drunk at the feast she gave. The next morning he rushed us out towards Hugellia, not wanting to speak of that night again. If you think his relationship with Malina was long and thought out, think again. She was a drunken fling and nothing more. Had she not gotten pregnant, I doubt Edward would have ever thought of her again."

"So you're saying it was an accident?"

"I'm saying it was a mistake that still plagues him," Marcus said. "He knew he betrayed Antoinette's trust, and between you and me, I'm unsure if he will ever forgive himself for it. Guilt is something not easily cast aside, and when it affects the ones you love, it binds itself to you."

Bernie's face was softer now, and she tilted her head. "You sound like you know this from experience."

Marcus lowered his head, thinking back to his father and the ridicule he endured for his scandalous birth. "Not on my own, of course," he said quietly. "But those close to me have gone through similar events."

The princess narrowed her eyes, but said nothing.

"I do not ask that you think well of the king," Marcus continued, looking back up and changing the subject. "Your sister has been betrayed and it is only natural that you come to her defense. But I ask you, Your Majesty, to realize that not all who sin are proud of what they've done. Edward may have hurt Princess Antoinette, but if he truly didn't care for her, he would not have beaten her husband so senselessly and sent his own bodyguard to watch over her little sister."

He watched as Bernette's expression changed, and she became quiet, turning her gaze back to the window as if in deep thought.

# Chapter 6: Love or Loss

Emmerich sat quietly in the corner of the Reinsbruch Tavern, eyeing the crowd around him carefully. The noise and revelry of drunkards drowned out his thoughts, and he watched the door, waiting for Prince Arnold to come in like he promised and take him to his wife.

Emmerich sipped from his ale, abhorring the bitter taste it gave. Reinsbruch was a smaller town, but its fame for drink drew even the most distant patrons. He wondered if that was why Arnold insisted on stopping there – the local women, along with the alcohol, were more than enough to entice a man of Arnold's tastes. But Emmerich was never one for parties, nor was he one for revelry. He wanted nothing more than to sit in front of the hearth with his wife, dreaming the night away.

It had to have been an hour before Arnold appeared in the tavern, covered in a cloak of fine furs and greeting the two ladies who stood by the door waiting for potential customers. He winked at them, speaking a word in their ears, and after meeting Emmerich's stare, he waved his hand and ushered the girls out the door with a grin.

Arnold approached the table where Emmerich sat, glancing at the barely-drunken ale. "Not a connoisseur of fine beverages, are we?"

"Apparently we have different tastes," Emmerich muttered as he sat straighter in his chair, "in more ways than one."

"You don't know what you're missing," Arnold said as he picked up the ale and finished it, sitting across.

"So is this the part where you tell me there's a snag in your plan and I can't see my wife tonight?" Emmerich hated to be blunt, but Arnold's record of honesty was about as pure as fetid water.

"You sting me with your words," Arnold said as he waved a waitress down and ordered another ale. "I only came here to tell you that I am giving you my inn room so you and Antoinette can share the evening together. The location is just down the street, past the church on the corner. It's a quaint little place that will have no guards at exactly nine. That's when my distraction should happen." He held out the key, sliding it forward on the table. "Here."

Emmerich took it hesitantly. "Where will you be?"

"Sampling the local cuisine."

Emmerich rolled his eyes, Arnold's promiscuity disgusting him. "All night?"

Arnold smirked. "I'm a man with a hearty appetite."

Emmerich shook his head, ignoring Arnold's attempt at humor and going back to the plan. It was too good to be true. "So you expect me to believe that I'll just get the evening with my wife…alone…without any incident?"

"You're a smart man, you know," Arnold replied. "Always thinking ahead. I think that's why Antoinette likes you so much. You're right, however." He sighed, leaning back in his seat. "I'm afraid you'll have to be out of the room around five in the morning. The guards will be watching for Antoinette and

I to come out together to the carriage, but fear not! I have a plan for that."

"And that plan would be?"

"I shall distract the guards while you and I switch places."

"And how will you do that?"

"My friend, there's a reason why my charms are legendary back home in Liegen. I can get anyone to do anything for the right price."

Emmerich rubbed his brow, still feeling unsure over the whole thing. He wanted nothing more than to have another moment with his wife, to spend time with her in peace and quiet and actually have an entire night with her. But to trust Arnold, one of the most sniveling cheats he'd ever known, with his life was asking too much. Had it not been for Antoinette's insistence, he would've shoved the man out of the way and told him never to bother with them again.

"I get the feeling you don't trust me, Emmerich."

Arnold's words made him look up and scoff. "I don't. And do you blame me?"

"Not in the slightest."

"Then why do you expect me to?"

"You're a reasonable fellow," Arnold continued as the waitress brought him his drink. He took it with thanks, taking another gulp. "I assure you that there is nothing to fear with me. As long as I'm happy, I have no problem making you happy."

"Oh, I'm sure."

"This is nothing more than a business proposition. As long as Antoinette keeps quiet about my indiscretions, I will keep quiet about hers." He set the mug down, leaning forward. "But I'm not worried about Antoinette, if I'm being honest. She's a good girl, always minding her own manners. I'm more worried about you."

Emmerich beaded his eyes. "And what's that supposed to mean?"

"I know how you are," Arnold continued, his voice lowering. "Always wanting to be chivalrous and noble. Sneaking in to see your wife for one night is simple, but let's be frank. Susanna is still young and healthy. It will be a long time before you can be open about what's really going on here. Are you willing to be part of this little charade for the long haul?"

Emmerich remained quiet. If he had his way, he'd run with Antoinette and they'd start their lives anew. But he knew better. Antoinette had trouble walking away when they had the chance, and the future would be no different. It would be difficult, but a lifetime of deception would be the only option.

But that didn't mean Emmerich would enjoy it, and dealing with Arnold was already testing his patience. "I'll do whatever I can to make Antoinette happy," he replied. "If that means deceiving our friends and family, so be it."

"Even if it involves things you might not agree with?"

Emmerich frowned. "What kinds of things?"

"The queen is expecting Antoinette and I to have children," Arnold replied. "Now it doesn't take a genius to figure out that with you both expressing your devotion more...*maturely*...you may produce some unintended side effects."

Emmerich's face softened as he started to understand Arnold's meaning. *What if Antoinette gets pregnant?*

"We'll be careful." His response was quick and firm, but Arnold only chuckled.

"Oh, I'm sure. But accidents always happen," he said. "Let's pretend years pass by without a change, though. Even if you both are so careful and precise in your dealings, would you really deny Antoinette the chance of becoming a mother? And let's not even go into the fact that Susanna will become suspicious if her daughter fails to produce any children."

Emmerich's mind already was swirling with anxiety, thinking of anything and everything that could go wrong. *His children would be Arnold's in name and appearance. Would he be able to see them? Would he have a say-so in how they were raised? Would they even know he was their real father? And if they did, could they keep their parents' secret, too?*

A secret marriage was difficult enough, but a secret family?

"I see I have you thinking."

Arnold's words snapped Emmerich back to reality and he hardened his features. "You're not raising our children, Arnold. I won't share them."

"Even if you're sharing your wife?"

"I'm not sharing her. She's just tolerating you until I can talk her into running away."

"Of course," Arnold said with a smirk. "But remember that if you cross me, I will have no problem crossing you."

Emmerich stood to his feet, leaning close. "Try me," he said. "I've already lost my home, my livelihood, and my dignity. Cross me and you'll be dealing with a man who has nothing to lose, and you know what they say about those people."

Arnold nodded, giving a laugh that made Emmerich's face burn. "I've never met a man who didn't have something to lose, my friend." He paused, giving back his own glare. "You still have a wife, perhaps even children someday, and you have your life. Trust me...there's still much more you can lose."

Emmerich backed down, whatever hope he had in the secret marriage suddenly dashing. He couldn't risk Antoinette, couldn't risk his children...

"Good boy." Arnold smiled as he picked up his ale and took a drink. "Now run along. Your wife is expecting you, and I think she's wanting an encore of yesterday's performance."

Emmerich looked away, his hands on his hips. If loving her risked getting pregnant, even that might become another luxury he wouldn't have...

"What are you waiting for? Go! The guards won't be distracted long." Arnold gave him a wink, and it made Emmerich clench his fists in hatred.

He said nothing as he stormed out of the tavern, fear gripping his heart as he made his way to his wife.

---

Antoinette sat quietly on the bed, looking around the room in boredom. It was evening and Arnold told her he was going to fetch Emmerich at the tavern, but how her husband was going to be able to sneak into their bedroom was anyone's guess. She turned to watch the fire in the hearth cackle softly, the heat feeling comfortable against the cold on her skin, and she was reminded of the night before when she spent it with Emery.

The memory warmed her more than the fire. She'd never forget the way he held her close when he kissed her, the way he whispered all the things he adored about her as they rested in each other's arms. She wanted nothing more than his presence...his touch...and as her eyes went back to the window on the side of the room, she let the memory keep her company until reality could take its place.

She didn't have to wait long as a commotion sounded outside her room, and she hurried to the window, watching as a screaming woman chased an older man with a pitchfork, cursing and swinging as she threatened to skewer the poor chap like chicken over a fire.

Antoinette's eyes widened as the guards hurried forward, quickening to contain the madness happening in the street. She looked out the window, watching the chaos unfold, until a shadow at the door caught her attention. The door handle moved, and her heart skipped a beat, thinking a stranger was breaking in. After the door closed and Emery removed his hood, however, she felt relief wash over.

"You made it!" She ran, jumping into his arms as he attempted to catch his breath, and he clutched her back. The touch of his lips upon hers felt like Heaven, and she hesitated to stop.

"Barely," he muttered as he pulled away. "Arnold's distraction happened fast. I had to run to make it in time."

"His plan worked, then?"

"So far," Emmerich replied. "Though how long it'll last is debatable."

She nodded, helping him out of his cloak and taking his hands into hers. "I know this isn't the best option, but at least we can be together tonight." She smiled, inching forward as she put her hands to his hips. "*All* night, I might add, without any interruption. And I think I know how we can spend it."

She moved to undress him, but he caught her before she could work, taking her hands in his and putting them to his chest. "Wait."

"What's wrong?" It wasn't like him to not accept her advances. He was more than willing the night before, and she thought…

"I'm just…I'm just really tired right now, Antoinette…from all the traveling and…" He paused, lowering his head.

She knew when he wasn't telling the truth. He never could look her in the eye when something was bothering him. "What happened, Emery? Did Arnold say something to you?"

"He said a lot of things," he replied, lifting his head. "Most of which are not our concern, but there was one thing that made me think…" He paused again, swallowing hard as he lowered his right hand and graced her stomach. "What if you get pregnant, Antoinette?"

"Pregnant?" she asked, raising her brow. "Emery, what's this about?"

"Arnold mentioned us having children," he continued. "When the time comes to have them, will they be living a secret life, too?"

Antoinette's face fell at the realization. She had been too worried about her marriage to think about a family.

"Either we'll have to hide them or…" She stopped before she could speak the words. Her face paled at the thought.

"Or they'll have to be Arnold's," Emmerich finished for her.

She turned, brows lowered. "They will *never* be his."

"Then we'll have to hide them."

"We can find another way."

"Antoinette, do you realize there is no other way unless we run?" Emmerich rubbed his brow as Antoinette left his embrace, pulling the curtains to the window shut lest they be seen. "If we continue this secret and you get pregnant, our children will grow up in deceit! And if Susanna finds them out..." He shook his head, fear taking away his speech.

Antoinette covered her arms and shivered, lowering her gaze. If Emery's fate was doomed, then what would happen to their family?

"We could protect them."

"How? By making another deal with Arnold?"

"I don't know." She sighed, unsure of what else to say. "If we can't hide them and can't bring them in this deceit, then...maybe we shouldn't have children now."

Emmerich's eyes teared up at her voice. "What? No, we...we can't do that."

"We can't have our kids grow up in this environment, Emery. It's too dangerous for them."

"But you wanted kids...I wanted kids..."

"I know, but..." Antoinette sighed, wiping her eye. The thought of never being a mother...it pained her more than she thought it would. "Emery, I'm risking enough being married to you...I can't risk them."

"But…" He lowered his head, sitting on the bed and putting his face to his palms. No words came forth as sorrow overtook him, and Antoinette felt the water swell in her eyes as she watched him, her heart breaking.

"Emery, I'm sorry, I…" She didn't know what else to say, didn't know how else to feel. All she could do was sit beside him on the bed, taking him in her arms.

"No, you're right." He lifted his head, sniffling as he looked at her. When their eyes met and she saw the hurt upon his face, she couldn't stop the tears that streamed down, and her lip quivered. He took his thumb and wiped her eyes, kissing the places each tear fell. "We…" He stopped, his voice catching. "We have to do what we have to do."

He let go of her, clasping his hands and facing forward.

"Emery, we can still be together," Antoinette said as she put her hand on his thigh. "We can still sleep with each other. We'll just have to be really careful and…"

"It's still risky, though. If I'm not paying attention, if the timing is off…"

She exhaled slowly. "It's a risk we'll have to take."

"I'm not sharing our children with Arnold, Antoinette," Emmerich said firmly. "And I'm not having them grow up in this environment. I can't do that to them."

Antoinette nodded, knowing what they would have to do. "I can't either."

"We only have one option, then."

They couldn't sleep together. Not now, not tomorrow…not until they were free.

Antoinette frowned, her lip quivering again. "That isn't fair."

Emmerich looked more pained than she as his shoulders dropped. "It isn't."

"But it's the only way." The words felt like a curse upon her lips, and she couldn't help but mourn. Despair for the future overcame her, and it seemed almost overwhelming until she felt Emery's hands gather her close.

"We can still be intimate," he whispered, kissing her softly.

"How?"

"We'd have to get creative," he answered, forcing a small smile. "Which could be a little fun, actually."

His grin, however fake it might be, gave her comfort, and she snuggled more into his embrace. But the ache in her heart remained, and she doubted it would ever go away.

"I'm sorry we can't have a family," she said as she placed her forehead against his neck.

"We have a family, Antoinette. It's you and I."

"Maybe...God willing..." She paused, forcing a flicker of hope. "Maybe we'll still have children one day. Time can change things and Mother may yet come around. Do you think?"

"My parents thought it'd never happen for them, yet time proved them wrong," he replied. "If God wills it, we will have children one day. But whether it happens or not, I will still be here. I love you, Antoinette. Even if every hope and dream is taken away, I will still be by your side."

His answer made her long for him, and she touched his face, pressing her lips together as she moved forward. "You always have a way of comforting me, don't you?"

He leaned forward, his breath mingling with her own. "I do try to please you."

She felt his hand upon her leg, moving upward, and she longed for his touch. She couldn't stop the words as they left her mouth. "Then please me some more."

What started as a simple kiss quickly deepened, and it was a matter of moments before they were on the bed nearly overwhelmed with passion for one another. As Antoinette took hold of his shirt to remove it, however, he stopped, panting as he moved away from her.

"This is harder than I thought…"

Antoinette laid on the bed, not wanting to give up the moment. "Did you think it would be easy?"

He gave her a look as he sat up. "Truthfully? I was hoping it would be."

"Sweetheart, there's nothing wrong with what we're doing."

"But if it leads to…"

"Don't worry," she said as she sat back up, hugging him from behind and massaging his chest. "We'll know when to stop. Besides, you said yourself that this is a chance for us to get creative."

He nodded, putting his hands atop hers as he turned his neck to face her. "I'm sorry, my love. This entire night has just been difficult. I…"

She smiled, forcing her hurts to the back of her mind as she held him tight. "I know. It's hard for me too. But let's not waste this moment together, Emery. We are husband and wife. We mourn together, yet we can also comfort each other. Let me comfort you as you comfort me."

He exhaled slowly, leaning into her embrace, her touch bringing peace to his troubled soul as they held each other for the rest of the night.

# Chapter 7: A New Problem

Edward sat amidst the house of nobles, barely listening as he rested his cheek on his palm. On and on the men bickered and complained over trivial things, and never had Edward been so bored. They complained of taxes when they had plenty of coin remaining. They complained of unfairness as commoners suddenly started demanding better wages. They complained of the weather, the market, the overcooked beef served at lunch, anything...and all Edward wanted to do was ignore them.

Did they not see how foolish they sounded, whining over money and power? Could they not be content with what they had? Their lands were fertile. Their money overflowed. Their workers were productive. Their health was good. They had anything and everything they could ever want, yet still it wasn't enough.

No, unless they suffered loss, they would never be thankful for their gain. Edward learned the hard way in his life when the woman he loved left.

And as he sat in the house of nobles, trying to pay attention but failing, his mind was overrun with thoughts of Antoinette.

*Was she safe? Was Emery with her? Had Arnold hurt her in any way?*

Though Marcus had only been gone for a week, Edward found himself glancing every so often at the door, waiting for a word on Emery's return or news on Antoinette. Petty squabbles regarding coin and trade were nothing compared to her safety.

"Your Majesty, what say you on this matter?"

A nobleman's voice woke Edward from his stupor, and he looked around, noticing every eye around the room was on him. He gulped, sitting up in his chair and clearing his throat, trying desperately to remember what the men had been talking about. He hadn't a clue.

"I...uhm..." He paused, giving a quick grin to hide his growing panic. "I'd much rather hear what you all think before I make a decision."

"We just told our opinions, Your Majesty," another nobleman said, his voice sounding perturbed. "So do you agree or not?"

"Uh...agree?"

Another nobleman stood to his feet, his face red. "YOU THINK I SHOULD GIVE HALF MY CATTLE BECAUSE I WAS LATE ON A TAX PAYMENT?"

Edward widened his eyes as the man fumed, another nobleman lifting his finger and shaking it.

"See! I told you, Sir Winifred...if you hadn't spent so much on your wife's jewels, we wouldn't have this problem."

"*But I paid it the day after it was due!*" he yelled before smacking his hand on the table. "And it wasn't my fault! Those stupid peasants didn't pay their taxes to me on time!"

Edward blinked, unsure of whether he wanted to laugh or shake his head. "Wait...you think he should give half of his cattle because he was a day late on taxes?"

"That's what we all agreed upon, Your Majesty. If we show mercy on one late payment, others would take advantage and then never pay their bills." The other nobleman rubbed his nose as he sniffled, thinking it no big deal. "Isn't that what you agreed upon?"

"The peasants should be punished, *not me!*" Sir Winifred yelled back.

"Hold on." Edward held up his hands, urging them to quiet. "Let us back up a moment. I change my mind. I agree that this is a harsh penalty. You will not give up half your cattle, sir."

Winifred settled down as he returned to his seat, nodding in approval. "Thank you, Your Majesty. I'm glad one of you sees reason! Now I shall punish my workers instead. Extra hours and a higher tax rate for a month to make up for any losses."

"And what did you lose?" Edward asked, cocking his brow. "You were a day late on a payment. It is forgiven. Move on."

"But Sire, my workers took advantage of me!"

"Your workers paid *you* on time, sir. It was *you* who paid late. But the matter is forgiven and should be dropped."

"But – "

"Drop it, Sir Winifred. I have shown you mercy, so show your workers mercy in return."

"I must disagree, Your Majesty! I..."

Before he could continue, however, a messenger came into the room, approaching the king. Edward motioned him forward, listening as the young man bent over and whispered in his ear.

"Your Majesty, your mother wished to inform you that your wife is very ill. She wants you to attend to her."

Edward nodded, thanking the messenger as the man exited the room. Edward sighed, rubbing his brow. He didn't want to deal with a sick Malina, and he wondered if it was an attempt by his mother to force him to spend time and thought on the woman who was his real wife instead of the one who got away.

He turned to the nobles, apologizing for having to leave. "We shall convey at a later time," he muttered in frustration as he stood to his feet. "I must attend to my wife, but I will see that dinner is served to you for this inconvenience."

The nobles nodded, some looking at the king in concern over Malina's illness, but he ignored their questions as he left the room to find his wife.

---

Malina didn't know how long she had vomited, but it was enough to make her never want to eat again.

She clutched the bowl in front of her as she hurried back to the bedroom, a group of maids following in concern. Once she reached the bedroom, however, she shooed them away, demanding her privacy. If she was going to vomit again, she wanted to do it away from prying eyes. It was too demeaning for them to see her weak, and if she was to be frail, she would be frail alone.

She slammed the door as she trudged to the bed, moaning as she sat upon its soft covers, feeling the nausea starting to settle. She still clutched the bowl to her chest, however, afraid the nausea would start again any moment. As she breathed in and out carefully, trying to calm herself, the sound of footsteps approaching made her heart race in fear.

"You're ill."

She looked up to find Malum, his arms crossed and forehead creased as he approached, glancing at the bowl in front. Malina shrugged, not in the mood for banter as she mumbled, "Something I ate, I'm sure."

"How long have you been ill?"

"A little queasiness for a few days, but this was the first time I..." She paused, not wanting to admit weakness. Heavens, how it frustrated her seeming so helpless in front of Malum! She shook her head, her body tensing. "I'm fine, though. I can handle it."

Malum was unrelenting as his stare remained. "Have you been with Edward?"

Malina scoffed. "What?"

"Have you been with Edward?"

"On occasion," she lied, though the truth was it had been since before Calimus' birth. He feared sleeping with her once her pregnancy advanced, afraid of harming the child. Since Calimus arrived, his mind had been pre-occupied with anything but her.

Malum narrowed his eyes. "You lie."

"I don't see why I would lie on such a matter."

"Save it. You have been with Vacius, haven't you?"

Malina looked to the side, not wanting to admit the truth. "What of it?"

"Could you be pregnant?"

Malina laughed as she set the bowl on the bed, shaking her head. "Of course not! I just gave birth three months ago. These things do not happen so quickly."

"They can and have before, Malina. There is no one else sick in the palace."

"Darling, you fret over little things."

Malum grabbed her wrist, pulling her up from the bed to face him. At first she was delighted that he would take her in his arms, but after seeing the look of fury in his eyes, she realized he was not holding her out of romance. He was angry.

"If you are pregnant, this is a great change of plans."

"I'm not pregnant, Malum."

"But we cannot take a chance, can we?" He let go of her wrist, turning his head towards the door as if listening for something. The faint sounds of footsteps could be heard in the distance.

Before he hid in the shadows, he pulled Malina close one last time. "Seduce your husband, Malina, and be his wife. For if your pregnancy is noticed and you have not slept with him, he will accuse you of adultery."

The knob on the door turned and Malum hurried away, hiding in the darkness of the room. Malina sat back on the bed, her mind reeling at all that was happening, and watched as Edward peeked in.

"Mother said that you were ill."

Malina's eyes went to the shadows where Malum hid, and she knew he was watching. She wanted nothing more than privacy, but that moment was gone, and she had a job to do.

If she was pregnant again, it had to be hidden. She had only been with Vacius, but to keep her and her lover safe, she had to pretend the child was another's. She looked back to the door, softening her voice and slumping over as she spoke.

"I'm sorry, Edward. I...I didn't mean to interrupt anything. I just..."

Edward rolled his eyes. "I left a meeting of angry nobles because of you. If you're sick, I will fetch a nurse. If you're not, then I will leave you be."

She didn't say anything at first, and as Edward huffed, starting to shut the door, she called out to him. "Wait."

"What?"

"I just wanted to see you," she muttered, giving a small pout. "Will you stay with me Edward? We've barely had any time together and I thought..."

Edward laughed, shaking his head. "Whatever you're trying to do, it's not going to work. Now stop trying to make me look bad to the nobles and leave me in peace!" He then slammed the door shut, leaving Malina and Malum alone in the room.

Malum approached from the shadow, his face hard. Malina didn't know what to say as she gave a small laugh, trying to downplay the matter, but Malum only leaned in close before walking away.

"Fix this," he seethed. "Or I will fix it for you."

# Chapter 8: Of Bears and Bernie

Bernie laid quietly on the ground, her blanket too thin for comfort as she tried to wrap it tighter around her body. Her escort had stopped early for the night after just crossing the border into Edeland thanks to an early rain and fog, not to mention a broken carriage wheel that got stuck in the mud, and with the nearest town a three hour ride away, there was no other place to camp but the forest.

It was the part of traveling that Bernie hated the most. She appreciated nature, but didn't want to live in it. And cold, spring ground that had barely dried wasn't the best bed she had ever slept on.

She'd been "asleep" for a half hour as the other guards got a fire going, keeping quiet as she tried to rest. Her back was turned away from them and she kept her distance, almost uneasy having to go to sleep surrounded by men.

Not that Mother would disapprove. Bernie could never attract a prince, so maybe a royal knight would be a nice backup.

"Do you think she's awake?" she heard a guard whisper. Her ears perked, and she suddenly became curious. A question like that was typically an invitation to gossip.

"Princes Bernette?" another guard softly called out.

She refused to answer, pretending to be asleep. Curiosity got the best of her, and she wanted to hear what they had to say.

"I think she's out."

"Good." Bernie heard the eldest of them sigh. "Blasted back is killing me not having a bed tonight. How long until we reach Staalberg?"

She heard some shuffling as if one of the men was getting out a packed snack. "About a week, maybe more if this fog keeps up."

"Ugh." The knight paused, giving a grumble. "That's practically a month away from home! And all for what? Having to escort a girl."

Bernie frowned at hearing the complaint, and she almost turned around to throw a rock and tell them to shut up. But then she heard another shuffle, as if someone was walking across the camp, and she heard Sir Peterson speak.

"Quit complaining, Sir Graug. It is our duty as knights to protect the innocent. Princess Bernette was done very wrong by being left behind, and I'm sure if it were your daughter or sister, you would wish to have the best protection for her."

"It's not like anyone would hurt her," Graug replied. "You think a bandit would want to kidnap that?"

Bernie lowered her brow. Any confidence in her protection suddenly flew away in that fog...

Sir Peterson was quick to respond. "She is a princess. Her title alone makes her vulnerable."

"But look at her!" Graug laughed. "Royal or regular, she's not attractive. You could offer her free to a man and they'd offer her back! Why else would her family leave her behind? Probably wanted to be rid of her just as much as we do."

Another knight chuckled alongside. "Too much fat on the meat, if you get my drift!"

Bernie's lip quivered at hearing their words. She never thought herself pretty, but from the way they talked, she was hideous. Their words cut through to the bone and she wanted nothing more than to cover her ears and hear nothing else.

"You shame yourselves." A low chastise from a distance made Bernie calm, and she was shocked to hear who it was defending her. She could hear Sir Peterson stop in his walk, scowling. "You are knights of King Edward and you dare mock his guest in such a terrible light!"

"It's not like it isn't true," Graug replied. "Plus it's not like she can hear us. We can talk about whatever we want."

"Even if she's asleep, you shouldn't mock her."

"But what if it's true?"

"I don't care," Sir Peterson reprimanded. "If I hear *any* more jeers from you, your positions in the guard will be terminated." He paused, and Bernie heard him sling a pack upon his shoulder. "Now I'm going to scout the trail ahead to make sure we are on the right path. I want all of you to get some rest while you can and stay quiet. Noise in the forest is unwise as it will attract the edelbears, and we do not need to endanger ourselves or the princess in their territory. Sir Graug will take the first watch and I will relieve him when I return. Understood?"

The men grumbled an agreement, and Sir Peterson began to walk away. As he stepped in front of Bernie, however, he stopped and turned to face the men. Bernie made sure she kept her eyes closed tight, still feigning sleep. "And for the record," Sir Peterson said softly, "Princess Bernette is a beautiful woman just like her sister. It is a shame you are all too shallow to see it."

Bernie couldn't help but open her eyes as she watched him walk down the road into the fog, his bow and quiver on his back and eyes ahead. Did he just call her beautiful?

Because surely the man didn't mean it. He *hated* her, just like she *hated* him. Their relationship was as friendly as a cat and dog. He wouldn't be attracted to her by any means, right?

She scolded herself for ever thinking such a thing. Of course he wouldn't. He was the typical chivalrous knight, always defending the weak. She could be a blob of jelly and he'd still reprimand the guards for mocking her.

But the thought warmed her nonetheless. Even if it was just his manners, it was welcoming to hear she wasn't repulsive.

She lay facing the road, her eyes now open and watching ahead, searching for any sign of him as he scouted. Calmness and peace entered her heart, and she couldn't help but smile as she replayed his words in her head.

It didn't take long for her thoughts to be interrupted as the guards went back to their speech.

"*Hmph. 'You shame yourselves' and all,*" Sir Graug muttered as the others set up their beds. "He thinks he's so prestigious when he speaks."

"Lad probably fancies her," another knight replied. "Why else would the king send him?"

"Nah," Sir Graug said. "I think he's annoyed with the princess as much as we are. He just won't admit it because he's so *noble*."

Bernie's heart sunk at hearing the words. *There. Of course he doesn't like you. He was only being good because Edward wanted him to be.* She suddenly felt so tired again, wanting to do nothing but sleep the disappointment away.

"He thinks he's so perfect, but I know better," the other knight continued. "I hear his entry into the guard was under mysterious circumstances."

"What do you mean?"

"I mean if it wasn't for the king's favoritism, he'd still be in Circh working the smithy like his father."

"I knew he wasn't a noble." Sir Graug gave a yawn, stretching. "Shame his birthright didn't keep him where he belonged."

The other knight cleared his throat. "It gets better than that. Apparently a knight had to sponsor him just to be allowed into the knighthood, and he got special permission from King Arden because his father was involved in intrigue."

"You don't say."

"I do. Apparently Sir Peterson's illegitimate, the son of a man and his whore."

It all started to make sense as Bernie remembered her conversation with him in the carriage. *He stood by Edward because his father did the same thing!*

Sir Graug chuckled. "And the king actually wants rabble like that leading us? No wonder the country's gone to the chamber pot!"

"You give a pauper the right of a noble and they think they're suddenly better. As if he were any braver or smarter than us!"

Bernie listened to the men as they went on and on discussing rumors and facts. At first she was hurt by their ponderings regarding her appearance, but once they started gossiping about Sir Peterson, her hurt suddenly turned to anger. Sir Peterson wasn't her favorite person in the world (Heaven knew he annoyed her), but to hear that Sir Graug chap mock him for his background was infuriating. So what that Sir Peterson didn't have a proper birth. So what that he grew up poor. So what that Edward had been helping him out. It didn't make Bernie angry that he was in charge. Rather, she felt sorry for him. His only issue was that he was different from the others, and she wasn't about to let him be made fun of for that!

She turned around, not caring that she revealed herself as being awake to the men, and stood up, throwing her blanket to the ground and stomping towards the now-surprised knights.

"Hey!" she sneered in a not-so-nice voice. "You might want to try listening to your boss and keeping it quiet! There's bears out here, you know, and they follow noise! And besides that, you know what you boys remind me of? A bunch of gossiping old ladies! Honestly, my mother doesn't even trash people this much!"

Sir Graug's eyes widened in embarrassment, and he looked to the ground.

"Now listen, because I'm only going to say this once!" Bernie continued, putting her hands on her hips. "You want to make fun of me? Fine. I'll be glad to throw some insults at you, too. But I don't want to hear you make fun of anyone else! Sir Peterson may be annoying, but at least he's doing his job! Instead of talking, *ladies*, maybe you should be getting rest or keeping watch!"

"Your Majesty, forgive us. We didn't expect you to hear our conversation," the other knight mumbled.

"I don't care. It doesn't make it right!"

Sir Graug suddenly sat up, looking behind him. "Uhm...Your Majesty..."

"No! You're not interrupting me! Now as soon as Sir Peterson gets back, I want you all to tell him you're sorry for -"

"Your Majesty!" Sir Graug gave a shout as he stood to his feet, sword at the ready. "Be quiet!"

Bernie gulped as she saw Sir Graug's sword pointed high, backing away. "Uh...let's not be hasty now. I mean, if you boys want to talk, just keep it down so I can sleep and...uh..."

"Not that! Listen!" Sir Graug put his fingers to his lips, and Bernie quieted, looking around.

There was a sound of shuffling, plus a set of low rumbles.

Bernie felt her heart stop as she turned to Sir Graug. "What is that?"

"I don't know," he stammered. "It sounds like..."

"BEARS!" The other knight gave a shout as two large, burly bears roared through the trees, rushing through the camp. The three guards pulled out their weapons and began to shoot arrows at the bears, but after a few misses and a broken bow thanks to a bear's paw, swords soon became the only option, and the camp was nearly overrun.

The three knights fought valiantly as Bernie backed near the fire, taking up a loose torch and lighting it as a weapon. She held it out in front of her, swinging to keep the bears at bay, but after seeing the first knight fall after a claw to the head, she suddenly felt panicked. Two edelbears against two knights and a princess weren't great odds, and with Sir Peterson in the distance with the only bow left, the odds were even worse.

*I'm going to die here...* Bernie felt her heart pound and her breath speed up, and as another knight fell to mauling with only Sir Graug left, her world seemed to stop as her eyes met the knight's.

It only took a second for his words to make her quake in fear. "RUN!"

She shook her head. She'd be alone in the woods...a fog-filled maze in the middle of nowhere and...

"I SAID RUN! GO NOW!"

It was the last words the knight ever spoke before he was overwhelmed, and suddenly the bears were eyeing her.

One glance was all it took before Bernie turned and sprinted as fast as she could, torch in hand, through the trees. The only knight left was somewhere out there, and she prayed to God that somehow he'd hear her.

"MARCUS!" She prayed her voice carried past the roars that now chased her into the darkness.

---

Marcus cursed to himself as he trudged through the fog. It was thick and heavy, like the mud he nearly got stuck in thirty feet back, and his visuals were limited. He could barely see the road ahead of him, the winding and narrow path that was difficult enough to see in daylight. He stopped, looking around and taking a breath, wondering if the group wouldn't be better off sleeping in and traveling once the fog was gone. The forests of Edeland were treacherous to get lost in, and many an inexperienced man died after losing the trail and never finding a way back.

But Marcus was not an inexperienced man, and he carefully marked the tree trunks of the path that he followed in case they had to travel in the fog. After a quick glance ahead, he brushed the bark off of his knife and sheathed it, ready to travel ahead until he heard a piercing sound.

He stopped, turning and looking behind to figure out what he had just heard. It sounded high pitched, frightened... an echo amidst the other nightly noises given by animals who made the night their day. At first he thought he misheard, his mind playing tricks from exhaustion, until he heard the scream again, this time with a familiar word.

"MARCUS!"

His heart started to race as adrenaline surged, and he ran back towards the camp. Bernie's voice was unmistakable and sounded terrified...pained...and a million thoughts of what could be happening to her entered his mind.

*Has she been attacked? Did the guards hurt her? Were we followed?* He'd be lying if he didn't think back to the shadows he felt in Verloris, how terrified he was being watched by the Velori and wondering if they were going to strike.

But at the sound of an animal's roar, he realized it was no man that threatened her. It was an edelbear, the violent predators of Edeland's forests always searching for their next meal.

Faster and faster he pushed himself to run, calling out for her to answer. "YOUR MAJESTY! WHERE ARE YOU?"

He heard her say his name again, this time sounding closer as a faint light showed up ahead.

The fog illuminated what he figured was a torch, but where exactly it was, he couldn't tell. The haze splattered the light in different directions, and he had to check his hearing to make sure he was going the right way. "Keep talking!" he called out. "I can't see you, but I can hear!"

"I'M BEING CHASED BY BEARS! HOW CAN YOU NOT SEE THAT?"

"It's the middle of the night and it's foggy out!"

"SOME EYESIGHT YOU HAVE!"

He shook his head as he hurried along, jumping over fallen trunks and dodging loose branches. After what seemed like an age, he finally saw the torch in a clearer light, and he paled when he saw Bernie come into view.

She was being chased by what looked like two bears - big, brown, and burly - fresh from a winter-long hibernation and undoubtedly hungry. He looked around, noticing the other guards were nowhere near, and a terrible realization overtook him. Either they had abandoned the princess or they couldn't protect her because…

He stopped his thoughts as he took aim with the bow, calling out to her. "To me!" he shouted. "Don't stop running!"

"Not a problem there!"

He let the first arrow fly, hitting the right bear in the shoulder. The animal shrieked, but charged even faster as pain fueled his hunger.

"*Can't you aim?*"

There was no time for banter as Marcus picked another target on the right bear and released the arrow, hitting the animal in the eye and knocking it to the ground.

"Don't forget the other one!"

The second bear was nearly upon her, and Marcus released an arrow, hitting the animal in the neck. It continued to charge, and Marcus shot another to the bear's cheek. Still it continued to chase. Marcus released two more arrows – one of which missed, the other which hit the bear's leg - but none of them caused it pause. And as Marcus reached to his quiver, realizing he was out of arrows, he knew he had only one option.

He drew his sword, a short blade typically mistaken for a long knife, and rushed forward. "Run!" he said as he passed Bernie, and as the adrenaline in his veins hit its peak, he pushed the sword forward into the bear's chest.

"*What are you doing?*" Bernie yelled as she stopped, running back to him.

But he didn't have time to answer as he felt a heavy weight slam against his head.

He could feel the claw slash at his ear and cheek, a deep wound that burned as he was knocked to the ground, his neck nearly snapping at the force. Dizziness overwhelmed him, the pain from the hit pounding his body into weakness, but he forced himself up as he took his sword, swinging it at the bear again.

"NO!" Bernie's yells were the last thing he heard as the bear's claw nearly caught his head again, but he dodged it in time as the pain now dug into his shoulder, the force of the hit nearly ripping his arm off.

He grunted, the pain being ignored as he took all of his strength and forced it into his left arm. The blade went up, and as the bear was about to pounce, he plunged the sword towards the bear's head. With a final roar, the beast went down, and Marcus was left heaving in the muddy grass.

The adrenaline started to fade and the haze of its effect overwhelmed every muscle and bone. Marcus stumbled, his vision making everything uneven, but he forced himself towards the princess. He had to make sure she was safe…had to make sure she wasn't hurt or frightened.

"Your…Majesty…?" His words were barely audible, but he saw her approach, her face pale and mouth open from gasping for air. She looked at him, and he saw her lips move and make a sound, but he couldn't tell what she said.

He squinted, trying to make sense of the world swirling around, but then a wave of weariness overtook him, and he knew no more.

# Chapter 9: Lost

Bernie didn't move, didn't dare to speak. Who knows how many edelbears could still be out there, and with three knights dead and the other one out cold, there was nothing else to do but think.

Her first thoughts went to Sir Peterson, lying unconscious on the ground, half of his face and left shoulder bloody and torn from fighting the bear. She'd heard stories from guards who traveled with her family through the forest about the animals, how they weren't like normal bears and would rip a man to pieces if given the chance. The fact that Sir Peterson had even survived an encounter with two edelbears was nothing short of a miracle, but his injuries looked blight, and if he wasn't taken care of, he'd be a midnight snack for any other animal that still ran loose.

She thought to move, but found herself frozen and standing still. She looked down at her feet, still planted in place, her legs feeling like lead and too heavy to lift. Her eyes went to her hands and she saw that they were shaking, and if she listened past the sound of her panting gasps, she could hear the faint echo of a whimper coming through her throat. Was she crying? She couldn't tell. Her mind was in such a heightened state of panic that every sense overwhelmed her and all she could do was shake.

But after seeing Sir Peterson a second time, she knew she had to gather her wits. The man would die just like the others if she didn't get moving and protect him. She looked back down at her legs, urging them to go, and after a few baby steps forward she soon fell into a stride, bending down to the knight's body and putting her fingers to his neck to check for a pulse.

A steady rhythm throbbed as his chest rose and fell. Good. He was still alive and breathing. At least something was going right that night.

"Marcus…" Her voice was like a frog's croak, and she cleared it, trying again. "Marcus…"

He didn't stir, and she felt a new panic begin to sink in.

*What if he doesn't wake up? What if he's really hurt?* She stuck the torch from her hand into the ground, putting both hands to the knight and gently touching his face. He looked so peaceful as he slept, so serene though his body had been mangled. She tapped his cheek lightly, giving his good shoulder a shake. He had to wake up. She couldn't lift him and get him to shelter.

"Sir Peterson?" She shook a little harder. "Marcus…"

*Please don't be hurt, please don't be hurt…*

She was about to slap the man awake, but after one final call of his name, he suddenly opened his eyes, meeting her terrified stare.

"Your Majesty?" he asked weakly. "Are…are you…alright?"

Her words were nothing more than squeaks as she nodded. "I'm okay."

He sat up slowly, grunting as he put his hands to her arms to keep himself steady. He was woozy, either from the blow to the head or the fallout from the adrenaline rush, and blinked as if trying to find his bearing.

"Where...are the others?" He struggled to speak as he leaned forward, breathing steady.

"They're dead."

He looked up, gaining clarity. "What?"

"The bears caught us by surprise."

Marcus was silent for a moment, his face showing hurt, but he immediately became stoic again as his fingers gave her arms a gentle squeeze.

"You're shaking."

She was? She couldn't tell. Her eyes lowered to her arms, and she noticed the slight tremor possessing them. She tried to shrug it off, not wanting to seem scared. "Just...a little tired from...all that running..." She faked a smile, giving a startled laugh. "I mean, I'm not in the best of shape and all, but...I think...I think I did pretty good outrunning two edelbears. How many...other people can do that in a dress, right?"

He didn't laugh at her jokes, nor did he say anything in response. He only lifted his good hand to her face, taking his thumb and wiping the tears that streamed down her cheek.

She looked at him, confused, until she realized what was going on. She had been crying the entire time he'd been awake, and she was just now noticing it.

"It's alright," he said quietly. "You're safe."

She rarely cried unless it was serious, always trying to hide her emotions behind a stony façade, but being so close to death...seeing three men she was talking to just moments before being mauled right before her eyes...

All she could do was nod as the emotions suddenly flowed out, and Marcus gathered her to his arms, holding her as she sobbed.

---

It took a few minutes for Marcus to regain his strength. Adrenaline was a wonder when used in the heat of battle, but after wearing off, it often left its user feeling exhausted, lightheaded, and emotional. It was why he passed out after slaying the edelbears and why Princess Bernette had been crying after nearly being mauled to death. But as their strength started to return and their minds became clearer, Marcus realized that they had to get up and move. They achieved nothing simply sitting there in the dark.

"We need to go," he muttered as he stood shakily to his feet, pulling the princess along with him. She hastily complied, holding on to his arm, still sniffling.

"Where?"

"I'm not sure yet," he answered. "Do you think there are any more bears?"

"Maybe," she replied. "But I only saw two."

He nodded. "We'll be vigilant, but I think we're safe for now. We need to check the camp to see what we have left," Marcus continued, sheathing his sword and slinging his bow and empty quiver across his shoulder. He stepped forward, heading to the bears and trying to pluck whatever arrows he could scavenge.

Bernie stayed close beside him. "But…you're bleeding…"

Marcus turned to his shoulder, fingering the wound and noticing a small trickle of blood coming from the side of his head. He'd forgotten his injury, only now starting to feel the sharp pains of being clawed. "It seems I am..." he muttered, perturbed. The last thing he needed to deal with was being hurt, especially when he had a princess to protect.

"I...I think there's some cloth and herbs back at the carriage. We can get them there."

"It's a plan. Let's go." He put his arm around her back, urging her to go forward, but she refused to budge just yet.

"You're bleeding pretty bad," she said, frowning at his injury. "Maybe we should patch it up now just in case. Animals would be able to track us because of it."

"What would I be able to patch it with?"

She looked around for a moment before lifting up her skirt. "We can improvise."

"Not yet," he said with a shake of his head. "It's not far to the camp. I can hold off."

"But what if we get lost?"

"We won't get lost."

"Did you mark the trail?"

Marcus paused. He hadn't had time to mark his journey to the princess when she needed saving. "I...I marked some of it near the road..."

"It's dark and foggy out and we're far from the trail. I know these forests, Marcus. My grandfather and my uncle both died here getting lost. And with no trail..."

Marcus turned to her, defiant towards defeat. He was a knight of Audlin and head of the royal guard tasked with protecting a princess of Edeland and bringing back the king's cousin. He refused to let a grove of trees fail him. "We'll find the trail and our camp if we leave now."

"But you can bleed out…and the animals…"

"If I'm feeling tired, I'll let you know," Marcus interrupted, urging her forward. "But we shouldn't tarry here lest more bears come to find us. Come, Your Majesty. We can find the camp if we hurry."

He reached down, taking the arrows that could be saved, and picked up the torch, tracing his steps through the trees.

They walked on in silence, not saying a word, as Bernie occasionally glanced up at him. He knew she was worried, afraid her only protector would leave her stranded and alone, no doubt. But he had to be strong. Had to fight the pain and exhaustion that was throbbing in his body, telling him to stop. And when the lightheadedness started to drain his energy, he pushed all the more. He couldn't be weak, couldn't fail his country and king.

"You're not looking so good," Bernie said as they slowed in their walk after a while.

"I'm fine," he muttered.

"But you've been bleeding for a while…"

"It hasn't been long."

"We just passed that same tree with the owl glaring at us…twice!"

He looked back at the tree, nearly pausing in his steps. It did look familiar…

"I know where I'm going," he muttered

"You're barely awake and we're walking in circles."

"I'm awake, Your Maj-" He felt his feet give way and a wave of dizziness overcame him as he tumbled to the ground. Bernie's hands grabbed hold of his arm, trying to keep him up, but her lack of strength made her fall with him.

He groaned, struggling to get back up, but the world was spinning once more and it was difficult to get his balance.

"You're losing blood, Marcus."

"The bleeding stopped a long time ago."

"You're still dripping, mosquito man. Now stop walking and let me see if I can stop the bleeding."

He didn't have time to waste and he started to get up, but after a quick "Oh no you don't!" scold from the princess, he felt himself being pushed back down. Soon he heard a rip, and Bernie (with a chunk of her dress missing by the calf) held two pieces of cloth in her hands, one going to his cheek and the other to his shoulder.

"The face should be okay, but the shoulder is still going," she muttered. "If we had some needle and thread, I could stitch it."

"But..."

"Look, you can be noble and heroic all you want, but if you're going to bleed to death, you'll be no help to either of us."

"I'm not going to bleed to death."

"This wound is nasty, Marcus. That bear clawed you good."

He let out a grunt, frustrated he was delaying them. If he could just get up and go a little further, the camp was surely just past the trees ahead and...

He gave a wince as she pressed the cloth further into his shoulder. "Sorry," Bernie interrupted as she gave a smirk. "Didn't mean to hurt you. Good news is I think the bleeding is slowing down. It's not as deep as I thought."

"Then let's bandage it up and get going."

"It needs to be cleaned, though. It could get infected if we're not careful."

"Is there any alcohol?"

"None. I don't drink."

Marcus sighed. "Neither do I. I never thought wine could be so helpful until now."

"It'd help if we had some water," Bernie continued as she patted the wound with her cloth. "I'll clean it as best I can, but we need to watch this. If you start getting sick, you need to let me know."

"I won't get sick."

"Probably not, but I want you to tell me just the same."

He wanted to shake his head and ask what she could possibly do to help him were the wound to get infected. With no civilization for miles and no access to a doctor, any disease or sickness would become a death sentence where they were at.

Which was why they had to find the camp. The longer she wasted in treating his injury, the harder it would be to find their way out of the forest.

"Is it bandaged?"

"Almost…" She did a quick tie around his arm with the cloth and nodded. "Okay, done."

"Thank you. Now let's go." He tried to stand, his legs feeling shaky, but he forced himself up. He couldn't give up, not now or ever.

As the ground wobbled beneath his feet, he found his steps uneven at first, but before anything could be said, he felt a hand slip under his arm, holding him steady.

He turned to find the princess holding him up, walking alongside him at a steady pace through the foliage.

"You need to rest."

"We can't rest yet."

"Marcus, we're not going to find the camp in this fog."

"If we keep going, though…"

Bernie huffed in frustration. "We've been walking for two hours already! If we haven't found it now, we're not going to find it! We're lost."

"We're not lost."

"We haven't seen any sign of the trail and we're going deeper and deeper into the forest. Until this fog clears up and daylight comes, we won't be able to see anything. We need to stop right now and wait until everything clears. Besides, you look exhausted."

"I'm *fine*." He turned to move, but she pulled him back. He glared at her, narrowing his eyes. "Your Majesty, we need to go *now*."

"No, we don't!"

"Yes, we do!"

"I'm an Edelandian, buddy!  I know what getting lost in the forest looks like!"

"I understand that, Your Majesty, but as head of the king's guard, I am trained for protection and survival," he argued back.  "With respect, I ask that you trust my instincts.  We need to keep going."

Bernie let go of his arm with a push.  "Fine!  Be such a know-it-all!  But if you go collapsing in the middle of nowhere, don't say I didn't warn you!"

With a stomp of her feet, she stormed off in the direction he had been wanting to go, and he hurried alongside, desperate to keep his balance as they hiked through the trees.

# Chapter 10: The Jealous Lover

Vacius didn't know how long he waited, but it felt like a lifetime.

He stood in the shadows, watching for her. Malina was scheduled to dine with a group of noblewomen, but afterwards would be free for the rest of the evening. As the king busied himself with other duties, that would leave the queen unattended and free, letting Vacius finally have a moment with her *alone*.

Not that the royal guard made it any easier for him. Even with that pathetic Sir Peterson gone, Sir Rikert managed to keep everything like before. Guards in every hallway, protocol being followed by the letter. It made his job difficult, almost impossible when trying to have time with his lover. Over the past week he had barely seen her, and that made him wonder what was going on.

The door down the hall opened and Malina exited the parlor she was in, faring the ladies well and hasting away as she touched her stomach. Her face had been pale over the past few days and Vacius heard rumors of her being ill. Perhaps that was why she stayed away, though he hoped she knew he was proper comfort.

She nearly passed him before being pulled into the other room, surprise on her face as he quickly shut the door and locked it.

"Vacius!" Malina said, though her tone was more harsh than pleased. She lowered her brow, pulling her arm away. "What is the meaning of this? I have business to attend to!"

"I wanted to see you," he said. "You've denied me all week. What must I do to gain your attention?"

"The days have been busy, my lover. I must do much to keep the nobles pleased."

"You've made time for them. Why can't you make time for me?"

Malina sighed, looking away with a shake of her head. "Because I must make time for Edward. Things...have become more complicated."

"Complicated?" Vacius' eyes flared with fire hearing the name he hated most. "Why?"

Malina paused, almost as if she didn't want to answer, but after a change of face, she lifted her chin and scoffed. "I am the king's wife, Vacius. He will become suspicious if I ignore him constantly."

"Suspicion didn't make you ignorant before."

"It is different now. Our child has been birthed and Edward will have need of me."

"Calimus is three months old. You did not waste your time after the birth."

"That was because I told Edward my body needed recovering. Now he expects me to share his bed." She shook her head in frustration. "You must be patient, Vacius. I cannot hold your hand every time you whimper!"

Vacius leaned forward, his voice near a growl. *"I have been patient long enough!* You've gone an entire week without even glancing at me!"

"I am with you now, aren't I?" she said, almost forcing the flowery words from her lips. "There will be moments in our lives together when we must be apart, my lover. I do not like it any more than you do, but if we wish to take this throne, we must be vigilant in our endeavors. Your job is to watch over me and protect; my job is to seduce the king and his people so that I can steal his crown. You must be content with this agreement if you wish to be free of the Velori."

"You did not say I'd have to wait this long."

"I told you it would be a long road. If you cannot handle it, then be gone with you!"

Vacius was about to retaliate with more than just words, but the sounds of footsteps outside the door stayed his hand. Both he and Malina turned, overhearing Edward talking to a servant.

Vacius' heart burned with rage. *"I will end him now."*

Malina put her hand on his chest, clutching the fabric of his tunic. *"You will not.* I shall handle this."

"Malina, I forbid it!" he seethed, grabbing her arm. "I will not be denied you!"

"You let your lusts control you, fool." Her voice was like venom as it hit his ears. "Now release me or I will go to Malum."

Vacius kept his hand on her for a moment before letting go. No matter what, she would have to get her way. If she went to Malum now, he would be killed for disobeying the Velori. If

Vacius stopped her, Malum would become suspicious and kill him for not protecting Malina as was his duty.

"We will speak of this again." He pushed her arm away, stepping back from the door.

Malina only glared as she turned and walked out, hurrying to Edward as the servant he was speaking to left to run errands.

Vacius watched from the darkness as Malina approached her husband, her hands going around his waist and her body pressing against his as she stopped him in his tracks.

"My love, I need a moment of your time," she cooed.

He looked disinterested. "What is it?"

"Come to our bedchamber with me. I have something I wish to speak to you about."

"Can it wait?"

"No," she said, fingering his shirt. "I daren't say it can wait even a second. Come now." She leaned forward, brushing her lips against his and letting her touch linger.

He took her by the arms and gently separated himself from her. "Malina, I'm not in the mood."

"But I am." She gave him a smirk, a playful turning of the lips that Vacius once thought was only meant for him. His lungs burned with fire as his breath began to heave.

"You haven't wanted my company since before Calimus' birth," Edward said. "Why now? Unless there is something you want."

"Do you think everything I do has an agenda behind it?" She laughed, taking her finger and touching his cheek. "My body is recovered from Calimus' birth, Edward. It is ready for you."

"And what if I don't want it?"

"Silly boy," she said, pulling him close. "I will not be denied the marriage bed. If I want something, I get it."

Edward rolled his eyes. "Then go to one of your other lovers."

"You know I have none."

Her denial was smart, but it pained Vacius hearing it. Even if it was unwise, he wanted her to tell Edward the truth. He was the real lover, not that wannabe king!

"Oh Edward," Malina continued after seeing Edward turn his head away. "Have I not seen you pine over the loss of Antoinette these past weeks? She is gone, my husband... bound to another. What would your mother say if she knew you had an adulterous heart, denying your wife the love of your body?"

Edward looked back up, frowning. "You have spoken to her?"

"She has spoken to me, encouraging our relationship because she worries you will not let go of your past."

Vacius was unsure if it was true or not. He hadn't seen Queen Maria speak with Malina in private, nor did he hear of any conversation about the marriage. But it wasn't like he saw much of Malina anymore. Perhaps, in the moments he was sleeping...

"Do not deny me my wants, Edward," Malina said, her voice suddenly firming. "I will go to the nobles and tell them of Stephen's true fate. Your name will be tarnished and you will be removed from the throne."

Edward let out a huff. "Are threats all you have?"

She glared at him, almost perturbed he'd challenge her, but then her face softened. "No. But I can remind you of what you have. You made your choice, Edward, to marry me. You made a commitment under oath. I should not be denied my wants, as simple as they are. I only ask for a moment to be with you, and that is not an unreasonable request of a wife. Now be my husband, Edward, and follow me to the bedroom." She smiled as her hands went across his body. "You cannot tell me you don't desire this. Let me soothe you, and I promise any longing for another woman will be far from your mind."

He closed his eyes, holding his breath at Malina's touch. Though he said nothing, Vacius knew the man's desire was rising. Even if he was not attracted to her, he had urges like any other.

"Fine," Edward muttered beneath his breath as he faced his wife. "I will go with you."

Malina smiled, taking him by the hand as she led him towards their bedroom, shutting the door.

Vacius could only watch with clenched fists.

---

"Come closer, Edward."

He looked up, wanting to scoff as Malina took him by the hands and pulled him towards the bed. She looked desperate, poor girl, and he wondered for a moment if she really was being denied the physical love she so deeply desired. After meeting her gaze, however, he could only think of one thing.

*She loves on me because she has to. There is no intimacy here.*

He didn't know what she wanted, but he was sure it was about to reveal itself sooner or later.

He'd have to humor her for the moment. Between his mother hounding him on letting go of Antoinette and the fact that he really did desire some sort of physical love, it was best to get the inevitable over with. At least he'd have a respite from the nobles and their unending demands.

She urged him forward and he followed, forcing his hand to her face in a caress. Her smile widened as she closed her eyes, arching her head back, and he leaned forward.

"This is wonderful," Malina whispered. "I haven't felt your touch in so long, and I..."

He wanted to roll his eyes at her words. Whether he was becoming wiser as he got older or he was just used to her lies, her playacting in desire made him want to laugh. It would be so difficult getting through everything without showing the humor.

"Kiss me."

He obeyed...until he had to stifle a gag. Bile managed to climb up his throat after touching her lips, and he had to force himself to remain still as she pulled him closer.

As much as he tried, loving her was proving difficult. But she was his wife, and it was his choice to marry her. He had to live with the consequences for the rest of his days.

He gathered her in his arms, fighting the urge to push her away and run out of the room, brushing his lips to the corner of her neck. She moaned in delight, grabbing hold of his shirt and attempting to take it off, and he did the same with her dress.

But through every touch and every kiss, every sound and every whisper, Edward felt nothing but emptiness. Though his body was getting the pleasure he craved, his heart was still yearning to connect. He felt neither desired nor wanted, and though he was about to make love to his wife, he knew that love would be left wanting.

*You married her, and this is the cross you must bear.*

He was flat on his back as Malina moved forward, her hands grazing his chest and attempting to remove his last covering. He laid there and watched, attempting to enjoy the show, but feeling little pleasure from it. As she was fiddling with his belt, however, a knock was heard at the door, and he sat up, Malina refusing to get off of him.

"Ignore it," she ordered.

"It may be something important."

"I don't care. I want you *now*."

The knock continued and Edward moved away from her grasp. "It can't wait." He was almost glad for the interruption, and he straightened his pants and belt as he approached the door, leaving Malina on the bed to hastily cover herself.

"What is it?" he asked through the wood.

"We have a situation, Your Majesty. Someone has just broken into the treasury."

Edward lowered his brow. "What was taken? Is Calimus safe?"

"Your son is safe, Your Majesty. As for the robbery, we don't know much aside from the fact that it just happened.

We're afraid an intruder may be in the palace." The knight on the other side cleared his throat. "With apologies, Your Majesty, but the royal family is needed. We will escort you all to the safe room until the guard has cleared the estate."

"Very well. We'll be right out."

Edward reached for his shirt, donning it quickly as he turned to his wife. "Get dressed. We need to head downstairs."

"Whatever for?"

"There was a breach in the palace defenses. The guard wants to move us to a more secure location without windows in case of any intruders."

Malina shook her head, scoffing. "Edward, we are two stories up! Unless the intruder is a bird, no one can get here!"

"I'm sorry, Malina. This is a protocol we must follow." He picked up her chemise and a robe near the dresser. "Now put this on. We must get Calimus and make sure he stays safe."

"But Edward..."

"If we don't leave now, the guards will come in and force you out, and I doubt you want to be dragged into the open with nothing but a bed sheet." He paused, giving a snicker. "Although I'm sure you would enjoy the attention."

She snarled as she grabbed her chemise, putting it on.

Once dressed, Edward opened the door and they were led by the guard down the stairs into a room designated for safety. Malina said nothing as she crossed her arms, perturbed that her moment had been ruined, but Edward could only smile as Calimus was brought to him safe and sound.

For the rest of the night they were under guard until the palace was deemed secure, and the shadow that watched in delight went unnoticed.

But unbeknownst to him, another shadow was watching, and he was far from pleased.

# Chapter 11: Wandering

"So...find the camp yet?"

Marcus grunted, foregoing words as he and Bernie continued to hike. He didn't know how long they'd been walking – searching – but it had to have been hours. The sun was just starting to rise above the horizon and the birds had long been singing their morning song.

And despite the journey, marking trails and following what he thought were signs, the camp eluded them. The fog was still thick and showed little sign of letting up, and whatever they could see remained the same: trees. Hundreds and hundreds of them for miles around.

He hated to admit it, but they were lost, and the princess had no trouble reminding him.

"Awe! Look at that. There's the same chipmunk we saw scurrying about an hour ago!"

He didn't know how she could tell the difference between that chipmunk and the hundreds of others they saw, but he wasn't about to ask. She was goading him, trying to make him feel guilty for getting them lost, as if he didn't feel guilty enough.

His first test of leadership and already he was failing. Three guards were dead under his watch and a princess of a neighboring country was wandering in the woods with an injured bowman as her only protection. And from the way Bernie talked, any chance of escaping the forest would be a miracle without a trained guide.

Still, despite the fact of being doomed to death, she was handling everything well. No panic or anxiety...just unending sass. Of course, that caused him panic and anxiety, but he couldn't let her know that.

"Can we take a break? I haven't slept all night."

He sighed, stopping and turning. Looking at her, the poor girl looked exhausted, just as much as he, and he felt more guilt creep up at making her walk for so long. He had been so worried about getting back to camp to make sure they weren't lost, but...

"Are you okay? You don't look so good."

He shrugged at her words, setting his quiver and bow to the ground. "I'm fine. But here – let's rest. I...I don't think we're going to find the camp until this fog clears up."

She sat on the ground, resting against a tree trunk. "Told you."

"I...admit that you were right." He lowered his head, sitting beside her. "Forgive me...I was hoping to get us to the camp before daylight."

"Even a guide can get lost in these woods. It could happen to anyone."

He knew she meant to be kind, but it didn't help him feel better. Failure was unacceptable in his line of work, and when other lives were at stake...

"How's your shoulder?"

He looked at it, noticing the wound was looking a little red underneath the bandage. He frowned, knowing from what little medical training he had that red could indicate infection. Without water or herbs to clean it, such a wound could kill him if he wasn't careful.

Bernie leaned forward in concern when she noticed him not speak, and he didn't want to worry her. They were in enough trouble as it was and he refused to add to it. "It's looking better," he lied, giving her a smile.

"Are you sure?"

"If it's bad, I'll tell you."

She gave him a look that showed she didn't believe him, making him wish he was stuck with someone who wasn't so clever.

"So..." she continued after a moment of silence. "We're lost."

He nodded solemnly. "It looks that way."

She smirked. "Thanks for being honest about that."

"Why wouldn't I be?"

"Typically guards like to pretend everything is perfect when it isn't."

"That's because we don't want to worry you."

She let out a laugh. "So you don't mind worrying me?"

If that were the case, he would've told her about his aching shoulder. "I'd rather not worry you, but you're a smart girl. You knew we were lost even before I did."

"That was just my pessimism talking. Truthfully, I wished we found the camp."

"We still may."

"Once this fog clears up, at least."

Marcus rested his back against the tree trunk as well, feeling so tired all of a sudden. He didn't know when the fog would clear, but he did know that he and Bernie couldn't overwork themselves. Though he hated to plan for the worst, experience taught him that fate favored the prepared. If they didn't find the camp, they would have to survive the forest until they could be rescued, and that meant living off the land.

"Get some sleep while you can," he said quietly. "We'll need to search for a water source."

"What about food?"

"We can hunt with the arrows I have and gather plants."

"Sounds like a plan," she said. "What about you? Aren't you going to sleep?"

"I'll watch for any predators," he answered. "Now get your rest. We need to save up our strength for when we need it."

---

Bernie didn't know how long she'd slept, but the crick in her neck told her it was too long. She groaned when she got up, too sore to move and feeling a gnawing pang in her stomach that begged for food. Her throat was dry, too, and she realized that it was the worst she'd ever felt when waking up.

"Ugh..." she moaned as she leaned forward, turning to the knight still sitting beside her. "How long was I out? I feel like I slept on rocks."

She noticed he was looking a little flushed when he met her gaze. He barely moved, nudging his nose upward to point to the sky. "The sun has already moved above us. It should be past noon by now."

She widened her eyes, not expecting him to let her sleep that long. Either she looked really tired or he was too tired himself to rouse her. "Alright, I got enough rest. Now it's your turn. I can keep watch."

"I'm fine," he said, pushing himself up to stand. "We need to move anyways. Water is the next priority."

"Where do you think we'll find it?"

"Where the animals go, water should be near."

He clutched onto the tree trunk to help him stand, but she noticed his balance wavered. He nearly stumbled over when he stood, and she reached out to hold him steady.

"I'm alright," he said softly. "Just a little weak, that's all. Probably from being tired."

"All the more reason you should rest," Bernie replied.

"I can rest when we find water."

He wouldn't take no for an answer, so she let him lead the way. But Bernie noticed his pace was much slower than before, and if she looked really close, she noticed he was starting to shiver. It was cold out, certainly – an Edelandian spring was rarely warm – but it wasn't enough to bring a chill to the bones.

As they walked about, looking for animal tracks in the ground, Bernie decided to take a quick look at his shoulder. Though the bandage was still over the wound, she thought it was starting to look a tad swollen, and the shreds in the fabric around it showed glimpses of red skin underneath.

She wasn't a doctor, but even she knew that wasn't a good sign.

"Your shoulder looks pretty bad."

Marcus looked up, raising a brow. "It's been clawed by a bear. Did you expect anything less?"

"No, I mean it doesn't look right," she clarified. "You don't think it's getting infected, do you?"

"The redness is just dried blood. Once we find water, I can clean it and it'll look better."

She shook her head, wondering if he was just lying to keep her from worry. "You're not feeling feverish, are you?"

"No."

"Would you tell me if you were?"

He looked at her, snickering. "Sure."

Why did she not believe him? She could only scoff internally at his answer. Men…always having to prove themselves the strongest!

They walked some more in silence, and after a half hour, Bernie started to feel bored. Others would find a quiet walk in the forest relaxing, but feeling thirsty and hungry alongside a sore body and aching muscles made her want to get her mind off of things.

"So…how'd you learn to shoot a bow so good?"

Marcus looked at her, seeming thankful for the conversation. "My father taught me."

"Was he a knight, too?" Grant it, she overheard the other guards say he was a craftsman, but she wanted to give Sir Peterson a chance to give the truth. She'd seen a lot of knights in her day, and none of them had craftsmen for fathers.

"Almost..." Marcus said, as if unsure of his answer. "He...left the program to raise his family."

"All the other knights have families too. He shouldn't have to leave just because of that."

"We weren't nobility. Opportunities were few for us."

"Oh." She knew not to press further, remembering back to the guards' accusations of him being illegitimate. She could tell Marcus was not one willing to talk about it, but at the same time she was curious. Perhaps in time, he would tell her more. "Still, your father must've been very talented. Seems he taught you a lot."

"He taught me much," Marcus said, his face warming. "He was the best father a son could ask for."

"Was?"

"He died a few years ago, just before I came to Reigal to serve King Arden."

Bernie frowned, not meaning to bring up such a painful moment. "I'm sorry to hear that," she said. "What happened?"

"He had been ill for a while," Marcus replied. "Heart issues, according to the doctors. He had some pains while working at the smithy that worsened, and he died there."

"You didn't get to say good-bye?"

"No, but my father knew I loved him and he made sure I was taken care of."

"At least you parted on good terms. How did your mother take it?"

Marcus frowned, nearly stopping in his walk as if debating on whether to speak. Bernie looked at him strangely. Even though he was of questionable birth, some woman had to have him.

"My mother..." Marcus began, looking to the ground. "She was...I mean..." He paused, looking back up. "Forgive me, Your Majesty. My mother is someone I rarely talk about."

"Are you not close to her?"

"No."

Bernie stepped alongside him, curious to hear the story though she figured he wouldn't tell it. "I'm not close to my mother, either. Sometimes I think she hates me."

He looked at her, his expression hurt. "Why would you think that?"

"Have you heard her? All she says to me is that I'm fat and ugly and that I need to change." Bernie paused, smirking. "Not that I listen, at any rate."

"It sounds like it bothers you, though," Marcus said. "And rightly so. A mother should be kind and uplifting to her daughter."

"She should, but she isn't," Bernie said with a sigh. "And until I'm pretty enough for her, I don't think she'll ever change."

"She might think that way, but I'm sure others don't. You're a princess. Many must be vying for your hand."

Bernie let out a laugh, making Marcus frown. She didn't care, though. The poor man hadn't been around long enough to know that she was the joke of Edeland. "I wish!" She chuckled again. "I mean, you heard your guards last night. If there's one thing my mother's been right on, it's that I'm not exactly the prettiest princess in the palace!"

She laughed some more, but his frown remained, and after a moment, he shook his head in disgust. "I was afraid you heard them. I'm sorry that they mocked you."

"Don't be. Not like I don't hear it from everyone else."

Marcus met her glance with his own gaze. "You won't hear it from me."

"That's because you're polite. Most people don't have your chivalry." She smirked, looking ahead to the trees. "At least you keep your comments to yourself. It's been refreshing not hearing how ugly I am for a day."

"And what makes you think I'd see you as ugly?"

"Everyone does."

"Your sister doesn't."

"Yeah, but she doesn't count."

"Why not?"

"Because she's nice."

Marcus nodded, a hint of sarcasm in his movements. "So tell me, then. How do you see yourself?"

Bernie raised her brow. "What do you mean?"

"Do you think you're pretty?"

Bernie scoffed. "No."

"Why?"

"Have you looked at me lately?"

"I'm looking at you right now," Marcus answered, suddenly stopping and crossing his arms.

She stopped in front of him. "And?"

"I see a beautiful young woman."

Bernie snickered, rolling her eyes. "Marcus, you don't have to be fake with me. I know I'm not your favorite person to be around."

"You're a bit of a wild one, I'll admit," he said with a grin. "But…in my honest opinion…you are just as beautiful as any other woman I've seen."

"You must not get out much."

"I've been a lot of places, Your Majesty. There isn't much I haven't seen."

"So you mean to tell me all women are beautiful?"

"I do. It was something my father taught me."

Bernie wanted to say that his dad sounded like a flirt who was just happy to get a girl, but out of respect for the dead, she held her tongue. "You must like women an awful lot, then."

"I think you misunderstand me," Marcus said, continuing their walk at a slower pace. "Thinking a woman beautiful and being attracted to her are two different things. If I'm attracted to a woman, I find features in her that I don't see in anyone else, and these are features that I find myself drawn to, complementing the needs and wants in my life."

"Like a skinny waist and voluptuous curves?"

"Like a loyal heart and brilliant mind."

"Ah," Bernie said, nudging him in the arm. "You must be single." Either that, or he was lying through his teeth, because *all* men went for women with looks.

He smiled at her response, continuing in his speech. "Unfortunately true, but that is another point. Beauty is different from attraction. It is the unique appearance of every individual that sets them apart from someone else."

"So everyone is beautiful?"

"Yes."

"I think you'd find people disagreeing with you on that statement."

"It doesn't make it any less true," he continued. "My father once said that people are like flowers. All unique, all different. Some are tall, some are wide, some are short, and some are thin. Some smell good while others not so much. Some are vibrant while others are plain.

"He then said that beauty is best explained by the flowers. One day, while I helped him in the smithy, he asked each customer what the most beautiful flower was. Some said roses. Others said carnations or tulips. By the end of the day, over twenty different flowers were named, all with each person saying their flower was the most favored of them all.

"My father then went on to explain that even though people had different opinions on what was the most beautiful flower, all of them were still beautiful. Though one thought the rose was hideous, another swore its beauty rivaled a sunset."

"So what does that have to do with people like me?" Bernie asked.

"The point I'm trying to make is that though some see you as a dandelion, others see you as a rose," Marcus answered. "Likewise, someone else may see me as a rose, but others...probably you...would see me as a dandelion."

He smirked at her, and she wondered if that was his attempt at a joke. She couldn't help but laugh in response.

"So regardless of whether we are roses or dandelions, we are always beautiful in someone's eyes," he continued.

"You know, for the record," Bernie said with a blush, "I like dandelions."

"You know what?" Marcus added, smiling back. "So do I."

# Chapter 12: By the River

"Have we found water yet?"

Marcus grunted as he trudged on, barely hearing Bernie's persistence. Thankfully the fog had dissipated and they could finally see where they were going. They had been walking through the forest following animal tracks for hours and had yet to find any water, but the way she talked, it was as if they were going on a carriage ride and waiting to arrive home.

"No," he muttered, his body feeling so weak he felt as if he could collapse.

"I'm really thirsty."

So was he, but his mouth was too parched to say it.

"I'm hungry, too."

He guaranteed the gnawing in his stomach was more painful than hers.

"You'd think finding water would be easier than this."

The survival texts he studied in Circh made it sound simple, but he was starting to see that reality was more difficult than words from a book. He was exhausted from two days without sleep. He was hungry and thirsty from no food or water. He was sore and achy from the edelbear attack. He was cold, lightheaded, feeling terrible from who knows what...

A wave of dizziness overtook him and his words were stopped as he tumbled forward, hitting the ground hard with his knees. He heard Bernie call out his name as she rushed to him. "Whoa! Are you alright?"

"I'm fine." he muttered, releasing himself from her grip as he stood back to his feet.

"That's…not very convincing…" She put her hand on his arm, stopping him as he tried to move again. "Maybe you should rest."

He pulled his arm away. "I'd rather find us water." He stumbled once more as he tried to walk, and before Bernie could catch him, he fell back to the ground.

"Something's wrong," Bernie said.

"It's probably dehydration."

"But…"

"No, we need to keep moving." He forced himself up and went forward, his steps shaky as if on uneven ground.

"Are you dizzy?" Bernie asked as she stayed near him.

He was, but it wasn't anything he couldn't handle. As long as he could walk, he would be alright. "I'm fine."

She gave him a stare, beading her eyes after looking at him, and she muttered, "That bear hit your head, right?"

He nodded.

"Do you think you have a concussion?"

He wouldn't be surprised if he did. Bears weren't known for giving little pats with their paws. "There's not much I can do if I've got one."

"You'd need to rest. You're not letting your brain recover."

He smirked, glancing at her. "Are you an expert on medicine, Dr. van Echt?"

She chuckled. "No, but I can read. I went through a phase when I was thirteen and read anything and everything medicine related."

He was about to say something again until his feet gave out from under him, and he stumbled once more. "This isn't working," Bernie muttered as she grabbed hold of his arm. "You really need to rest. When was the last time you slept?"

Two days, though in the past week he'd slept for a total of five hours…maybe…

"You've barely slept, haven't you?"

He shrugged, not wanting to answer.

"You know that can kill you, right?"

"That hasn't been proven," Marcus replied.

"Well I'm hoping you're not volunteering to prove it because your body can't function without rest." She sat on the ground, urging him to stay down. "We're stopping *now*. You need to sleep."

"We have to find water first, Your Majesty. We can only go so long without it before dying of thirst."

"But…"

"I appreciate your concern, but we have to keep going." He moved to stand up, but she immediately pulled him down again.

"I'm not moving until you rest."

If there was one thing he both admired and hated about Princess Bernette, it was her stubbornness. She could be more loyal than a parent, but she'd ignore reason just to get her way when she thought herself right.

"If you won't take care of yourself, then I'll make you! I'm not about to explain to Edward why I let you get yourself killed."

Marcus let out a sigh, but as he was about to retaliate, he thought he heard a strange sound.

"So what we need to do is make a bed with these leaves..." Bernie continued as she started making a pile. "That'll keep you warm. If you lend me your bow, I'd be happy to keep watch while you sleep and..."

"Wait." Marcus put his finger to his lips, quieting her as he felt a faint rumble from the ground. He put his free hand on the dirt, feeling for more vibrations in the earth, listening intently. He could hear the faint sound of a river, and as he looked ahead, he could see a small group of deer in the distance.

"I think we've found it."

"Found what?" Bernie asked.

"Water." He forced himself up, using whatever adrenaline he could gather to move, and he rushed to the left, Bernie following close behind.

They made their way down a small hill and past a thick grove of trees, but once they stepped past the last branch, the most wonderful sight beheld them.

A fast-flowing river, clear and unpolluted, was ahead.

"Oh, thank God!" Bernie rushed forward to the source, Marcus trailing close behind.

"Wait! Check it before you drink to make sure it's not foul."

She bent down, scooping her hand into the water and putting it to her nose. "There's no smell and it's clear and cold," she said, taking a sip. "And it tastes good! I think it's alright."

Marcus knew even fresh water could carry sickness, but with no pots to boil the water in and no guarantee they would find another water source, there were few options. They would drink and pray no sickness would come.

He bent down beside her, drinking what he could, the coldness of the liquid putting a chill in his bones. He thought the water would be more refreshing than it was, and though Bernie had already drunken what seemed like a gallon, he barely managed a few sips, his body not wanting to drink.

The pain in his shoulder worsened, and he glanced at it, noticing it seemed redder. "Keep drinking. I'm going to clean my shoulder."

"I can help."

He knew she meant well, but whether it was embarrassment for having to take his shirt off in front of her or simply because he was too tired to deal with it anymore, he knew he'd rather be alone. Besides, they needed to find food now that they had water.

"Finding food would help me more. Do you know which berries and plants are edible and which aren't?"

"Yes."

"Then stay near the river and gather some. I'll join you once my shoulder is cleaned."

"Can you reach it alright?"

"I'll be fine."

She nodded, almost hesitantly, but scurried to the distance, looking around the trees for food.

He bent down towards the water, taking a piece of his tunic and ripping it off for a cleaner rag. He carefully removed the bandage Bernie had put on him, slipping off half of his shirt and outer tunic to get a better look at the wound. Once he saw it, however, he felt his heart fall to his stomach.

The wound was red and his shoulder had already swollen considerably. Red streaks could be seen making its way down his arm, and as he started to chill harder from being exposed to the air, he began to realize he was running a fever.

Infection had already set in, and there were no herbs to cure it.

Marcus said nothing, dipping the rag into the stream and cleaning the wound as best he could before re-dressing it and going to hunt so he and Bernie could have dinner.

---

For the first time in what seemed like ages, Bernie felt good.

Her throat was no longer parched. Her belly was (somewhat) full from the roots and cooked rabbit Marcus had hunted for earlier. She felt rested and alert. Her body was warm from the gentle fire that cackled near, and the wind was blocked away to keep out the cold, the small shelter she and Marcus made out of sticks and leaves doing its job well in protecting them.

For being stranded in the forest two days, things weren't so bad.

Marcus had insisted he take the first watch, letting Bernie rest for a few hours before allowing her to switch places and let him sleep. The poor guy hadn't slept since before they stopped at the trail, and she could only imagine how tired he was. He looked terrible, almost as if he was ill, and she didn't doubt that exhaustion was what made him feel that way.

That was why she didn't wake him when she was supposed to. Sure, he'd be mad about it, but the least she could do was let him sleep. She sat the rest of the night away, glancing up at the stars and going over constellations, eventually getting to watch the sun rise. When hunger called, she headed out of the shelter (borrowing Marcus' bow and arrows, which she was sure he'd be willing to share) to hunt for breakfast. After about an hour of missing every squirrel and rabbit in the forest (and getting an arrow stuck in a tree), however, she decided to go back to her gathering for roots and plants and berries. Once she ate, she drank more from the stream, finally heading back to the shelter.

As she approached, she expected to find a livid knight wondering why his precious bow was missing, but to her surprise, Marcus still remained on the ground, the fire in the pit long out. She thought it strange he was still sleeping after so many hours, but she shrugged it off, thinking his exhaustion went deeper than she thought.

She went on to patch up the shelter, covering any holes and gathering tinder for their fire. Once the sun was directly overhead and noon rolled around, she noticed Marcus still had not roused.

"I know you're tired, but man...that's a lot of sleeping." She went back into the shelter, peeking in to see if Marcus was awake yet. He laid still, his cloak tightly around him as he remained on his side, and she noticed that his face was looking flush.

"Marcus?" she asked.

There was no response, and she bent down to face him.

"Marcus?" she called again, and when she put her hand to his cheek, she jerked it back. He was burning.

She glanced at his shoulder, noticing it was twice its size compared to when she last looked at it, and as she gently moved the bandage out of the way, she reeled back. It was red, practically oozing in some spots, and she knew what it had to be.

Infection.

"Marcus, wake up." She hated to rouse him from the sleep he undoubtedly needed, but she had to know what was going on. Had to know his symptoms, had to know how long he noticed his shoulder getting so bad. She cursed to herself, wondering if she should've been more forward about his injuries instead of relying on him to tell her when he felt bad, but it was too late for regrets as survival became everything.

He moaned as she shook him, and soon she began tapping his cheek harder with each passing moment. It only took a second before he opened his eyes, squinting amidst a glassy haze, looking at her.

"Did I oversleep?" His voice was barely above a whisper, raspy, and Bernie felt a new panic enter.

"Marcus, your shoulder is starting to get infected. I think you're running a fever."

He closed his eyes, looking disappointed. "I…I know…"

Her face started to burn as much as his, anger surging through her veins. "Why didn't you tell me?"

"I didn't want to worry you."

"Well I'm worried now!"

"I'll...I'll be okay."

"No you won't. Not without medicine." She began to think of all the herbs she had studied during her botany phase when she was twelve. Some plants had healing properties, able to treat infection when used right...

"There aren't any doctors out here, Your Majesty," Marcus muttered.

"You won't need one," Bernie replied with a grin. "You just happened to get stuck with a person who studied botany, so I'm going to make you better."

"Botany?" he asked, shutting his eyes again.

"Yep! Now you rest here. I'm going to get you some water and then I'll go searching for herbs to make you better, alright?"

He moved to sit up, but dizziness soon overtook him. "I can help..."

"Not this time, buddy. You saved my life, now it's time for me to save yours."

She meant it as a joke, but after he closed his eyes once more, resting his head on the ground and shivering harder, she realized he was in no mood for banter.

She had to get his fever down and she had to work fast. She gathered some large leaves outside of the shelter, pulling out threads from her dress to make a bowl that she could hold water in, taking another strip from the dress to use as a rag.

She hurried to the river, hoping and praying that somehow God would give her the strength to help Marcus survive.

# Chapter 13: Return to Staalberg

"Ah! Home!" Arnold took in a deep breath as he stuck his head out the window of the carriage, the sight of the palace straight ahead. "You know, this quaint little city is starting to grow on me. All that fresh pine air…"

Antoinette only turned away, thinking of her husband. Though she had been fortunate to spend some nights sleeping in his arms, being away from him during the day had been difficult. She missed him – missed his voice, his smile, his laugh, his touch – and now that she was back home again, that meant returning to secrecy with Mother, having to make over Arnold in public just to keep people believing she was married to him.

Arnold still promised her evenings, but it didn't feel like enough, and she doubted it ever would.

"Cheer up, my dove. As soon as we arrive, I shall insist your mother give us our own home. Within the week you will be able to live with your man in peace. You should be thrilled!"

"I'm still living a lie, though."

"I know!" Arnold gleamed. "Isn't it fun?"

She lowered her brow and pouted, not wanting another argument.

As the carriage pulled to a stop in front of the palace steps, Antoinette gave a sigh of relief. She may have had to put up with Arnold, but at least her days were relieved with her sister. Bernie had been forced to travel with Mother since Audlin, and she could only imagine how eager she was to be reunited with the only family member she got along with.

Antoinette peeked out the window to wave, but after looking at the steps, she noticed only her mother, father, and brothers approach.

She squinted, wondering if she was having trouble with her vision. "Where's Bernie?"

"Hmm?"

She turned to Arnold after not seeing her sister, her voice firm. "I said where's Bernie?"

"Oh I don't know," Arnold replied with a shrug. "Didn't she ride with your mother?"

"That's what you said."

"Then maybe she's in the palace."

"No," Antoinette muttered as she looked back, the door being opened for her. "She would be out here, even if she was ill."

She didn't wait to take the guard's hand as she jumped out of the carriage, hurrying to Mother.

"Welcome home, child! I trust you had a safe journey? Arnold told me he was taking you the scenic route so you could spend some time together."

There was no time for pleasantries as she stopped in front of them. "Where's Bernie?"

"What?"

"*Where is Bernie?*"

"I thought she was with you."

Antoinette felt a panic rise in her heart. She turned as Arnold approached from behind, giving the queen a friendly wave before being nudged in the side by his "wife".

"You said Bernie rode with Mother!" Antoinette hissed.

Arnold looked around, cocking his brow. "You mean she didn't?"

"Does it look like she's here?"

"What's this all about?" Mother asked.

"Bernie's missing," Antoinette replied.

"*What?*" The queen put her hands on her hips, shaking her head in disgust. "Once again that girl has gotten the best of my nerves! Where did she run off to this time?"

"She didn't run off, Mother! She was left behind!" Antoinette glared at Arnold, but he put his hand on her shoulder, giving it a gentle squeeze.

"My dear, you worry so much. I'm sure it has all been a little mistake," he began softly. "Your sister told me she was going to ride with your mother, but I'm sure she had another plan up her sleeve. She was the one who put the bugs into the dinner back in Reigal, right?"

Antoinette nodded.

"Well I saw her with another jar when she spoke to me. Doubtless she was going to pull the same stunt again for breakfast! She probably only told me she was riding with your mother because she didn't want me to snitch on her!"

Antoinette sighed, rubbing her brow as her mother stepped forward. "This does not surprise me. When she was fourteen, we visited relatives in the west and she did the same thing! We had to turn around and go back."

"I know, but Audlin is so far away and she's all alone..." Antoinette felt her stomach sour in worry. Surely Edward would send her back to Staalberg with an escort...

"I wonder, though..." Arnold said after a pause. "And...forgive me for saying this, Your Majesties, but...what if King Edward purposely kept Lady Bernette in Reigal to force us to return to Audlin for her? I wouldn't put it past the man to do such a thing."

The queen lowered her brow, her face firm. "After what he did to you, my dear son-in-law, I would not be surprised. We shall send a letter at once to make sure such a thing has not happened, and if it has, we shall threaten with action!"

Antoinette's eyes widened. "But Mother, surely..."

"Not to worry, child. I shall handle it. For now, I only want you and your husband to rest from your travels." She held out her hand. "Come. I should like to hear all about your trip from Reigal."

"But..."

"It was a wonderful journey, Mother," Arnold interrupted cheerily. "The scenery, the rest, the...romance..." He wiggled his brows as he took Antoinette's hand in his, kissing it. "I daresay I am falling in love with my wife more and more each day! You wouldn't believe what good care she gave me."

"I should like to hear all about it!"

"And I shall be happy to tell," Arnold replied, and off he went.

Antoinette took one final look outside before being led into the palace, and as she turned to the gardens, she saw Emery hiding in the trees, watching her.

She gave a low smile, sending her love through a glance as the door was shut behind her.

---

The crickets were already sounding by the time Emmerich sat down on the grass to rest his legs.

He had watched Antoinette be escorted into the palace with Arnold, following the king and queen for an update on their trip. At first Emmerich thought the talk would be quick and Antoinette would join him in the apple grove like they had planned, but after minutes turned to hours, he was unsure if his wife would ever make it out.

He leaned back against a tree trunk, Waffles quietly grazing and sniffing for any apples hidden by winter.

Emmerich felt a nudge near his knee and gently lifted Waffles' nose away from the ground. "You won't find any snacks," he whispered. "Last time we were here, you ate everything in sight!"

Waffles snorted in frustration, looking around the grove.

"Well if you weren't so hungry all the time..."

Waffles started to neigh, but after a quick hush from Emmerich, the horse quieted down.

"You can't be too loud here, Waffles. If we're caught this time, we'll be done for!" Emmerich sighed as he looked out ahead towards the palace, the windows barely lit from candlelight. "Although, if I'm being candid...I almost would risk getting caught if it'd let me see my wife sooner."

He closed his eyes, thinking back on their last night together, sleeping in one another's arms and waking to the sight of beauty incarnate. His heart longed for Antoinette's presence, and he prayed that he'd be patient enough to withstand the wait.

There was a weight that suddenly became heavy upon his shoulder, and at first he thought it a burden from his thoughts being manifested physically upon him until he opened his eyes and found Waffles resting his head on Emery's shoulder.

Emmerich gave a chuckle as he patted the horse's cheek, hugging him back. "I know, I know," he said. "You're good company, too."

Waffles neighed in delight, but suddenly quieted at the sound of rustling grass in the distance. Emmerich sat up, urging Waffles to remain silent, and stood to his feet, edging closer near the bushes to see who it was on ahead.

At the sight of a young rabbit suddenly appearing (and then disappearing) through the leaves, Emmerich let out a sigh, sitting back on the ground again.

"It's just an animal," he muttered to Waffles in disappointment.

Waffles lowered his head, going back to sniffing the ground for any food.

Emmerich leaned back against the tree trunk, feeling exhaustion from all the travel flow through his veins. Though anticipation kept him awake and alert, he'd be lying if he said he didn't long for sleep. The nights between Reigal and Staalberg were spent with Antoinette or traveling, and instead of resting like he normally would, he would either stay up and chat or love on his wife, taking advantage of whatever moments he could have with her. Though it gave him only around four hours of sleep a night, the sacrifice seemed well worth it.

But his body still begged for rest, and as he waited in the grove watching evening turn into the middle of the night, he rested his eyes, his thoughts overtaking his mind.

*He'd never forget the first time he met Antoinette. Four years old, shy like no other, stuck on a trip to Edeland because his father had to discuss a trade agreement with the newly-crowned King John. Emery remembered being so terrified during the trip, feeling homesick and uncomfortable staying in such different territory. Instead of hills, there were trees closing all around him, making him feel trapped, and instead of the coolness of summer, the weather was hot and humid and sticky. Either the heat or anxiety made it difficult for him to breathe, and he remembered never wanting to let go of his mother's hand when they stepped out of the carriage and into the palace.*

*But he'd never forget what he saw after walking inside. King John and Queen Susanna introduced their young family, and as Emery looked around and glanced upon each of them, he remembered feeling more terrified than ever. He couldn't help but be reminded of his cousins, so mean and constantly bullying him. Would these children be the same? Would they make fun of him, steal his toys, and push him into the mud when the grown-ups weren't looking?*

*He was almost afraid to look them in the eye for fear of being seen. But something drew him to lift his head after pushing it back down, and the first set of eyes he met was of a young girl his age. He squinted, unsure of what he was actually seeing. Was she…smiling at him?*

*All he could do was stare back, unsure of how to react. He couldn't remember the last time someone smiled at him besides his parents.*

*The moment was short-lived as the grown-ups immediately went to work, talking about boring things and eating fancy dinners that Emmerich didn't find very fun at all. Pretty soon he was sent to a parlor to play while the grown-ups talked in the next room, and he found himself in a comfortable, familiar abode: alone with his thoughts and toys, not a soul disturbing him as he quietly kept to himself.*

*For a moment he was all alone, being watched by a governess at the end of the room, but then the door creaked open, revealing that same little girl that smiled at him earlier.*

*He looked up, frozen from his play and holding tight to his toy animals, wondering if she was there to take them like the other children he knew did.*

*"Hi," she said sweetly, stepping inside. "Why are you here by yourself?"*

*Emmerich gulped, not willing to tell the truth in that he was afraid of being bullied. "It's quiet here."*

*"It's quiet out there, too," she said, pointing to the window.*

*He nodded, looking back down at his toys. What could he say to her? Why was she there? Surely she didn't arrive just to be nice to him, right?*

*Her words interrupted his thoughts as she plopped down on the floor in front of him, showing that familiar smile. "Want to play?"*

*"Play?" he asked, confused.*

"Yeah. Play together with our toys or maybe run outside," she answered, holding out her doll. "We can play house."

He looked down at his own toys, a fabric set of stuffed horses being all he had with him. "I just have animals."

"Then we can play farm."

"How do you play farm?"

Her eyes widened. "You've never played farm before?"

He wanted to say he typically never played with anyone except his parents, but he never heard of "farm", whatever that was. It had to be an Edelandian game, he thought.

"It's really easy. My doll can be the farmer," she said, holding the toy up, "and your horses can be the animals. Then we can pretend what they do."

He nodded again, unsure of how to play, but wanting to learn. "Okay."

She smiled again, and he found himself smiling back.

They went about setting up their toys, the young girl taking some old books off the shelf beside them to create a stable for the horses. As they were setting up their play farm, he heard her speak again.

"What's your name?"

"Emmerich," he answered quietly, hoping she wouldn't make fun of it like his cousins had.

"Emmerip," she repeated.

"Emmerich," he clarified.

"Emmerish."

*He smirked, shaking his head.  The girl paused for a moment, scratching her chin, until she held up her finger and said, "How about I just call you Emery?"*

*He never heard himself get a nickname before, but he couldn't deny that he liked it.  Emery – it was a name that fit him well.*

*"Okay.  What's your name?"*

*"Antoinette."*

*"Ant…uhm…Ant…"  He blushed, embarrassed he couldn't say her name properly.  Even though she had messed up his name, he hoped he'd be able to pronounce hers well so she'd like him.  Now that he couldn't say her name right, she'd surely be mean to him.  He lowered his head, unwilling to even look at her, afraid of what she might say.*

*"You know what?  You can just call me Anty," she said, making him look up in bewilderment.*

*"Anty?" he asked.*

*"Yeah," she answered.  "My sister calls me that all the time."*

*He didn't want to remind her that her sister was only two and practically a baby, but at least he wasn't in trouble.  He watched, amazed that the girl in front of him was still around being nice to him.  Maybe…just maybe…he could open up and be nice to her back.*

*"Here," he said, holding out one of his plush horses.  "This is Waffles.  You can play with him so your farmer has a horse to ride."*

*"Waffles?" Antoinette giggled as she took the horse in her hand.  "That's a funny name.  What's it mean?"*

*"I named him after this new food I tried with my mommy and daddy on a trip. It was really good!"*

*"I like it!" She took the toy horse and gave it a hug. "Hello, Waffles! You seem like a very nice horse."*

*"He's very nice. He won't bite or anything like that."*

*"What about the horse you have?"*

*"Garlic? He's a wild horse. He likes to run a lot, but he always leaves a stinky trail behind." He hopped the toy around the floor, pretending the horse was racing through the fields, pinching his nose in play.*

*Antoinette held the toy horse close to her chest, still hugging it tight. "Thank you for letting me play with the nice horse."*

*"Sure," he answered.*

*They went on to play with their toys, the governess watching quietly with a smile in the distance. Emmerich didn't know how long they'd played, but he remembered feeling so happy having someone else his age spending time with him. It was something he rarely experienced, only getting to play with his cousins Edward and Stephen during holidays when he saw them.*

*But even they weren't as pleasant of company as Antoinette was. Stephen always wanted to be left alone and Edward never liked to share or do anything other than what he wanted. Antoinette, though…she was different. She enjoyed his company, wanted to share and play and do things they both wanted to do.*

*And in the midst of their play, he heard her say three words followed by four that would change his life forever. "I like you," she said, facing him. "Want to be friends?"*

*He couldn't tell her no one ever asked to be his friend before. He almost wondered if he'd ever have one. His smile widened and he scooted closer to her, giving a nod. "I'd love to be your friend."*

*She took his hand in hers and held it. "Friends forever, then?"*

*The touch of her hand around his felt so warm, and he never wanted to let go. "Forever," he repeated.*

*The rest of the day was spent together, and they practically had to be forced apart at bedtime because they were having so much fun playing. But that day was truly the beginning of forever for them, and Emery would never forget the first friend he ever made.*

*He didn't know it back then, but he wondered if it was the first time he knew he loved her, too.*

His thoughts became dreams and his wife filled them, everything from her touch and smile to her voice and laugh lifting his soul as he slept. In his dreams he was there with her, full of so much joy in being free to express his love to her in the open. She was in his arms, passion keeping them warm despite the cold around them, and as he spoke sweet words in her ear, he suddenly felt her hand upon his face, turning him and speaking in a soft voice.

"Wake up, sweetheart."

"I'd rather not," he muttered.

"Emery," she repeated, her voice becoming quiet. "Wake up." Her words continued until he finally realized he was dreaming, and he slowly opened his eyes, seeing his wife caressing his face and meeting his gaze.

He tried to sit up after smiling at her, noticing her hooded and cloaked form glistening in the moonlight. "How long was I...?" he asked, stifling a yawn.

"Not long," Antoinette answered, sitting across from him. "I had to wait until everyone in the palace was asleep before I could sneak out."

"What time is it?" he asked.

"Two in the morning."

He closed his eyes again, feeling so tired and wanting rest. "It is later than I thought."

"I'm sorry, Emery," Antoinette said, her touch waking him back up again. "I would've come earlier, but Arnold and Mother wouldn't leave me. We were working on sending a message to bring Bernie back from Reigal."

"Bernie?" He blinked, concern coming across his face. "What's wrong with Bernie?"

"She was left behind in Audlin by accident."

"*What?* How did that happen?"

"It was a misunderstanding, apparently. Mother thought she was riding with us and we thought she was riding with Mother."

"Is she alright?"

"I hope. Mother has sent a message to make sure she comes back safely. This did happen once before, so..."

"She wouldn't leave you alone, though," Emmerich replied with a frown. "Not with Arnold."

"I know," Antoinette said with a sigh. "But she was adamant about getting that bug prank done a second time…"

His face softened after seeing the heaviness in her eyes. He was sure Bernie was fine, despite the nagging worries. It was best not to get his wife concerned. "It's alright," Emmerich answered as he gathered her in his arms, kissing her gently. "I'm sure Edward has sent her here with an escort after we left."

"I still worry over her, though."

"I know. But I know my aunt. She will make sure your sister is well protected on her way here."

Antoinette smiled. "That comforts me."

"If you're comforted, I'm comforted."

She snuggled close beside him, resting her cheek on his shoulder. "You seemed like you were having a pleasant dream."

He smiled, feeling the warmth of her body on his. "I was. I dreamt of us."

"What were we doing?"

"The one thing we can't do."

She frowned, understanding too well. He gave her a gentle squeeze, massaging her back with his hand, hoping for her smile to return. "Before that, though, I was thinking of a memory."

"What of?"

"When we first met."

"That was a long time ago. I'm surprised you remember it."

"I'd never forget meeting you, Anty."

She gave a chuckle, closing her eyes and hugging him tight. "That nickname…"

Emmerich laughed beside her, knowing how much she grew to hate it. Though his nickname stuck, eventually being used by everyone close to him, her nickname faded because she eventually thought it made her sound like an insect or aunt.

"Speaking of ants…" Antoinette said after squirming to the side, rubbing her leg. "I think I just got bit by one. These woods are crawling with them."

"We can go further out if you'd like," Emmerich said. "There's a private spot in the grove with not as many trees or intruders."

"I like the sound of that," Antoinette answered.

"Alright," he said, standing up and helping her to her feet. She held his hand and they walked through the grove, leaving Waffles tied to the tree as he quietly slept.

# Chapter 14: A Night Under the Stars

Antoinette had always enjoyed a walk between the trees, but she had never done it in the middle of the night.

Call it fear of the dark or fear of ghosts that frightened her during childhood tales, but she typically took her walks during the day when she could see where she was going. But now, in the middle of the night as a full moon shined amidst a sea of stars in the sky, she found that the darkness wasn't as frightening as it used to be, and her husband's protective embrace only added to the feeling of warmth that enveloped her in the cool, spring air.

"This is lovely," she said as they stopped in the middle of the grove's opening, looking up at the sky. "I've never seen this many stars."

"It's a clear night," Emery added as he held her close, pointing upwards. "You can even make out the constellations." He drew the lines of the Big Dipper after he took her hand in his, lowering them when finished.

"You know what, though?" she said, looking around. "We've been here before. Do you remember?"

Emmerich glanced about. "It is familiar."

"It's the same place we danced in the rain," Antoinette said with a smile, facing him as he held her in his embrace. "Right after we came back from Reigal last summer. We danced all day…"

"I remember well now," Emery said as he held her hands and began to move around the grass in a familiar dance. "We waltzed right over here…"

He twirled her around, making her laugh, and they moved about the grove, the stars swimming around and making streams of light above their heads. Antoinette arched back, looking up as they spun, the stars and intimacy of the moment making new memory.

"Remember that time we danced at your aunt's wedding?" Emmerich asked.

"We were ten, right?"

"Around that age."

"Bernie got jealous and you had to dance with her." Antoinette chuckled at the memory.

"She also stepped on my foot a lot," Emmerich added, laughing.

"Thankfully she's better now."

"Probably because she had a good teacher." Emmerich pulled her close in a slow dance, his lips nearly touching her ear as his voice lowered to a whisper. "You were always good at this."

"Now you're just flattering me," she teased.

"Flattering would be dishonest," he said as he lowered her in a dip, his gaze resting on her face. "Although, I'll admit you're getting more flexible."

She grinned, batting her eyes. "I've had good practice recently."

"Oh really?" he asked as he lifted her up, beginning a tango. The feel of her knee going up his leg gave him a shiver of delight. "With doing what?"

"Dancing." she said, getting close and nearly touching his lips with her own. "Though it's a bit different from this kind."

"Oh?"

"A bit more…intimate…"

"Hmm…" Emmerich's hands went up her back and to her face, cupping it. "You're intimate often?"

"Only with my husband," she said with a smirk, a twinkle in her eyes.

"He's a lucky man."

"A very lucky man, just like I'm a lucky woman," Antoinette added as she touched his jaw line with her fingers. "Though I think he still has a lot to teach me."

"I think he learns more from you than you do from him." Emmerich fingered the fabric by her shoulder, gently starting to tug it downward.

She copied his motions, untying the small string on his shirt to loosen it. "You think you can teach me some things he can't?"

"Now you're just being flirty, Mrs. van Ketten," Emmerich said with a grin.

"Oh?" She inched closer, pressing her body close to his. "Maybe I should be more direct, then."

She kissed him, her touch deep and loving as he took her in his arms and held her in the moonlight. Simple movements soon turned to passion, and it wasn't long before they were both pulling at the fabrics covering them, lowering to the ground.

They were soon headed into forbidden territory, married though they were. Antoinette lied on her back, pulling him forward, ignoring the pain of the twigs and pebbles digging into her skin. She wanted her husband more than anything at that moment, and the desire that flowed through her veins had never been stronger.

She knew in her mind that if they made love, she risked pregnancy, but she didn't care. Reason was abandoned as she took hold of his clothes, helping him remove them.

Cool air met her skin, making goosebumps rise, but she got more of a shiver from his touch as his lips started warming her.

"We shouldn't be doing this..." he said between breaths. "You...you could get pregnant."

"I won't, Emery."

"Are you sure?"

"I know my body." She pulled him closer, kissing him for a long time. "Just like you know yours. We'll be careful."

"I...I don't know."

"Emery...do you want this?"

He let out a sigh, kissing the crook in her neck. "More than anything."

"One time won't hurt us, then." She held him close, running her fingers through his hair. "Be my husband, Emery, and let me be your wife.  If we're going to give up each other's bodies, then at least let's have one final time before having to wait."

"One last hurrah?" he asked.

"Hopefully not," she said with a smirk.  "But until we can do this again, let's make it the best night yet."

He smiled, and she met his gaze with a fluttering of her heart, enamored by his body bathed in cool moonlight.  He lowered himself, kissing her before going back to their passion, and as he moved in the darkness, Antoinette could only bask in ecstasy, her spirit swimming in a sea of stars.

---

"Your Majesty, you're positively *glowing*."

Antoinette looked up at the two noblewomen she was drinking tea with, lowering her head in embarrassment. Though she was exhausted, not getting back to sleep until dawn after spending an entire night with Emery, her body was still full of energy and excitement that she doubted would go away soon.  Though she had no previous lovers or experience to compare her "last night" with Emery to, she couldn't imagine anyone else making her feel the way he did.  Her body felt like a mixture of cooked pudding zapped with lightning, and the thought of everything he did during the night made the heat rise in her neck.

*Lying in his arms, starlight as their covering.  The feeling he gave overwhelming her soul.  His touch was so warm and gentle, every move meant to please her and her alone...*

*She couldn't help but cry when they were done, her emotions flooding forth.  And when he held her so close, panicking in thinking he'd done something wrong, she laughed as she touched his face, telling him she had never been happier.*

*But the truth was, she never felt so loved. After Edward walked away, she didn't think it possible someone could adore her so much, and Emery had proved her wrong.*

*And she had no problem showing her appreciation.*

"I know that look," the woman said after taking a sip of tea. "From all the yawning she's doing, I'd say she had a rather busy evening with her husband."

Antoinette pressed her lips together, hoping to stifle a smile. "I'm not one to discuss private affairs."

Lady Applebridge faked a grin, putting more sugar in her tea and tapping her spoon a little too hard against the porcelain rim. "Yes, let's keep bedroom talk *private*."

"But look at her! I've never seen her like this," Lady Greendale replied with a laugh. "You look different, Your Majesty. Radiant, even."

Antoinette didn't think she looked as different as before, and even after her wedding night no one complimented her demeanor. Perhaps it was because the night after she first slept with her husband, she had to be separated from him, fearing she'd never see Emery again for a long while. But if she were to admit it, something *did* feel different about this time. Though his lovemaking was the same (a little clumsy yet full of devotion...plus a twig or two that poked her in all the wrong places because the ground was not nearly as comfortable as a bed), there was something...unique...about this last time. She couldn't quite tell what it was, but for some reason, she felt happier.

Which was strange, considering it was the last time they'd be intimate until pregnancy was no longer a concern.

"I'm just having a good day, is all," Antoinette said as she sipped from her tea, a light breeze blowing through her hair. Her eyes glanced in the direction of the wind towards the grove and she felt a warmth as she looked to the trees. She wondered if Emery was there watching over her, though she couldn't see him yet. They promised to meet each other in secret after the gathering for tea ended, and she couldn't wait to see him again.

"Your Majesty, did you hear what I just said?"

Antoinette blinked, turning back to Lady Greendale apologetically. "Forgive me. What was it you were saying?"

"Look at her! She's even in a daze!" Lady Greendale gave a laugh as Lady Applebridge rolled her eyes. "I was just asking how your trip to Reigal went, but apparently you didn't hear me!"

"I'm so sorry, Aurora. I didn't mean to ignore you." Antoinette stifled a yawn, hoping the tea would keep her awake until evening. "I'm still tired from the trip."

"I heard rumors Reigal was unkind to you," Lady Applebridge interrupted. "The queen says King Edward acted foolishly and attacked Prince Arnold. Is this true?"

Antoinette kept the tea cup to her lips as she nodded, hoping to drop the subject.

"Oh my! What intrigue!" Lady Greendale exclaimed. "Why did King Edward do such a thing?"

Antoinette shrugged, wishing she could blab Arnold's infidelities. "I'm not sure. I only arrived after it happened."

"And where were you? Why weren't you with your husband?" Lady Applebridge demanded.

"I was at the toiletry doing what all ladies do," Antoinette said with lowered brow. "I was gone for only a moment. Edward arrived during that time."

"Awfully convenient timing," Lady Applebridge muttered under her breath.

"But don't you understand, Candace? It sounds like the king was jealous!" Lady Greendale clapped in delight, Antoinette wanting to laugh at the young girl's obsession with gossip. "Oh, what it must be like to have a former love still pine for you! I bet he attacked Prince Arnold out of envy!"

"And you'd better believe that I fought back!" Antoinette turned to see Arnold arrive, his voice sounding nasally as the spring allergies started to settle in and his damaged nose healed. "I had the king nearly in tears when I was through with him!"

"How romantic!" Lady Greendale said with a sigh. "To have a man so valiantly defend you! I envy you, Princess Antoinette. What a joy it must be like to be married to such chivalry!"

"It's a pleasure," Antoinette muttered as she sipped more tea. If she could only tell them what *really* happened...

"Look at her, Prince Arnold! Have you ever seen her in such a state?" Lady Greendale gave a snicker. "I daresay I've never seen your wife so happy and so lost in her thoughts."

Antoinette yawned again, excusing herself as she lowered her eyes in embarrassment. "Well, we had a late evening," Arnold continued as he put his hand on hers, sitting beside her on the bench. "And of course, all the travel..."

"I heard you took the long route back to Edeland," Lady Applebridge said. "Ten days instead of seven? That's an awfully long journey."

"We stopped at a few places to have some alone time," Arnold said matter-of-factly. "Although, if I'm being blunt, I didn't feel so alone with the love of my life in my arms."

"Awe!" Lady Greendale exclaimed, though Lady Applebridge only rolled her eyes.

"You flatter me, Arnold, but I don't think we should bore them with the details of our trip," Antoinette replied.

"My little dove, you must forgive me," Arnold said, caressing her hand as he leaned forward. "I can't help but be overwhelmed by your beauty. It's as intoxicating as these spring flowers blooming their scent!"

"Oh, Prince Arnold! You show such affection!" Lady Greendale exclaimed. "If only my husband adored me as much as you adore Princess Antoinette."

"It is a shame he is so ignorant of you, My Lady," Arnold replied. "But I have a remedy that could help make him better, and you must tell him he has to do all three of these things to make the perfect marriage."

"And what are they?" Lady Applebridge asked.

"First, you tell your spouse that you love them." Arnold turned to Antoinette, touching her cheek and whispering, "I love you." She couldn't help but nearly choke on her tea.

"Second, you must compliment your spouse daily." Arnold then touched Antoinette's shoulder, caressing his hand down her arm. "You look lovely as always, my dear."

Antoinette faked a smile, but she was secretly hoping he'd quit.

"And lastly, you must give physical love every evening, whether it be in the fullness of the marriage bed or the tenderness of a kiss." With that, Arnold quickly turned

Antoinette's chin and planted his lips on hers, slipping his tongue into her mouth and trying to get it past her now-clenched teeth.

Antoinette gave a moan, but not the happy kind that made her sound wanting, and after a few seconds of not letting up, she soon grabbed Arnold's hand, digging her nails into his skin to make him stop.

The man had a large pain tolerance as he continued to kiss her, and rather than risk being found out, Antoinette forced herself to bear it. She closed her eyes, attempting to pretend enjoyment, but after Arnold lowered his hands to her hips, she soon pushed him away, giving a nervous laugh as Lady Applebridge gave a concerned look.

"Forgive us," Antoinette panted as she tried desperately to keep herself from throwing tea at Arnold's face. "My husband gets carried away at times." She turned to him, gritting her teeth. "You know we must not show such displays of affection in public, *my dear*. It's much too improper."

"Of course! I forget at times. In Liegen we express our love freely and openly." He turned to the women with a bow. "You must forgive me, ladies. I meant no offense. I just can't help but express devotion to my wife!"

"No offense taken!" Lady Greendale said dreamily. "I'd gladly take the embarrassment if my husband would make over me that way."

Lady Applebridge gave a scoff as she turned back to Antoinette. "Your glow seems a bit dull now, Your Majesty. Perhaps we've tired you out after all."

"A rest will do me good," Antoinette replied.

"Then come, Lady Greendale. We've overstayed our welcome as the princess must rest." She stood to her feet, the other noblewoman following, and she bowed to Antoinette and Arnold. "Good day, Your Majesties. Have a pleasant... morning."

Lady Greendale gave a final wave after bowing, and the women left the courtyard, leaving Antoinette and Arnold alone.

Antoinette remained silent as Arnold gave a wave good-bye, turning back to his pretend wife with a grin. "My, that Lady Greendale is a treat! I should like to see her again."

Antoinette said nothing, standing to her feet and walking towards the grove where Emery waited. "Wait, my little dove!" Arnold called out as he chased after her, giving a motion to the guards to stay put.

He finally caught up and snickered. "My, I've gone and upset you, haven't I?"

"You went too far there, Arnold."

"Too far? My flirtations with Lady Greendale were rather tame this time."

"I'm not talking about her." Antoinette stopped as they entered the grove, taking her hand and giving him a swift *slap* across the face. Arnold groaned as he rubbed his aching cheek, lowering his brow in frustration. *"Don't you ever, EVER kiss me like that again! We agreed that you would never do such a thing!"*

"Darling, it had to be believable," Arnold replied. "If we're constantly cold with each other, then people will think something's amiss. I'm only trying to help you keep this deception going."

Antoinette frowned, wondering if he was right. The way Lady Applebridge was so accusatory towards her, the way she looked as if every word said wasn't to be believed...

"Like it or not, Antoinette, but everyone thinks you're married to me. If you can't convince strangers, then you'll never convince your mother."

A rustling sound of crunching twigs was heard, and Antoinette looked to find Emmerich stomping towards them, his eyes glaring and fixed on Arnold. Waffles trotted behind, somehow looking as angry as his owner, and before anything could be said, Emmerich took a swing of his fist, knocking Arnold in the nose.

*"I told you what would happen if you touched my wife."* Emmerich picked the man up by his tunic, shoving him against a tree trunk. *"Now which would you like cut off first? Your slithering tongue or your groping hand?"*

"Emery, don't." Antoinette gently pulled her husband back, wrapping her arms around his chest. She could feel the pounding of his heart, knowing that his anger was at its highest.

"You're defending him?" Emmerich asked as he turned to his wife.

"No. I'm only protecting you."

*"But he was inappropriate with you, Antoinette!"*

"I know. And I have scolded him for it."

Emmerich's lip turned downward as his voice lowered. "A scold is not punishment enough."

"You two are terrible liars, you know," Arnold chimed in, rubbing the bridge of his nose and giving a sniffle. "Lady Applebridge was getting suspicious of Antoinette here and I stopped a rumor from being started. You should thank me for covering your tracks."

"We don't need your help," Emmerich sneered.

"Of course you don't, because you can fool everyone so well by being ignorant and distant."

"I pride myself for being an honest man, Arnold. It's a shame you do not share that trait!"

"You wanted to deceive Queen Susanna, my friend. This is how you do it. You want to stay married to your wife and keep your head? Then everyone must think she is married to me."

"Deception is one thing, but it can be done without you perverting yourself with my wife!"

"Stop it! Both of you!" Antoinette stepped between them, holding her hands out. "Fighting gets us nowhere!"

"Tell that to the hothead who doesn't appreciate fine theater!" Arnold sneered.

"*I'll show you hothead!*" Emmerich moved forward with fists clenched, but after a call in the distance, all three of them suddenly froze.

"Oh thank heavens! It's the queen." Arnold breathed a sigh of relief as they watched Susanna approach the grove, a letter in her hands.

"You'll need to go back further into the trees and hide," Antoinette said as she turned to Emmerich, touching his arms.

"But we were supposed to spend the afternoon together," he said softly, his face showing hurt.

"I'm sorry, sweetheart. I don't think that's possible now."

"But…"

"Go, Emery! Please hide so Mother doesn't find you."

He frowned, but after a gentle shove from his wife, he took Waffles and started to move back into the density of the trees. Before leaving, however, he pointed to Arnold with beaded eyes. *"We're not finished with this,"* he muttered.

"We never are," Arnold said with a sigh.

Emmerich went back into the trees, giving a final look to Antoinette as Susanna's voice became clearer.

"Antoinette? Prince Arnold? Where are you?"

Susanna was just about to approach when Arnold took Antoinette by the arms and pulled her into an embrace. "At least pretend to enjoy it this time," he said before kissing her again.

Antoinette wanted to vomit, but at the sight of Mother in the corner of her eye, she forced herself to act, closing her eyes and wrapping her hands around Arnold's chest, though it didn't stop her from having a morbid look on her face as the kiss was happening.

"Oh! I didn't know I was interrupting! Forgive me," Susanna said as Arnold pulled away, keeping his hands around "his wife".

"No apologies are needed, Mother," Antoinette said, her voice somewhat shaky as she could feel Emmerich's breaking heart through the trees. She knew he saw what had just happened, feeling the ache in his chest from being unable to do anything about it.

"It is I who should ask forgiveness, Mother," Arnold replied as he drew Antoinette closer, kissing the top of her head. "I'm afraid my desires got the best of me. We went out to take a walk and I was overwhelmed with love!"

"You needn't apologize, Prince Arnold," Susanna gleamed as she looked to Antoinette. "Your wife seems quite pleased with you. I daren't say I've ever seen her face so radiant! But that is not what I came to talk to you about." She held up the letter in her hands. "I've got news from Reigal."

"About Bernie?" Antoinette said, her eyes wide as she stepped forward to see the letter. "That was fast! I thought you just sent the letter."

"This was sent the day after we left Reigal, so they were aware she was left behind. The message is from a Sir Rikert, letting us know that the royal guard is escorting Bernette back to Staalberg," Susanna said flatly. "Apparently she was caught in the kitchen and did not know we'd left. I can't say I'm surprised much. I knew I should've put a lock on that girl's door! Always stuffing her face…"

Antoinette still thought the situation suspicious, but she wasn't surprised Bernie was in the kitchen. She did mention something about an "encore" of the bug incident at dinner. Perhaps she was putting the insects in the morning pastries…

"Did they say when she'd arrive?" Arnold asked.

"The messenger said he rode ahead of them, but they should be a day or two's ride away. Apparently there was a patch of fog near the border that delayed everyone."

"But the royal guard is with her, right?" Antoinette asked, her worry still remaining. "She's not alone?"

"Sir Rikert said that Edward sent the head of the guard…a Sir Peterson, I believe…with three others to protect her."

Antoinette breathed a sigh of relief. Though she didn't get to know Sir Peterson as well as she liked, she remembered King Arden singing his praises when he first arrived. He was a prodigy from Circh, one of the most talented men to ever wield a bow. If anyone could keep Bernie safe, it would be him.

"Can we ride out to meet her?" Antoinette asked. "I've missed her so much..."

"No, child. I've already sent a royal escort to find her and hurry her along. I'd rather not have to deal with any more rabble from Audlin, even if it is a group of knights." Susanna smiled. "Besides, I've got a pleasant surprise for you. Prince Arnold mentioned you and he wanted your own home, and I have found the perfect manor for which you can settle in and start a family!"

"How delightful!" Arnold said with a grin. "I do hope it's close to the palace."

"Very close, my prince," Susanna replied. "It's just down the road!"

"How wonderful! Come, my dove. Let us go and look at our new home!" Arnold tugged at Antoinette, and she inwardly groaned, shuffling her feet as she wanted to spend the afternoon with Emery like she planned.

"Come along, child! You mustn't be so slow!" Susanna urged.

Antoinette sighed, nodding as she picked up her pace. Before she left the grove, however, she turned back to the trees one last time, meeting Emmerich's frowning gaze as he watched her leave.

"I love you," she mouthed to him when her mother wasn't looking. "And I'm sorry."

# Chapter 15: The Princess and the Guard

Marcus was shivering as he huddled closer to the fire, never feeling so cold in all his life. Though his shoulder was looking better thanks to Bernette and her obsession with keeping it clean, he felt his fever worsen. His body ached, his chest was burning, and over the course of a day he suddenly developed a terrible cough that practically choked him every time he breathed.

"Here. Drink this." Bernette held out what used to be a shoulder pad of armor now being commissioned as a cup since her leaf bowl would burn at the first touch of the fire. Marcus lifted his head with a grunt, eyeing the dark, sour-smelling liquid with a grimace. Whatever it was made his nose burn, and it had to have been bad because he was congested!

"What is it?" he asked.

"Edelroot, mushed and made into tea." She made sure she was steady when handing it to him, and he nearly dropped it once it was his. "Careful! Not a lot of herbs here. Don't want you wasting it."

"You want me to drink this?"

"There's no choice in this, buddy. If you want to get better, you drink."

Marcus wondered if he'd be better off being sick. Nausea was never a feeling he was very fond of, and he was certain there wasn't a stomach around that could handle what she was offering him.

"What does it do?"

"Seriously?" Bernie rolled her eyes in frustration. "Edelroot is an herb that helps fight infection. It'll clear up your shoulder, fight off whatever bug you have, maybe even lower that fever of yours." She paused, biting her lip. "It's also used to relieve constipation, but we won't worry about that side effect for now."

At the mention of being guaranteed a chance to mess himself and being the furthest away from any sort of bathroom, Marcus turned his head away. "No. I'm not drinking that."

"Why not?"

"I'm sick enough as it is."

"What? You're afraid of pooping?"

Marcus cocked his brow. From the way she talked, that tea would make him explode, and he was embarrassed enough in being ill.

"You know, people poop. I poop, you poop, my sister poops..."

He cringed at hearing her talk, unsure of whether to laugh or be embarrassed further. "You're rather blunt, you know that?"

"I'm just saying what you're thinking." Bernie smirked. "But trust me when I say the runs are the least of your worries right now." She held it out again, urging it towards his lips. "Now drink it."

"The shoulder's getting better, Your Majesty. In a few days this fever will be gone and I'll be better."

"You've been getting worse, Marcus. The herbs you've had helped your shoulder, but I think what you have now is different. You're sick…like, pneumonia sick."

He scoffed. "I'm fine."

"You barely slept before this trip, so your body was run-down to begin with. It's spring and there's still disease out there, and if your body wasn't properly taken care of, it can become susceptible to illness."

Marcus lied back down, covering himself with his cloak. "How do you know so much about medicine?"

"I went through a medical phase, remember?" she said, taking his cloak and pulling it off of him. "Learned a lot about stuff, like why you shouldn't keep covering up with every blanket you have when you're running a fever."

"But I'm freezing."

"And you're making your body hotter by keeping it hot. Now stop whining like a little baby and take your medicine!"

Marcus coughed again, his lungs burning harder than before. He started to wheeze, feeling the fluid build in his lungs. He never felt this terrible, even during that bout of influenza when he was a child and was bedridden for an entire week.

"Marcus, you won't get better unless you let me help," Bernie said softly. "You took care of me, so now it's time for me to take care of you."

"You don't have to," he said quietly. "It's not your duty."

"I know it's not. But you know what? Not every act of kindness is out of duty. Some people help because they want to."

Marcus smirked. "I thought you didn't like me very much."

"Well, you annoy me," Bernie replied. "But...I wouldn't say that I don't like you."

"Is that an attempt at a compliment?" He chuckled.

"That, or an attempt to make you drink your tea." She kept it close to him, inching it towards his lips. "Now stop stalling and drink it."

He gently put his hand out, moving the drink away. "I thank you for your kindness, Your Majesty, but I'm fine. I'm not that sick."

"Marcus, I think you have the flu or pneumonia. If you don't take care of it now, it'll get worse."

"I'll be alright." He took the cloak back from her hands and covered himself. "I just need some rest."

The princess frowned as she set the shoulder pad back to the ground, muttering her disappointment beneath her breath.

---

Bernie had gotten a pitiful night's sleep. She tossed and turned for hours, worry getting the best of her as Marcus' breathing became raspier and raspier. For a moment he was improving after she first took care of his shoulder, but after what she swore was pneumonia setting in, she noticed he no longer wanted her care. Call it pride or fear of drinking Edelroot tea, either way his stubbornness would come back to bite him. She knew it well. All she could do was pray throughout the night that somehow, someway he'd see reason or a miracle would happen and his fever would break and his lungs would clear.

But as dawn started to approach and she was just starting to get to sleep, she heard a soft voice calling for her.

"Your Majesty…"

The voice was so soft that she almost didn't hear it, but Bernie got up and hurried to the knight, noticing him lying on the ground, shaking.

"What's wrong, Marcus?"

"I…something's wrong…I don't feel right…"

She put her hand to his forehead and quickly pulled it away. He was burning hotter than ever before, and his eyes were so glassed over and watery that he was practically crying without knowing it.

"Your fever's too high," she muttered as she forced the cloak off of him. He gave a groan, shaking even more, but she forced his complaints from her mind as she pulled him to his feet.

"Get up. We need to get to the river."

"Why?"

"I need to bring your fever down now."

"But…"

"If I don't, you'll die."

He didn't say anything as he nearly fell into her arms, barely able to walk. "Work with me, Marcus! Stay awake and at least make it to the water."

"I…" He paused, giving a cough. He nodded, unable to say anything as he forced himself to move.

They barely were able to walk as they headed away from the camp and towards the river. Bernie was thankful there was enough light coming through that they could see where they were going, and the river wasn't too far away. She urged him forward, practically shoving him towards the water, and when they finally reached the bank, she sat him down and began pulling off his boots.

"What are you doing?" he asked after collapsing to the ground.

"Something you're not going to like."

He closed his eyes, trying desperately to stop shaking.

She pulled his legs forward, rolling up his pants and taking off his boots and putting a rag to the water. Once it was drenched, she put it to his feet and calves, and he gave a jerk, practically sitting up as he tried to pull himself away. "That's...that's so cold..." His voice shook as his teeth started to chatter.

"It's not as cold as you think." She dipped the rag into the water again and soon began rubbing his face and neck with it. He shuddered, keeping quiet as she worked. She took a scoop of water in her hand and then wet his hair down, taking a tug of his shirt.

"Why are you doing that?" he asked after she tried to pull it off him. He pulled his shirt back down, giving her a glare.

"It's not what you think," she said, holding up her newly-dipped rag. "I need to cool off your back and stomach. Either I get your shirt all wet or we take it off, I cool you down, and then you get a dry shirt back on."

"I'd rather you not take off my shirt."

"Marcus, I have two brothers. It's not like I haven't seen a man's chest before." She pulled at his shirt again, but he pulled it back down.

She wanted to curse his manners. Didn't he realize she was trying to save his life and not seduce him? What kind of girl did he think she was?

She rolled her eyes at him, and after a moment of tense silence, he finally caved. "Fine," he said with a groan.

"You'll thank me later when I save your life." Then she slapped his hand away and yanked his shirt off.

Now if she wasn't in the midst of playing doctor, she would've admitted that Marcus really did have a nice chest...perfectly built and muscular that was firm to the touch...but she had to stay focused. She needed to help, not gawk at him.

But bless it, if it wasn't so difficult...

She ignored his handsomeness for a moment as she dipped the rag again and moved to his back, Marcus remaining quiet the entire time.

"I'm going to go over you once more, alright? I think the water's bringing your fever down." She washed down his legs and feet before going back to his chest, back, and arms. She then finished with his face and neck before scooping up some more water and washing his hair down.

"There. That should help," she said. "Now try and drink some water. The coolness of it will bring your temperature down from the inside."

Marcus nodded, lowering his shaking hand into the river and sipping the cool water slowly. "It's...very...cold..."

Bernie put her hand on his shoulder, attempting a comforting touch. She normally wouldn't force cool water on him because it risked sending him into shock, but his fever was so high and needed to be brought back down…

"Do you…do you still have that tea?"

Bernie nodded, feeling thankful she kept it instead of dumping it like he wanted her to. "Yeah. It's back at the shelter."

"I think I'll…have some now…"

He had to have been really sick to be willing to drink the edelroot tea, but Bernie was thankful he swallowed enough pride to accept help. She put his shirt back on, keeping the outer tunic off so only his undershirt remained, and helped him to his feet. "Come on. Back we go," she said.

He nodded, leaning in to her as she led them back.

---

Marcus had never tasted a more foul concoction in his life.

Edelroot tea was sour at first, turning bitter once it trickled down the throat. He nearly coughed it up after swallowing, but in desperation to survive whatever illness plagued him, he forced it down, hoping his burning stomach wouldn't regurgitate whatever it was now churning inside.

"This is terrible," he muttered.

"Well, I've never been known for my cooking skills."

"I think a chef couldn't make it any better."

"Stop talking, more drinking. I want this whole thing gone."

Marcus nodded with a grimace, forcing the rest of it down in a quick gulp. He nearly gagged after finishing, but it was finally gone, and he set the armor cup beside him, lying back down atop his cloak.

"When will it start working?" he asked.

"I don't know. You let your fever get pretty high so it might take a little longer." She paused, taking her leaf bowl and dipping a rag into it, wetting it with water. "I'll keep your fever down, though."

He tried to stop the shaking that wanted to overtake his body as she wrapped his feet in the wet cloth. "That's...freezing..."

"The water's lukewarm, Marcus, and it's nice outside. You're just running a high fever still."

He wanted to curse at his rotten luck, repeating the same prayer over and over in his mind as illness nearly overtook his sanity. *I can't be sick, I can't die. I'm supposed to protect the princess and bring Emmerich van Ketten back to Reigal. I have to protect Edward and Calimus. Please, God in Heaven...don't let me die...*

He knew he should've drank the tea before his fever worsened, and now...as he lied in the middle of a forest all hungry and dehydrated and feeling so sore he thought he had been beaten...he began to wonder if he'd ever be well again.

It was possible the fever would kill him, leaving Princess Bernette stranded in the forest alone.

His heart pained at the thought of her being by herself. Though he didn't doubt she'd survive longer than most, eventually hunger or the elements or animals would end her. It was a terrible way to die, especially for a woman...a woman who deserved to have a wonderfully long life.

As he watched her take more edelroot and fix it into tea, he started to realize that maybe he was wrong about Bernette. Though vibrant in personality and somewhat judgmental, he noticed that deep down inside, she really was a good person. Her personality showed a love of joy and honesty. Her judgments masked a fierce loyalty to those she loved. Her love of books and knowledge made her practical and able to adapt to situations, keeping a cool head under pressure. Her hard work in caring for him showed that even to her enemies she could show kindness, and she was not one to give up without a fight.

She was smart, faithful, caring…practically everything he had ever wanted in a woman that he could never find in anyone he'd met before.

"I know you won't like it, but I'm making you some more of that tea," she said, giving it a quick stir with his hunting knife. "Not that I'm going to make you drink it right away, of course. I'll let it get cool so it won't bring up your temperature and you can drink it at the end of the day once the stuff you just had wears off."

"Thank you," he said quietly. "I'll trust your advice."

"About time," she said with a chuckle. "Now let's wipe you down once more and then you can rest, alright?"

He nodded, watching as she took the rag and dabbed it on his face gently, going down his neck and towards his chest.

He tensed when the water touched his sternum, and he wondered if she'd have him undress again. Thankfully, however, she allowed him to keep his shirt on, saying nothing as she dabbed around his shoulders before going back to his neck and head.

He was shivering hard by the time she was finished, and he hadn't felt so terrible in his life. She propped up his cloak in a folded wad to make a pillow for him, and gently laid him atop of it, stroking his damp hair.

"I want you to rest now, alright? I'm going to go find some berries and plants to scrounge up for food and I'll wake you when it's time to eat." She moved to get up from the ground, but he gently took her hand, pulling her back.

"Wait."

She looked at him curiously. "Everything okay?"

Perhaps it was fear finally taking hold of him, but in case he went to sleep and never woke up again, he wanted her to know. "I must speak with you. Just for a moment."

She nodded, sitting close beside him and placing her free hand atop his. "Sure. What is it?"

He swallowed hard, feeling terrible his shaking was so bad it was even affecting his voice. "I wanted to ask your forgiveness."

She snorted. "For what? You didn't do anything wrong."

"No, my lady. I've been very wrong and wish to make amends in case I no longer have the chance."

"Hey." She lowered her brow, leaning close. "No sad talk with me, you know. I'm praying hard for you to recover and you better believe you're going to get better!"

He smiled, the thought touching him. "I didn't know you were praying for me."

"Just because I don't shout it out loud doesn't mean I don't pray," she said. "Trust me; if I didn't think God could make you better, I wouldn't bother asking!"

Her faith astounded him, and he gave her hand a gentle squeeze. "Then I should tell you what's on my heart, regardless of my circumstances. I wished to tell you I was wrong."

"About what?"

"You."

"Marcus, I'm pretty sure you were right about me," Bernie said with a chuckle. "I know I can be annoying."

"No, my lady. I was wrong. I was judgmental and thought you a wild woman without a care for anyone other than yourself and your sister."

Her smile faded and she lowered her head, making him pull her hand closer to his heart as he continued to speak.

"You must forgive me, Lady Bernette, for my pride and lack of judgment, for I have never been so wrong about a person in all my life."

She lifted her head, looking at him curiously.

"I have met many people – both men and women – who do not have even a pinch of the kindness you possess." He paused, coughing for a moment. "I...I don't think anyone besides my father has ever given me such care."

"You're an easy patient," she said with a smile.

"Now that I've listened," he added, smiling back. "I should've drunk that tea earlier. I would probably not be as sick as I am now."

"But you'll get better."

"Perhaps," he said, his face becoming more serious. "But if I don't...I just wanted to say that I'm glad it is you who will be with me, though I am sorry for failing to bring you back home."

He could've sworn he saw her lip quiver at his comment, but she forced a smile, clasping his hand hard. "You and I are *both* going home. As much as you want to see your dad, I don't think he wants to see you just yet. You've still got a lot to do before it's your time to go."

He smirked, looking away for a moment. "If I wanted a long life, I wouldn't have become a knight. I don't fear death."

"Sure," she said. "But you're young, you know? You've got a lot going for you, so you can't give up. You've got Edward and...whatever his kid's name is...to protect, not to mention a whole royal guard to lead! And what about your mom? You don't want to leave her all alone, do you?"

He frowned, thinking of his mother. "She wouldn't be alone."

"Well she'd still be upset if you went."

He almost wondered if she would. Chances were his missing status would soon be listed as a casualty, and his name would be listed among the soldiers who were killed in the line of duty. With being head of the guard, word would spread quickly through Reigal of his death. When she heard his name, what would her reaction be?

Or would there even be a reaction?

His heart ached at the thought of it.

"I don't know if she'd even be aware," he said quietly, turning his head.

"What do you mean? Of course she'd know!"

"Your mother is not like my mother, Your Majesty," Marcus replied. "Mine left right after I was born. She didn't want me, so my father raised me alone."

Bernie was quiet at first after he spoke, but after a moment of silence, she moved around to face him, her features firm. "But she'd still know you're there. She's your mother. She still cares."

"My heart hopes that she would, but...my mind tells me that she wouldn't." He paused, thinking back on the memories. "The last time I saw her was a year ago, and it was by accident that we met. Before then, I saw her last when I was a baby."

"What happened?" Bernie asked.

"I was in the market buying food. I came across a little girl who was lost and looking for someone. I helped her, asking what her name was and who she was looking for. She said her name was Rose and that she was looking for her mother.

"I went about the market searching for this mysterious woman, and after a few minutes of wandering, I finally found her. Rose ran to her mother, jumping into her arms as the woman wept and held her daughter, terrified something had happened.

"It was when the woman calmed and stood to look at me that I recognized her. Though I hadn't seen my mother since I was a baby, my father had always kept a painting of her, and I recognized her face. And when she told me her name, I knew it was her, for my father's friend said she remarried and was under a different name."

"She asked me who I was and I told her. At first she looked at me funny, but after a moment she only laughed and thanked me for saving her daughter. She barely said a good-bye before going back to her husband and never speaking to me again."

Marcus paused, the pain of the memory almost unbearable, and he watched as the princess looked at him with pity. "Sometimes I wonder whether she really didn't recognize her own son that day, or was it that she did recognize me but didn't want to acknowledge it?" He shook his head, scoffing. "Either way, if I die…she doesn't care. No one would. I have no family and very few friends. There would be little mourning for me."

"If I died, I think Antoinette would be the only one to miss me," Bernie replied sadly. "But don't say that you wouldn't be missed. I'd…I'd miss you."

He almost didn't believe her when she said it, but the look in her eyes told him she was being truthful. She could be an honest woman, never afraid of hiding the truth when she meant it.

"If our roles were switched, I'd mourn for you as well," he said, noticing their hands were still clasped together.

"Then I suppose we should both survive this little adventure, huh?" Bernie said, her smile warmer than the small fire going near them. "Can't have a sad knight and sad princess being all mopey in the forest, right?"

He smiled back. "No, I suppose not," he answered. "But may I ask you one more thing before I rest?"

"Anything," she said.

"Whether I depart this world or stay in it, I wish to be on good terms with you." His eyes met hers in a simple gesture. "Despite our differences and past, can we be friends from this day forward?"

She smiled. "Absolutely. But..." She pursed her lips, pausing for a moment as if unsure whether to speak. "Okay, if we're friends now, then...I guess I should come clean."

"About what?" he asked.

"It was me who put the bugs in the dinner salad back in Reigal."

He lowered his brow playfully at her. "I knew it."

"Not a harmful prank, of course," she muttered. "Just a...you know, way to get back at Arnold, Edward, and Malina (and maybe Mother) for being mean to my sister."

He snickered, the laughter lifting his spirits. "I suppose I should come clean, too."

"About?"

"I knew there were worms in that pastry you ate. I only gave it to you thinking I could get a confession about the dinner."

She let go of his hand, putting her own on her hips and scoffing. "I knew it!"

"I promise I thought you wouldn't eat it," he said with a laugh that quickly turned into a cough.

"Well, you're lucky I'm in a forgiving mood," she said, putting her hand back on his. "Though don't be surprised if you get pranked once you're feeling better. I'm known for paybacks."

"As long as it doesn't involve drinking that tea again, I welcome the challenge."

"Buddy, you don't know what you just got yourself into."

"Either way, it'll be an adventure."  He smiled, the feel of her hand on his becoming the greatest comfort as he closed his eyes, finally going to sleep.

# Chapter 16: A Dire Message

"Darling, are you not hungry?"

Antoinette looked up from her dinner, the roasted venison and potatoes unappetizing as the plate remained untouched. She was far from hungry, her mind too concerned to eat. She scooted the plate forward, taking her napkin and placing it on the table. "I suppose not."

The queen gave a frown as she looked to Arnold, already on his third plate of food. "Are you ill?"

"Worried," Antoinette clarified. "Shouldn't Bernie have been here by now? It's been five days since we've sent out our escort to meet her near the border."

"I admit they're a little late," Susanna replied, sipping her broth. "Though I've heard the fog has been thick in the wooded parts. Traveling is slower in the spring because of it."

Antoinette leaned back in her seat. "That doesn't ease my worry."

"Fret not, my sweet," Arnold chimed in. "I'm sure all is well and Lady Bernette will arrive by the end of the morrow. She never was one to be on time for things, so why would she rush back?"

*Because she knows I'm stuck with you,* Antoinette thought to herself. She let out a sigh, a strange feeling in her gut that told her something was wrong.  She knew it, felt it…but couldn't explain why.

"If you'll excuse me," Antoinette said.  "I'd like to go for a walk."  She got up to leave, hoping to go into town where Emmerich stayed at Father Thomas' church until their new manor could be furnished.

"I shall go with you," Susanna said, standing to her feet.

"Mother, you needn't bother…"

"I insist, child.  There are things we need to discuss, anyways."

Antoinette nodded, feeling sorrowful that she'd be unable to see Emery *yet again*.  It had been four days since spending time with him, and she could only imagine the loneliness he was starting to feel, separated from his wife as he stayed hidden at the church.

Susanna led Antoinette out of the room, walking her down the hallway as a gentle rain fell and patted the windows to their side.  "Tell me – how goes married life for you?"

Antoinette kept her eyes up front.  "It's going well."

"And Arnold is pleasing you?"

"Very…much…"

"I am glad to hear of it," Susanna continued as she took her daughter's arm and hooked onto it with her own.  "For a moment I was starting to worry that you would never give the man a chance, but after seeing the way you stood by him in Reigal, I am no longer concerned."  She patted her arm, giving a warm smile.  "I am glad to see you caring for your husband. Once you have children, your bond will grow even larger."

"Children are still far off, though," Antoinette added. "I'm not sure I'm ready for a baby just yet." She paused after seeing Mother's brow rise. "I mean, I want to make sure Arnold and I have time with each other before a child adds to our stresses."

"Of course. I suppose I can see the reasoning behind that," Susanna said. "Though I hope you don't wait too long. Your clock is ticking and you have only so many years of childbearing left."

Antoinette wanted to remind her mother that she was only nineteen and had practically three decades to give birth, but speaking would only bring about an argument, and she was in no mood to participate.

"You know what I've been thinking?" Susanna said with a spring in her step. "Prince Arnold has brothers...one of whom is single. Perhaps we can arrange Bernette to marry him."

Antoinette was about to offer a rebuttal, but a sudden rush of guards stormed through, being closely followed by the king. Antoinette looked to her father, a strange panic in his eyes that she had never seen before. Her stomach fell to her gut as a strange, heavy feeling overcame her. Something was wrong. She could sense it.

"John, whatever is the matter? Why so many guards?" Susanna asked, approaching them.

"Susanna..." John stopped, his voice catching. "Something's been found near the Kurzwood. It's Bernette."

Antoinette's world slowed as she froze along with time, her heart starting to race as she listened to her father give the guard's report. Their words seemed to scatter amidst the fog covering her mind, and the glimpses of reality that came through only filled her with dread.

"We found bodies mauled beyond recognition."

"The carriage and camp were destroyed."

"It's was definitely Bernette's escort. We found her belongings in the carriage car, ransacked."

"We think it was an edelbear attack in the night."

Antoinette found herself shaking, ice suddenly flowing through her veins as she watched her mother quiet, face becoming pale and eyes becoming teary. "Was she there?" Susanna asked with a choke in her voice. "Did you find her?"

"There were three bodies, all of royal guards," John replied. "Bernette and another guard are still missing, though there were two sets of tracks leading opposite ways. A scout, no doubt, who had gone on ahead to mark the trail, and then Bernette's."

"Where did her tracks lead?"

"They were scattered, Your Majesty," the guard replied. "We...found bear prints beside them. We think she was chased into the forest."

A moment of silence followed, everyone too stunned to say a word, but Antoinette knew what was going through their minds. If Bernie was chased into the Kurzwood, only two things would have happened: either she was caught by the bears and mauled or she escaped the bears and became lost in the unending forested maze.

Either option meant death, immediately or soon.

"I want a search team organized now!" Susanna barked, taking a guard by the arm and shoving him towards the door. "Find any man able to guide us through the Kurzwood! I want my baby found *now*!"

"Yes, Your Majesty," the guard stammered. "We've already got a search party at the site looking."

"Then send more!" Susanna shouted, her fists tightening. "And ready my carriage! I want to leave within the hour!"

The guards nodded, scurrying away as the king took his wife in his arms and attempted to hold her.

"I'm so sorry, dear. We'll make sure the funeral is lovely," he said quietly, but Susanna pushed him away.

"No! My daughter is alive! I will not be told otherwise!" She glared her husband away, pointing to the door. "Now either get our carriage ready or move out of my way!"

The king only blinked, taking a step back with a sigh before walking away out the door to check with the guards.

Antoinette stood silently, holding back tears though her lip was quivering, and she put her hand on the queen's arm, tugging it. "Mother..."

Susanna turned and faced her daughter, her features scrunched up as if enduring pain.

"Mother, I want to go with you..." Antoinette stuttered as tears started to stream down her face. "Please, take me with you."

"It's not safe, dearest. You need to stay here."

"I don't care. I want to find my sister. You can't convince me otherwise."

Susanna nodded, her eyes looking away in worry as she put her nail to her lip and bit it. "My wonderful little Bernie..." she muttered quietly to herself. "All alone in the woods...for gracious knows how long..."

"She's smart, Mother. If anyone could survive, it'd be her," Antoinette encouraged, desperate for hope. "And they said another guard may be with her. She wouldn't be alone."

"That worries me, though," Susanna said quietly. "Not every knight is noble, child. What if the forest is not the only danger she encounters?"

Antoinette felt a shiver go up her spine from fear, and she desperately prayed that God would spare Bernie from such an ordeal. But Edward, if he still cared about the past, would surely send knights who were trustworthy to escort her sister. She thought of the men she trusted most in the Audlinian guard – Sir Rikert…Sir Peterson. Perhaps the latter was in the forest with Bernie for protection.

"Gather your things quickly, my dear," Susanna said with a sniffle, breaking Antoinette's thoughts. "We will leave within the hour. Go and inform Arnold."

"Yes, Mother." Susanna then hurried down the hallway, and Antoinette knew she only had a little time to send a message to Emery of what all had happened.

---

"Go, Waffles! Go!"

Emmerich wasted little time in speeding out of Staalberg towards the Kurzwood, his heart beating fast from adrenaline and his mind on high alert as he headed down the trail towards the site Princess Bernie was seen last. He had little knowledge of the matter as the message she sent through Father Thomas contained only a gist of what happened, but the words were clear.

*Bernie missing near the Kurzwood. Edelbears attacked their camp. Three dead plus another missing guard. Possibly lost in the forest. Mother and I are leaving. Please pray.*

Antoinette never had the chance to tell him to go, but he knew it in his heart that she'd want him to be there. He was a Hugellian, therefore an expert on living off the land, and if anyone thought like Bernie, it was him. They shared a common mind, able to think their way out of a situation because no challenge was too great.

But he knew the dangers of the forest. He heard of souls being lost in the Kurzwood, trapped in a maze of foggy terrain full of animals that could eat a man whole. He didn't doubt Bernie was brave enough to face the dangers there, but like Antoinette, he wished Bernie's courage would remain untested. Bravery didn't matter if an animal was hungry enough, and bravery did little against starvation and dying of thirst.

He hoped...prayed, even...that she was alright. Though he didn't have the pleasure to get to know her as well as he did Antoinette, he knew her well enough to call her his friend. Out of everyone, she remained loyal no matter what the struggle, and he could say from the bottom of his heart that aside from his wife, mother, and aunt, she was the only woman he truly loved.

Not that it was a romantic love, though if Antoinette had married Edward like planned, things with Bernie could have been. Rather, his love for her was of a familial sort, she being the sister he never had but wished for. And the thought of losing his sister, well...his heart was crushed enough. It couldn't bear to be shattered again.

*Am I entering the hurricane?*

Bohden's words came trickling back into his mind, and a fear entered his heart. No, this could not be his hurricane, but it would be Antoinette's. And what his wife suffered would become his suffering as well...

*God in Heaven, I beg of You...* His prayers were never prayed more fervently, and he could feel his wife utter the same words in her spirit. *Please protect Bernie. We can't take much more hurt. Please...keep her safe...*

He repeated the prayer, throwing the hood of his cloak over his head as the clouds above him began to thunder.

# Chapter 17: A Growing Sprout

Marcus took in a deep breath of the forest air, thankful for finally being able to breathe. Though the edelroot tea was foul (and caused a rather ghastly moment in which its wonder for constipation relief was demonstrated at a pine tree behind the camp), he couldn't deny its ability to make him better. His lungs, though not completely clear, no longer pained him, and his body aches were more dull than sharp. Even his fever, once thought to be the death of him, was going away.

"Hey! Dreamer boy! Berries are over here." He felt the *thunk* of a small berry hitting him on the nose, and he turned to find Bernie stifling a giggle.

"Didn't your mother teach you to not throw food?" he teased.

"Sure," she answered, picking up another berry from the bush and tossing it at him again, hitting him in the forehead. "But I never listened."

"Why doesn't that surprise me?" He bent down, ignoring the slight dizziness still plaguing his head, and scooped up a handful of berries that had fallen to the ground. He picked one up with his free hand, hitting her on the shoulder.

"Hey! Didn't your dad teach you to check your aim?" She threw another berry at him, playfully sneering.

"Of course. And I'm finding my target every time." He then threw a few more berries at her, pelting her arm.

"Oh no you don't!" She said, grabbing as many berries as she could in her hands. "This is war, buddy! You are so going to lose!"

"You know I'm a professional soldier, right?" he cackled, dodging her throw and nailing a target on her cheek.

"Yeah, but I'm the smart one of the family!" Bernie said as she chased him and threw a few more berries, hitting him in the back. "I never back down from a challenge!"

"Neither do I!"

They threw more berries at each other, some missing and some hitting their targets, splatters of color being seen all over their skin and clothes and hair. Out of ammunition, Bernie then did the next best thing she could think of: she scooped up the muddy ground, her fingers squishing dirt, and she took aim.

"Wait! That doesn't count!" Marcus stopped, lifting his arms in surrender.

"Too late!" She was about to throw it at him until he rushed forward, meeting his hands with hers.

He felt the gush of muddy dirt go between their palms as he slid his fingers between hers, clasping their hands together. "No fair!" she said, trying to fight his strength as he lowered their hands to her side.

"Told you." He smirked as he leaned forward, noticing the blush of her cheeks as she caught her breath. "I'm a professional."

"Well I'm known for getting vengeance." She gazed at him, suddenly quieting as he looked back at her.

For a moment they said nothing, simply staring into each other's eyes, a smile slowly lifting on their lips. Marcus studied her features closely, and he realized that though much of them mimicked Lady Antoinette, there were other parts – fuller lips, brighter eyes, cheeks that blushed pink instead of red, brown eyes like him – that were much more…beautiful.

"You're thinking something," she whispered, still meeting his gaze.

Would he tell her? Should he? He was never one to put his feelings out in the open for fear of them getting crushed. He couldn't end up like his father, dying young of a broken heart. The rejection was too much to bear, too much to handle and face…

"It's okay," Bernie said, her smile widening. "Tell me."

"I don't think words could describe it…" Marcus said, lowering his sight to her lips. The pink shades beckoned to him, and he felt his stomach flip in both nervousness and delight.

"Well, if you can't use words, show me." She leaned forward, and he found himself following, the desire to kiss her too overwhelming to stop.

He closed his eyes, parting his lips ever-so-slightly before touching hers quickly, pulling away just as fast to glimpse her reaction.

Did she accept it? Would she turn him away?

She said nothing, but her face showed more than what words could ever express. She gave a light pant from holding her breath, and she leaned closer to him, giving his hands a gentle squeeze.

He kissed her again, suddenly letting go of her hands and cupping her face as he pulled her close, ignoring the mud and dirt he undoubtedly smeared on her. She didn't seem to mind as she embraced him back, mud drying on his face as she touched his, too. But how he looked was far from his mind, and all he could think of was how right it felt kissing her, holding her in his arms and never wanting to let go.

Was this what love felt like? If so, then he never wanted it to end. No wonder his father loved his mother until his dying breaths, despite the pain she caused. The presence of a woman – her beauty, her voice, her touch, her love – it was worth giving up all sanity for.

"Marcus." He heard her say his name, though how she did it while still kissing him was strange.

"Marcus."

He paused, looking at Bernie as she caressed his cheek. How could she be talking when her lips didn't even move?

*"Marcus, wake up..."*

It was then he suddenly realized he was dreaming, and in a flash he opened his eyes, no longer being in the berry field, but in the darkness of their small makeshift shelter, the pitter-patter of rain gently falling above his head. Bernie had stretched his cloak as best she could to keep water from falling on them, and as he felt the pain of lying on brush and twigs to stay dry, he wished more than ever he was back in the dream.

He gave a groan as he sat up, looking to her as she held out another serving of edelroot tea. "Sorry to wake you, but you have another dose."

He'd been drinking the stuff for two days, hoping to feel better but finding little relief. He took it from her, downing it in one swift chug, being used to the bitter aftertaste it gave.

"Pleasant dream, I take it?"

He looked to her, cocking his brow. "What makes you say that?"

"You were smiling in your sleep." She smirked, taking the armor from him and setting it near their fire to make another batch. "I heard you laughing a bit, too. What were you dreaming about?"

He gulped, unsure if he wanted to tell her. Truth was, he wasn't sure of what he dreamed. Certainly, he enjoyed Bernie's company, but...*not like that.* Did he?

"I was feeling better in my dream," he muttered, looking away. "Yeah, I was just...uhm...running around the forest."

"With me?" Bernie asked.

His eyes widened. Just how much did he reveal of his dream while he slept?

"How'd you know you were there?"

"You said my name."

"Oh." He pursed his lips, clearing his throat and coughing. "Forgive me, Your Majesty. Uhm...yes, you were there."

"What were we doing?"

Kissing, making out... "Throwing berries at each other during a hunt for food."

She let out a chuckle. "Did I win?"

"I'd...uh...say you did."

"Huh." She nodded in approval. "Sounds like a good dream."

"Yeah," he said, lying back down. "It…it was."

"You know what?" She turned and approached, feeling his forehead. "You're sounding better."

Her touch made him uneasy at first, but he couldn't deny it felt…good…to him. "Am I?" He took a listen as he breathed, noticing his lungs weren't sounding as raspy.

"You feel sweaty," she said, wiping her hand on her dress. "But not as warm. I think the fever broke."

"Really?"

"Well you're not half-dead on the ground like you've been lately, so I'd say it's an improvement."

He breathed a sigh of relief. Though his body still ached and his lungs burned (likely from lying on twigs during a rainy day), he couldn't deny that maybe…just maybe…he was starting to feel better.

"Does this mean I'm on the mend?" he asked, smirking.

"I'd say so." She smiled back. "Though don't overdo it. You're still sick and you need your rest."

He looked at her, noticing the dark circles developing under her eyes. The poor girl looked exhausted, and through a combination of hunger and taking care of him, he could only imagine how worn out she was.

"What of you?" he asked.

"What of me?"

"You need your rest, too."

"I'll be fine."

"That sentence doesn't ring familiar." He gawked at her, making her eyes roll.

"You're just like my sister."

"Someone has to look out for you." He chuckled, patting the empty spot near him. "Here. You rest and I'll keep watch. I'll wake you when needed."

"But you need rest more than I do."

"I've been resting long enough," he said warmly. "I'm doing better now, so it's my turn to take care of you."

She looked unsure, though she straightened the pile of brush before sitting on it as if preparing to lie. "Are you sure?"

"Positive. Now get some sleep."

It didn't take her long to obey, and before a minute had passed, she was out cold, gently snoring as she faced him.

Marcus watched her as she slept, getting up and reaching for his outer tunic, draping it over her shoulders for some extra warmth since the cloak was being used as a roof patch. Despite the weirdness of the dream, he couldn't deny that she looked pretty in the firelight, her face so peaceful that he found it comforting despite the circumstances they were in.

He looked away, staring towards the small fire near their feet. It wasn't as if he hadn't been attracted to a girl before. Truth was, he fell in love quite easily. Whether it was because he grew up without a mother and longed for another woman to fill her void or he was just plain lonely, he didn't know, but he couldn't deny the dream he had was a reflection of what was growing in his heart. Princess Bernette, the girl he once thought the worst of her gender to ever exist, suddenly became the best, all in the matter of a week.

He shook his head, thinking it folly. Even if he was falling in love with her (which he was sure *he wasn't*, because what he saw was just a dream and dreams were often silly nonsense), the possibility of a match between them was practically foolish. She was a princess...a foreign one, at that...and he was a guard. Once she returned to Staalberg, he doubted he'd get more than a glimpse of her for the rest of his life.

The thought of it left a sour taste in his mouth, and he felt his spirit get heavy. He shook his head, thinking it the edelroot tea still having an aftertaste. Bless it, if he didn't have something edible besides berries and roots to get the taste out of his mouth...

He picked up his bow with the few arrows he had left, watching as the rain started to stop. He and Bernie had been starving enough, and they needed animal protein for energy. He looked back to her one last time, letting out a sigh as he watched her sleep just a second longer.

He turned away, standing to his feet and fighting the weariness that wanted to overtake him. No matter what his feelings to her, be it love or be it duty, duty always came first. He was a knight of the royal guard, and he was charged with her protection. That meant ignoring all personal feeling and doing what was best for *her.*

He stepped out of the camp, trudging through the mud to hunt for some game.

# Chapter 18: Uncaged

Rage. Malina could explain her feelings using no other word.

She stormed down the hallway, fists clenched and jaw tense, her heart pounding within her chest from fury. First it was the defiance, then it was the treasury being robbed (though nothing was taken and no burglar was found). After that it was interruptions. Letters clearly forged from nobles to keep Edward occupied throughout the night so he couldn't join his wife in bed until she was asleep. Never had she seen fate deny her a man's embrace, and never had it been more clear as to who it was that denied her.

She'd been trying to get Edward to sleep with her for three days, and every time there was an interruption or inconvenience. But not this time. Oh no, she would make sure of it.

She entered the small room tucked in the shadows of an empty hall, shutting the door and locking it as the man she wanted to see met her glare.

"Hello, my love," Vacius said, his lips curled up in typical hunger. "You wished to see me?"

"I did," she replied, though her tone was far from friendly. He approached, attempting to touch her, but she slapped his hand away. "How dare you meddle in my affairs, Vacius!"

He widened his eyes, confused at her anger. "What do you mean?"

"You've been stopping me from being with my husband. I do not appreciate it!"

"I have done nothing."

She scoffed, shaking her head. "You've broken in the treasury, forged letters…"

"You have no proof."

"I don't need it when the trail is clear as day!" she interrupted, her voice rising. "This ends *now*, Vacius. I am queen and must please Edward physically if I am to remain his wife and retain my crown!"

"He seems disinterested," Vacius said, his voice low. "Were he truly attracted to you, nothing would stop him."

Malina lowered her brow, knowing the truth of his words but ignoring them. What she was doing had nothing to do with *love*. It was about *power* and keeping it. If her pregnancy was caught, then Edward would know the child was not his, and Malum would be angry…so very angry…

"You know so little, Vacius," Malina said back, turning her head. "He has been tired and distracted of late. Anyone like that would barely have time for himself."

"It never stopped you."

"That's because nothing stops me," Malina said, stepping forward to him. "And that includes you, *my love*. Your jealousy was cute at first but now it annoys me and endangers our mission here. I am not through winning the people, and until we can gather enough support, you must be content to wait for your throne!"

"But I do not want the throne!" he said, voice seething as he bared his teeth. "I want *you*."

"You have had me, Vacius, more than any man," she said, keeping her voice in check. "But you will have me no longer if you cannot stifle your rage!"

"What are you saying?" His voice suddenly cracked, and panic entered his eyes.

"I'm saying I will choose another to be my king if you can't handle it," Malina answered. "I will not condone weakness and impatience!"

"But I am content to wait for the crown!" Vacius said. "All I want is *you*, Malina. You've never ignored me this much!"

"Then give me my time with Edward. Once I give him his desires, I can give you yours."

"But I can't share you," Vacius seethed. "*Not anymore.*"

"If you can't share, then you can't have me," Malina replied, eyes narrowed. "Now be gone with you. Unless you are useful to me, I want nothing more."

"But...Malina..." Vacius' face reddened, his rage nearly stifling the room, but Malina didn't care. She had a job to do, and to protect herself, she had to seduce the king no matter what the cost.

Even if that meant losing her favorite toy.

It didn't matter, though. Vacius would be gone, but surely Malum would be pleased with her handling of the situation. And once she had Malum, she would need no other.

She turned to leave, touching the door handle, but Vacius' voice caught her one last time. "NO! YOU CAN'T LEAVE! I FORBID IT!"

"Any louder, darling, and the guards might hear you," Malina said, facing him one last time. "And if they come here, I promise I won't stop them." She opened the door, her lips in a snarl. "Now do something useful for me or *leave*."

She then closed the door, leaving her lover alone with his fury.

---

Vacius would never forget the first moment he spent with Malina.

They were in Cathal, a cold winter's day upon them and keeping everyone indoors to stay warm. He had just finished a mission – taking care of an enemy of the king, at his late request – and he was heading back home before reporting to the Velori in the morning.

But she saw him in the hallway that night, smiling and beckoning for him to approach. He obeyed without question, wondering if she had a job for him like her father. Instead, she offered him much more.

The Velori were trained in secret, never being allowed friends or family outside their brothers-in-arms. That meant never having a wife or children, and until his night with Malina, he never thought such a thing was desirable. But once he had tasted, he wanted more than just a bite, and their relationship grew over the months before Edward came along.

The man's name was like vomit on his tongue, and Vacius spit to the ground to remove it. He watched from the shadows as Malina approached her husband, putting soft hands on his shoulders and massaging him as he sat at the dining table, finishing dinner.

"You seem tired, my love," he heard her say before planting a kiss on his cheek. Vacius burned with jealousy as he watched her kiss him again, this time on the neck.

Edward let out a sigh, the kiss he gave back as she leaned towards his face almost seeming forced. "I am tired," Edward answered. "It's been a long day."

"But a productive one, no doubt." She turned to him, leaning against the table. "I am proud of you, my husband. To work so hard and so diligently for your nation is commendable."

"I don't need a reward," Edward muttered, taking a sip of tea. "I'm only doing my job."

"But every good deed deserves an accolade," she replied. "Come with me to the bedroom and let me give you my own prize."

"At least let me finish dinner first."

"Darling, aren't I enough to fill your appetite?" She leaned forward, exposing a bit of her chest as she kissed his cheek. "At least save me for dessert."

Edward nodded, though the voice that followed sounded disinterested. "If you insist."

The scene was nearly unbearable for Vacius, watching his lover make over the king in such a manner. He remembered when Malina spoke to him like that, how she looked at him like there was no other man in the universe. Now, she only had eyes for Edward, but Vacius knew he could fix that problem. He killed before, and he could kill again.

But he wouldn't make it fast for Edward. Oh no, that would be simple. He would make it slow and painful, giving him time to speak to the king and tell him who Malina's heart really lied with.

Edward would die knowing the truth, and despair would be his final thoughts before entering eternity.

And with Edward gone, Vacius would finally have Malina to himself. The crown would be his, the throne would be his, his child and lover and everything he ever wanted would be in his grasp.

Nothing could stop him, and already the plan was going to be set into motion.

He watched as a servant opened the door and walked in with two glasses of wine, freshly poured and red as the blood about to be spilt.

"A gift from the house of nobles to Queen Malina, in celebration of her good favor."

Malina looked surprised, but delighted. She never turned down a good drink.

"Thank you," she replied. "But I'm unsure if I want any."

Vacius beaded his eyes. It wasn't like her to not want wine.

"Are you sure?" Edward asked, curious. "I've never seen you not want it."

"I'm more interested in you, dearest."

Edward muttered something beneath his breath, shaking his head. "Well, I'll need all the help I can get," he said quietly, taking the glass and drinking.

Vacius watched, curious as to why Malina didn't touch the wine. It wasn't like her.

"This wine is strong," Edward said, pausing from his drinking. "How can you handle this?"

"It does its job of putting me in a good mood."

"But you're always in a bad mood."

"Then perhaps I should drink more, but not tonight." She rested her chin on her palms. "Tonight I only want you."

He finished the glass, Malina watching him and barely touching her plate.

Vacius remained silent as they finished dinner, eventually leaving the room and heading towards their bed. It wouldn't take long for the wine to do its job, but he had hoped Malina would be drugged along with it. No matter. With Edward about to feel the effects within a few minutes, he'd be barely coherent to do anything but want sleep.

And that would give Vacius time to do what needed to be done: kill the king of Audlin.

# Chapter 19: The Assassin Strikes

Vacius would never forget his training, how in Verloris he was taught that a Velori was nothing but an animal, a hunter always seeking its prey. Like a grass lion, a Velori was a king ruling his kingdom through fear and control. If the masses obeyed and stayed out of the way, they were safe. If they crossed their paths, however…they became like the deer the grass lion hunted for sport.

And as he watched and waited for night to fall, he began to stalk his prey in hopes of a swift and sudden kill.

The effect of the drugged wine meant also for Malina began to already sway her husband. He seemed groggy, too tired to even move, and by the time they reached their bedroom, Edward was already denying Malina's advances for a hope to sleep. "Wait until the morning," he muttered as he shooed Malina's hand away from his waist. "I can barely keep my eyes open. I'm exhausted."

Malina gave a scoff as she crossed her arms, demanding her husband's attention, but Edward would have none of it and entered the room.

"Are you not even getting undressed?" Malina asked.

"I'm too tired. I…just want to sleep."

Vacius could guess what happened next by Malina's reaction. Edward collapsed on the bed, already nearly knocked out from the drugs, his head falling on the pillow from being so exhausted. But what was pleasant about the poison was that though it exhausted the king, it wouldn't allow him to sleep. No, that would be too easy for him and too pleasant an end. Vacius wanted Edward alert but immobile before he perished.

He watched from the shadows as Malina threw her hands up in disgust. "Why will you not be with your wife?"

"I'll be with you in the morning, Malina," Edward said. "I'm too tired."

Everything was going according to plan, and now it was time for its second part.

Malina let out a sigh, perturbed as she entered the room. Before shutting the door, she turned to the two guards standing watch in the hallway. "See that no one disturbs us," she uttered. "My husband will be...indisposed. I want no interruptions."

"Yes, Your Majesty," the guard replied, and watched as Malina shut the door.

Vacius would have to be quick, and as he stayed hidden in the darkness of the night, he planned how he was going to take out two guards silently. He would have little time and little room for error, but he had been in trickier situations. He only needed to wait a few seconds until the two reached his spot in the shadows, a small place untouched by the candlelight dimming the hallways.

Vacius held out two knives, dipped with a poison that instantly killed their victims at touch, and approached from behind as the guards stopped to look around.

"Edward, do not deny me. Not a second more."

Edward could barely lift his head off the pillow. Never had he felt so exhausted in his life. Certainly, he was tired after the day he had, but never was he so beat that he couldn't even move. And of course, his wife would want his company right at that very moment. Surely she wasn't in so much need that she couldn't wait a few hours to at least let him nap!

"Stop complaining," he murmured, snuggling his face deeper against the softness of the pillow. Heavens, how good it felt to rest his head for once!

"How am I complaining?" Malina sneered. "I have *begged* for your company, but you've done nothing but ignore me! Don't make me go to your mother and demand she make you love your wife."

"I'm not...trying to push you away, Malina," Edward said, feeling very faint. "I...I'm getting dizzy..."

Malina shook her head in disgust. "I am tired of your excuses. Either sleep with me or I shall reveal what happened to Stephen!"

"Malina..." Suddenly Edward could barely tell if he was awake or in a dream. Everything was so fuzzy, spinning round and round as if he was caught in the wind. He'd only taken a glass of wine – surely it wasn't so potent to make him drunk!

"*What?*" Malina asked, her voice full of fury, but after watching her husband turn his eyes to face her, his skin deathly pale, she softened.

"Edward?" she asked.

He could barely get the words out as he felt his heart starting to race. "Something's wrong..."

But before he could say anything more, he saw a shadow approach Malina from behind after the door was swiftly opened and closed back again. Malina had turned, opening her mouth to see who it was that had interrupted them, but soon found it stifled as an unknown assailant grabbed her, putting a cloth with a strange, sour smell to her face. She let out a gasp before collapsing on the floor, unconscious, and Edward looked ahead, the man approaching him coming into view of the candlelight.

It was a man he hadn't seen since Cathal, a Velori whose face he would never forget as long as he lived. Vacius, the shadow who trailed him all the way to Hugellia and Verloris...

"You..." Edward found his voice leaving, and his muscles felt numb. He could barely lift his hands or legs or head. "What...what did you do to me?"

"The Velori are known for many things, Edward," Vacius replied, edging closer to the bed. "One of the most famous being our poisons."

"Poison?"

"Not enough to kill you," Vacius said with a smile. "But enough to leave you weak until I kill you myself."

"I don't understand..." Edward struggled to breathe, struggled to think. "Why are you...doing this?"

"It was destiny," Vacius replied. "Everything you have belongs to me, and I am here to claim what is mine."

"You...have nothing..."

Vacius chuckled low, stepping in front of Edward. "Have I?" he asked. "Tell me, *oh wise king* – did you really think everything you've achieved was done on your own accord?"

Edward watched as Vacius pulled out a sword, fresh and clean, and he pointed it towards Edward's chest. "Your crown?" Vacius began as he circled the blade's tip around Edward's sternum. "Given to you *by me*. Who do you think it was that killed your father?"

"My father...?" Suddenly Edward began thinking back to King Arden's strange death. The timing, the circumstances, the mystery behind it all...

"Poison," Vacius said. "Once more, one of our specialties. Though I admit I had help."

Edward prayed he could somehow gain enough strength to move, but no matter what he did, he continued to feel weaker.

"Speaking of my help, let us talk more of her!" Vacius looked back to Malina, still unconscious on the floor. "Did you know I've been bedding your wife since you married her? Malina only stayed married to you to get your power and throne. But once she garnered enough support of her own, she was going to overthrow you and give me your crown!"

Of course, Edward could believe that. He figured Malina had been up to no good. But giving the crown to Vacius? Any hope of that was dashed once the man made her unconscious. "You're...delusional..." Edward said, his eyes going onto the blade that now neared his heart. "Malina would...never share...her power. You know this. If you didn't, you wouldn't...have harmed her."

"She gave me everything I ever wanted, *fool!*" Vacius then took the blade, slicing it across Edward's abdomen, creating a deep enough wound to make Edward shout in pain. No, it wasn't enough to kill him...yet...but it was enough to make his death painfully slow.

Vacius took Edward by the collar, lifting him up and making him cry out in pain again. "Your wife is my lover," Vacius seethed with a wicked grin. "A woman I defiled your bed with *countless* times. Not once did she ever find pleasure with you. It was always me. It will always be me!"

Edward felt the adrenaline surge through his body as it fought to stay conscious, to stay alive. He could feel his blood leaving him, and suddenly fear overtook any pain. He was going to die, and there wasn't anything he could do to stop it.

"She only lies there because I want to save her from being blamed for your death. But I will let you in on another secret," Vacius said as he dropped Edward to the floor, the king hitting the stone hard, putting him in a daze. Edward groaned, his body starting to shake from the shock of the impact (or poison, since he couldn't tell a difference), but his eyes glanced upward towards Vacius as he waved the sword around. "Your son," Vacius began, "the boy you believed sired from your body?" He paused, his smile widening. "He is *mine*."

'I...won't let you...take my son..." Edward struggled to move, but nothing happened. If only he had the strength...

"I only have to take him back," Vacius replied, "because it is you who took him from me." Edward started to hyperventilate as the realization of what Vacius was saying began to sink in. "Calimus never was your son. He has always been mine."

Edward felt his world stop. Everything he loved, everything he lived for...it was suddenly lost to him.

*Antoinette...Father...Calimus...*

Images of the baby he held on the day of his birth suddenly filled Edward with dread. Every look, every touch, every sound Calimus ever made was never meant for him.

*I'm not his father...*

Disappointment, fury, sorrow, hatred…emotions nearly overwhelmed him at the revelation, and all he could do was lie there in the floor like a dying animal, his body jerking and tears trickling down his face.

"No…" It was all he could say as his world crashed down around him. Surely Calimus was his son. The boy was his chance at redemption, a new start in life, the one good thing he had amidst so much loss and pain…

But Stephen's words from the past haunted him into the present. *"I told you this day would come…"*

*Your sins have found you, and now justice has come to collect.*

All Edward could do was pray as he lay dying on the floor. *Lord, have mercy…*

"With this truth, perish." Vacius held the sword high towards Edward's heart. "And know that you die an unwanted, despised failure with no hope of tomorrow."

Edward felt his consciousness start to leave him, and as he watched the blade come down, he suddenly heard a shout and some noise, but he couldn't make out any of it as he was suddenly plunged into chaos.

*He could see the swirl of images come at him fast. Whether a vision or dream or a mixture of both, he didn't know, but it was as if life suddenly flashed before him. He saw glimpses of the past, happy moments he once thought forgotten by time. Soft moments with Antoinette, play times with Emmerich when they were children, the one time he, Father, Mother, and Stephen all ate Christmas dinner together as a family. But as the past faded away and new images came forth, Edward found himself in the midst of things he did not understand.*

*A boy, young and full of personality, running through the forest with sticks as toys. The lad was practically a mirror image of him, and Edward chased him playfully, picking him up. The boy laughed down into his belly as Edward hugged him close, and the words from the boy's mouth gave him a strength he thought gone.*

*"I love you, Daddy."*

*Soon he saw an army, small yet effective, hiding amongst the trees and villages as they faced ironclad knights bred for battle. "Are you sure of this?" It was the voice of someone familiar, though it seemed older and wearier than before. "If it fails…"*

*"It will work." Another voice came from a man clothed completely in brown and green, his face covered by a hood but his stance and sound reminiscent of a king.*

*But then the images changed, and they flew by him as he heard himself speak.*

*"You will know pain…"*

*What he saw filled him with dread.*

*Kettensburg burning, the people within its walls running from an advancing army, Uncle Aldaric clutching his wife, telling her to run.*

*Antoinette falling into the snow, sobbing as she was being held by her sister, her face turning to the heavens as she screamed Emmerich's name.*

*He saw Sir Rikert trembling as he marched in front of a crowd. He saw his mother bedridden and trapped in despair. He heard mobs of rioters chanting, the sight of Marcus cupping the face of a woman and kissing her amidst the chaos. He saw so many more images pass by that he couldn't tell what they were anymore, until he heard his voice speak again.*

*"But your pain will serve a purpose, and you will know joy again."*

*Suddenly a peace overtook him, and at first he wondered if it was then that he was to enter the afterlife, to finally be with his father and brother and God.*

*But there were no angels greeting him with harps, no cherubs singing songs as he rose above the clouds to pearl gates. Instead, his vision became hazy, and all he could see was light as a distinct voice spoke.*

*"I love you, Edward, no matter what you did."*

*The voice was so familiar, so soft and soothing, and he could feel a touch upon his face. And though the haze was starting to become clearer and he could see himself in a garden, a woman in his arms caressing his cheek, her face was what stood out the most, and he suddenly knew who spoke.*

*Antoinette's face was firm, radiant, and full of hope. "Don't give up."*

*He spoke her name, though whether it was in the dream or out, he didn't know.*

*Darkness then overtook him, and he knew no more.*

# Chapter 20: Entering the Game

"Why are we doing these patrols?"

The young guard sounded bored, but Sir Rikert chuckled to himself. Orders were orders, no matter how silly they were, and just because Sir Peterson was gone didn't mean his scheduled palace patrols would be ignored. "We have a duty, Sir Thatcher. Sir Peterson scheduled these walks before the evening shift and we can't skip them."

"Yes, but usually *he* takes them."

"And until he returns from escorting Princess Bernette home, it is us who will do it."

Sir Thatcher frowned, already tired from working long hours. "There are guards down every hall. If something is amiss, they'll call for help."

"Rules are rules," Sir Rikert replied. "Besides, you can never be too careful. You never know when a surprise may – " He stopped as a servant came rushing forward, a letter in his hand.

"Forgive me, sir," the man stuttered as he bowed hastily. "A message just came for the king. It is a letter from his cousin."

Sir Rikert took the letter in his hand, looking at it. "Has it just arrived?"

"Yes, sir."

"Thank you." Samuel clasped the letter. "I shall take it to the king immediately."

"Of course, sir." The young man bowed, hurrying off towards other duties.

Samuel stared at the messenger strangely. For some reason, he looked as if he had seen the man before. "Who was that?" he asked Sir Thatcher.

"A new servant, I should think," he answered. "Probably the replacement for the one the king got rid of after that incident with Prince Arnold."

Samuel nodded, still unsure. New servant he may be, there was something familiar about him. He shook his head, turning back to the letter. Edward would want to hear word from Emmerich. Perhaps there was even an update from Marcus in it, too.

They turned around to head towards the king's bedroom. As they neared the hallway leading to it, however, a muffled sound was heard. "Wait..." Sir Thatcher opened his mouth to speak, but Samuel quickly shushed him, listening. He could've sworn he heard something, but now...

"Do you hear that?" Samuel asked.

"I hear nothing," Sir Thatcher replied.

One of many problems, Samuel thought to himself. At least the sounds of guards breathing or shuffling in their stance should be heard. Instincts kicked in and he found himself hurrying down the hall, and as he neared the king's bedroom, he found two things that set his heart on edge.

The first were the bodies of two royal guards lying lifeless on the ground near the shadows. The second was of a voice speaking in the king's bedroom, and that voice did not belong to the king. After hearing a stifled yell, Samuel began sprinting towards the door, turning to Sir Thatcher as he brandished his sword and knife.

"Get the guard! GO NOW!"

Sir Thatcher scrambled away as Samuel ran to the king's door, barging through into the darkness of the room. It only took a second to see that every guard's worse fear had come to life. The queen was on the floor unconscious, the king on the other side bleeding out from a wound on his abdomen. A towering figure stood over him, about to lower a sword into the king's heart, and Samuel only had a blink to react.

His running never stopped as he threw the knife towards the attacker, hitting the man's arm and stopping the blade from piercing the king's chest.

The attacker turned, giving out a yell as he pulled the knife from his arm, clutching it in his left hand and pointing it back at Samuel. The knight lifted his sword, ready to attack, and after a few swings and parries, Samuel managed to get closer to the king, ready to defend with his life.

"You waste your time here, knight!" the attacker growled as he swung again, Samuel blocking the blade with his own. His heart pounded, his body began to sweat, and already the adrenaline was coursing through his veins. He hadn't been in this close of combat since the battle near Braiden so many years ago, but he was just as fast now as he was then.

"I will not let you harm him," Samuel growled back. "Under the authority of Audlin and her royal guard, I demand you stand down!"

"A Velori never surrenders," the man seethed, and soon Samuel found himself in the fight for his life.

Samuel had heard stories of the Velori during his training days as a knight. A mystery they were, found more in legend than in life, but their stories still made the hearts of men tremble. They were agile, clever, strong, unbeatable…many even saying the men were immortal and unable to be killed. But Samuel knew better, and the Velori before him was no different from any man. Every person had a weakness, a limit. And if Samuel could hold on until reinforcements arrived, he was certain the Velori would be defeated by numbers alone.

But the fight wasn't easy, and Samuel quickly longed for younger bones that didn't ache as he fought with the warrior. Their blades spun through the air in a dizzying flurry, sparks from every clash bringing light into the room. Samuel cursed the darkness that made the room as dangerous as weapons, and he found himself nearly tripping over furniture or running into things. But the Velori felt at home, dodging every blow with a swift grace best described as more talent than training. Samuel found himself praying for strength, just the ability to hold out a little longer until the guard arrived, but soon his prayers were dashed as he felt a knife slice his arm.

Pain shot through him, and he felt a smack on his jaw, being knocked to the ground beside the king.

"You really thought you could defeat me?" The Velori laughed.

"Not really," Samuel replied, slowly lifting himself off the ground. "But I thought I could distract you."

He then lunged forward, giving the Velori a quick fight before being pushed into the wall once again.

Samuel found himself weary as he lifted his head from the ground, a throbbing pain being felt near his temple. But as the Velori approached, ready to give a final strike before death, the sound of rumbling through the floors and the shouts of war came quickly through the door.

It was Sir Thatcher and the royal guard, and the Velori found himself being backed into a corner.

"Surrender, intruder!" Sir Thatcher shouted as he lifted his bow. "You have nowhere to run!"

Samuel stood to his feet, lifting his sword as best he could through the pain. "It is over, Velori. Your mission has failed."

"Has it?" The man cackled as he neared the window. "The king cannot be hidden from me forever."

"You cannot win. Surrender now or face death!"

"I will do neither," he seethed, and as he moved to attack the king one last time, Sir Thatcher released the arrow from his bow, hitting the Velori on the shoulder. The knights rushed forward, swarming in front of the king, and before anything else could be done, the Velori jumped out the window into the cool night air.

Sir Thatcher rushed out, sticking his head through the broken glass to find the assailant. "He's going!" he shouted as he watched the Velori lower himself from a tree he jumped onto. "He's escaping!"

"Send a search team to find him *now!*" Samuel barked as he rushed to Edward, gently tilting his head to face him. The king was barely conscious, going in and out of a fainted state as he bled out from the wound in his abdomen. Samuel grabbed part of the bed sheets and pressed down, attempting to stem the bleeding. "Get a doctor! The king may not have much time."

Sir Thatcher ran out again to fetch one as a few other guards attended to the queen, lifting her and putting her on the bed. But Samuel paid them no heed as he gently tapped Edward's cheek, hoping to rouse him.

"Your Majesty," Samuel began. "Stay with me. It's going to be alright."

Edward's voice was barely a whisper as he fought with consciousness once more. "Vacius…"

"Is that who attacked you?" Samuel asked, but Edward fainted before he could answer.

Samuel held on to the king as best he could, keeping the fabric on the wound until the doctors arrived. He turned, looking as Queen Malina began gaining consciousness, and he frowned as anger surged through him. He knew little about the Velori, but there was one fact that was well-known throughout the land.

The Velori served Verloris, and there was only one from that dreaded nation who would have contact with them, and she was now a queen.

"Hang on, Your Majesty," Samuel whispered as he turned back to the king. "You have much to live for. Don't give up."

But Edward's face soon paled, and death looked as if it was about to claim him.

---

*Failure.*

Vacius ran into the night, staying on the side streets and alleys lest he be caught by prying eyes. His arm and shoulder burned and weariness threatened to overtake him, but he wouldn't give up. Edward had a chance to survive the wound, and if he did, everything would fall apart. He had to go back, had to kill the king even if it killed himself.

But how he was going to sneak back in unnoticed would be tricky.

How, *how* did the royal guard know how to find him? He had checked the halls and took care of the guards. Sir Rikert's patrol was scheduled for the lower levels of the palace at that hour, so why was he not where he was supposed to be? Something was wrong, going against him and his plans. Surely Malina would not have known Vacius was going to strike. She was a clever woman, but not a mind reader!

He stopped in an empty alley, attempting to catch his breath, the chasing guards already lost in their trail of finding him. While the men ran, he would go back and take care of the king before Edward could wake and speak the truth. It was the only way to complete his mission, the only way to get Malina back.

Vacius stood, enduring the pain as he turned back towards the palace. But as he looked up, he saw a figure standing in the shadows.

Was it the guard? No, no, it was only one man…

"What are you doing, Vacius?"

Vacius froze, his heart struck by a chill now flowing through his veins. He recognized the voice of his leader, and as the figure came into view under the moonlight, the face was unmistakable.

"Malum…"

"I asked you a question, Vacius. What are you doing here?"

"Protecting Queen Malina." It was a lie, but hopefully it would work. "You ordered me to do so, and that is what I've done."

"That is not what I see." He approached, touching a finger to Vacius' shoulder and arm. "You're wounded."

"I was nearly caught by the guard, but I escaped."

Malum's emotions didn't flinch. "You lie."

"I swear by my blood it's the truth," Vacius stuttered, and he found himself backing into a corner.

"That part is true, but you have slipped in your mission." Malum stopped as he faced Vacius, crossing his arms. "You attempted to kill the king."

"I..."

"Do not lie again, Vacius."

He lowered his head, gulping. There was no time for fear anymore. The Velori had controlled him long enough, denied him his wants and desires too much! There was nothing left to lose, nothing left to gain except the one thing he could still hold onto: freedom.

"I attempted to kill the king."

Malum remained emotionless. "Why?"

"Because he took Malina away from me!" Vacius stood tall, his fists clenched. "I was going to take back what was rightfully mine! The crown, my woman, my son..."

Malum chuckled, shaking his head, making Vacius fume. "You sound as if you planned this a while," he said. "But you know the consequences. A Velori must renounce all worldly pleasures for the sake of the brotherhood."

"That is impossible to do, Malum," Vacius replied.

"Our brothers have kept their vows for centuries, though you are certainly not the first to stray," Malum said. "And I doubt you'll be the last."

"So what are you going to do? Punish me?" Vacius spat. "Try your best, Malum! I am the Velori's greatest fighter. You know I can defeat you!"

"And what would defeating me accomplish?" Malum asked.

"I can be rid of you and your rules! I can finally be free and have everything I want!"

Malum nodded, stifling another laugh as he stood still. "You can't defeat me."

"You would really test it?" Vacius pulled out his sword and knife, readying in his stance.

"Fool," Malum said. "A test would be challenging, but fighting you is only play."

Vacius beaded his eyes. What was Malum getting at? Was it some sort of trick? Was he surrounded by his fellow brethren, secretly watching and waiting for him to fall?

He began to look around, searching for any sign of a fellow brother, but Malum only smirked.

"There is no one else but us."

"What game are you playing, Malum?" Vacius seethed.

"That has been the problem," Malum replied, stepping closer. "I haven't been playing, but now I think I'm going to join."

Vacius found Malum facing him, his presence nearly overwhelming and filling him with a dread he hadn't felt before.

"You have failed in your mission, Vacius," Malum continued. "You were hired to protect your queen and watch Edward, yet you have done neither."

"I regret nothing," Vacius spat as he clenched the weapons in his hands. "Everything I did, I did for freedom. I did it for my woman and son."

"And here you are, caught," Malum said. "Your work is finished, Vacius. The brotherhood no longer needs you."

"Then I die a free man!"

"You die a fool," Malum replied, and as Vacius moved forward to attack, Malum turned, stabbing him in the neck with a small needle. Vacius knew instantly when he was hit, and his body gave way, throwing him to the ground.

Another poison, one similar to what was used on Edward, only this one was more deadly.

"I…still die…free…" Vacius forced the words out as his body started to twitch, and Malum stepped over him, bending down.

"Before you go," Malum said, putting the needle back into its container, "I think you should know something."

Vacius only grunted, not caring what he had to say. He was proud of what he died for. He died for freedom. He died for honor. He died for love.

"Everything you wanted, everything you thought you 'earned'," Malum began with a smile, "I'm going to take from you."

Vacius' voice had nearly left him, and he cursed his lack of movement. *You cannot take anything, Malum. I will haunt you from the grave!*

"Your woman? She is my puppet," Malum said as he held up his fingers and twirled them. "She has been this entire time. And your son?" He lowered his hand and put it on Vacius' shoulder. "Malina whores with everyone, yet she was instructed to be careful with you. Did you really think he would be yours? The child looks nothing like you." He paused, whispering. "Why do you think Calimus only responds to Edward? Even a baby knows its own father."

Vacius felt his life starting to wane, but his spirit was being crushed. *Malina...Calimus...SHE LIED...*

He thought because the child had been born early that it meant Edward wasn't the father. But any baby could be born early, and Vacius knew in his heart...

*Calimus was never mine...he is Edward's...*

"As for your crown..." Malum stood to his feet. "It was mine from the start. You only thought you could have it."

He turned around, leaving Vacius in the cold street as he started to walk away. "I now go to fix the chaos you have started, Vacius, but do not despair. Though minimal, your contributions have sped up my plans. I suppose I should thank you."

Vacius said nothing as his heart started to slow. *No...Malina...she is mine. Calimus is mine...my crown...no...*

"Good-bye, Brother."

Soon his body began to convulse, and before darkness overtook him and breath left his body, Vacius could only think of regret.

# Chapter 21: A Common Life

"Why are we fishing?"

Bernie stood at the edge of the river, carefully balancing near some rocks as she held up a sharpened twig, searching for a fish to skewer.

"Because you nearly killed yourself with my bow."

She rolled her eyes at the guard as he waded in the shallow part of the water, pant legs rolled up and scooping his hand in the stream, flinging a fish onto the ground.

"I got us a ham dinner, though," Bernie reminded.

"Only because I stabbed the boar before he could trample you." Marcus paused from his fishing and gave her a look. "Reading a book on archery doesn't give you proper practice, Your Majesty. The bow is an art that only time can teach."

"Well how else am I going to learn unless I practice?"

Marcus chuckled. "Not on wild boar!"

"Fine," Bernie muttered. "What about a squirrel or deer?"

"Too fast and too easily startled," Marcus replied. "We can try a rabbit."

"Absolutely not!"

Marcus scoffed. "You wouldn't slay a rabbit? Why?"

"They're too cute to eat."

"And it's okay to eat a boar because it's ugly?"

Bernie shook her head, poking the stick in the water and missing yet another fish. She swore Marcus caught enough for a seafood buffet while she had yet to catch one. If only she hadn't inherited Father's skills in hunting. "That's not what I'm saying at all," Bernie replied as she started her search anew. "All I'm saying is rabbits are adorable, innocent little creatures who would never hurt anyone. Not unlike a boar, I might add."

"Clearly you've never had a garden."

"Well if you only plant carrots, what do you expect?"

"Fine. I'll teach you the bow, but only on practice targets like a bush," Marcus said after a sigh. "No heroics, mind you. There's still bears in these woods and boars past the trees and we wouldn't want a repeat of yesterday's theatrics."

"Admit it. You enjoyed the exercise." She looked up at him, smirking. Heavens, it was wickedly fun teasing him.

He smirked back, returning to his fishing. "So how many have you caught?"

"Uhm..." She paused, seeing a fish towards the deeper parts of the water. It was large, slow, and just waiting to be caught. She could almost smell the thing roasting over a fire, and her rumbling stomach was practically begging for a fish dinner. "You know what?" Bernie called out. "I think I just found one that counts as ten!"

"Oh?"

"This thing is massive! I'm going deeper for a better look." She hopped over a few rocks, still trying to balance as she edged near the deeper banks of the river.

"Be careful!" Marcus warned. "It's slippery and I'd rather you not fall."

"I know how to swim."

"That's not what I mean," Marcus said, standing up straighter. "If you fall and break your neck..."

Bernie scoffed. "I won't fall and break my neck. You saw yourself – I jumped out a window and I was fine."

"Your Majesty, please – don't repeat any stunts! You've nearly stumbled already!"

Bernie ignored him as she stopped near the fish, leaning over and taking aim. "Alright, fishy...time to become dinner!" But as soon as she spoke, the fish started to swim away from the rock.

"You're leaning too far out!" Marcus called, but Bernie paid him no heed as she reached further to try and catch the fish. She took aim one last time as the fish started to slow, but after she leaned forward a little more, slipping her foot on a wet rock and losing her balance, she fell straight into the water.

She barely heard Marcus yell her name as she went head first, practically smacking the fish with her forehead.

She scrambled up, feeling thankful the river was only up to her waist, but the current was fast and had already dragged her nearly ten feet downstream. She gasped for air as she stood, the cool spring wind feeling like ice upon her skin and wet clothes, and she started to shiver, her head feeling colder than anything.

She saw Marcus run up, not caring that his pant legs were getting soaked, but he suddenly stopped in front of her, his eyes wide.

It was then when Bernie realized what had happened. After falling forward, the stream rushed through her hair and pulled the hairpiece she had been so careful to keep on, off. She turned to her left, watching as the fake hair flowed down stream, and she felt herself freeze as her worst nightmare suddenly came true.

Her thinning hair, her bald spots, all of it...suddenly exposed and known to someone other than her sister or mother.

Marcus didn't say anything at first as he approached, and he gently put his hand on her arm, helping her out of the water. "Are you alright?" he asked after a moment of silence.

Her mind raced at how to answer. Should she downplay it and laugh? Should she act like nothing happened? Should she show what was in her heart and start sobbing at the embarrassment of having the one man on earth who didn't hate her find out that she was a balding woman? Bernie started to shake, more from nerves than from the cold, and after seeing Marcus look at her expectantly, she suddenly didn't know what to do.

She met his glance and her spirits fell. She had finally, *finally* got the guard to be her friend. But she knew better than to think that would last long. Now that he knew what she really looked like, he wouldn't want to have anything to do with her anymore. He'd be like the other guards, mocking her, and now he had more information than anyone.

But the thought of losing his affection...the thought of him no longer looking at her with that warm smile or that teasing glance...

All she wanted to do was hide, to never be seen again because the pain of rejection would hurt too much.

"I'm fine," she muttered. "I just...uhm...I'm going to go get dried off now." She gave a forced grin, hoping he wouldn't notice the tears welling up in her eyes, and she hurried back to the shelter, grabbing Marcus' cloak from the ground and putting the hood up over her head.

---

Marcus didn't know what to say when he first saw her come out of the water.

Her hair had disappeared, as strange as it sounded. One moment she looked normal and fell into the river and the next moment she came back up with as much hair as a newborn baby. Her scalp was clearly visible, large patches of baldness throughout her head, but it was the look on her face that shook him more, and he couldn't get it out of his mind.

She looked terrified, exposed, as if her worst fears and nightmares suddenly came to pass and she could do nothing to stop it. He didn't know any woman who had ever lost her hair before, and he wondered what had happened to the princess to have such an event happen.

She hurried back to the shelter, barely saying a word though he tried to get her to talk. After her continued silence save asking to use his outer tunic and cloak to replace the clothes now soaked by the river, he decided to go and finish his work, cleaning and gutting the fish and sticking them on skewers above the fire to roast for dinner. Once that was finished, however, he found Bernie huddled up near the corner of the shelter, the cloak around her body and the hood completely covering her head.

His heart surged with pity for her, and he couldn't imagine how embarrassed she must have been having such a secret be revealed so quickly.

He approached, sitting in front of her. "I've got the fish roasting."

She only nodded, keeping her head down.

"And I thought I'd make some edelroot tea. My lungs still burn a bit." He coughed, noticing she didn't look up. He could barely tell her facial expressions by the way the hood covered her, and after a moment of silence, he figured he should check to see if she was alright.

"Your Majesty, are you cold?"

"Well, I did just fall into a river."

Marcus nodded, noticing that even in his fevered state he never *completely* covered himself. At least he showed his face, his hands, his feet...

"Did you get my tunic?"

"Yeah, I've got it on." Bernie paused, her voice lowering. "Uhm...no pants, though, so don't mind me staying covered until my dress dries."

He nodded, smirking. He didn't doubt the tunic went down to her knees, but he respected her modesty. "Of course." He then paused, keeping his eyes on her. The hood she wore covered every inch. How was she even able to breathe? "Your Majesty...uhm..." He stopped again, hoping he wasn't sounding rude. "I...uhm...well, are you able to breathe?"

"Why wouldn't I be able to?"

"You have the hood completely over your head," Marcus stammered. "I…I'd rather you not suffocate yourself. Surely you don't have a reason to hide your face."

"It's fine," she said casually.

He knew better than to believe her. No one, not even a child, would cover themselves completely without some way to get air. "Your Majesty, you've covered your face with the hood."

"That's because my head's cold."

He pursed his lips, unsure of how to answer. Should he say something about her hair (or lack of it)? Was she baiting him? Was she wanting to talk? Or was she simply downplaying it? "I can build the fire if you wish," he said, hoping the answer would suffice. "But please, Your Majesty, at least uncover your face. Without proper air, you'll faint."

"Is dinner ready? Maybe you should check on it." She was trying to change the subject, and could he blame her? Already the conversation was getting awkward, and he wasn't sure how to respond.

"It should be ready in a little while. But I can check…" He paused, suddenly hearing a rumble of thunder. He turned to look outside of the shelter, and after a few sprinkles of warning, a downpour fell from the sky.

"Great," Marcus muttered as he turned back to Bernie. He hated to ask her, but knew if they didn't use the cloak as a second roof over their shelter, it would flood and the fire would go out. "Your Majesty, we need the cloak to help stop leaks."

She raised her head, but kept the cloak over her. "The rain won't last that long."

"Your Majesty, even if it doesn't, the fire's about to go out and our shelter's getting wet. *We're* getting wet."

"But..."

"Your Majesty, I promise your calves and feet will stay covered. Here." He bent down and picked up some brush, handing it to her. "It's not much, but until your dress dries, it's what we have. I'm sorry."

She paused, hesitating at first in giving him the cloak, but after feeling water already wetting the ground, she gave a huff of frustration, taking the cloak off and handing it to him. He thanked her, spreading it over the roof of their shelter as she covered her calves with the brush.

"There. That should keep us dry until the rains stop and you can have the cloak back." He turned back around to face her, but after meeting her glance, she quickly lowered her head, looking away.

"Your Majesty?" He squinted, noticing her face was red and streaked. Had she been crying?

"Yeah?" she asked, keeping her head down. He noticed she pulled her sleeves over her hands and put them to her head, pretending to look bored. In reality, she was trying to cover what remained of her hair.

He felt his spirit become heavy at the sight, and his heart surged with compassion. He bent down, sitting atop a makeshift mat, and faced her, lowering his head to meet her gaze. "Are you alright?" he asked softly.

"I'm fine. Why?"

"You..." He paused, exhaling slowly. He couldn't help but be truthful, to want to comfort her in any way he could. "You look like you've been crying."

"Oh? Uhm...yeah, that's just leftover river water getting out of my eyes, you know?" She gave a nervous chuckle as her head remained bowed. "I mean, I have allergies and stuff and river water is so polluted with all that animal junk, and when it gets in your eyes, it irritates them. And who knows? Maybe I'm getting the cold or flu you got. I mean, your eyes were pretty watery from that, too. Maybe I should make some edelroot tea." She moved to get up, but Marcus gently took her by the hand, keeping her near.

She kept her head down, and Marcus could hear her breathing becoming more sporadic. As he looked, he noticed her lip was starting to quiver, and he gently touched her chin, lifting it to look her in the eyes.

What he saw made his heart break, and he saw a tear fall down the princess' face.

---

*HIDE IT, HIDE IT, HIDE IT.*

Bernie had made sure she covered every inch of her head, every tiny little speck of skin that showed just how much hair she'd lost. Sure, it was hard to breathe covering up everything, but despite the faintness and heat, she couldn't be seen. She was hidden, invisible in plain sight, and no one could see her balding head. No one could see just how...hideous, as she thought...she was.

But then it just had to rain.

She didn't want to give up her covering, didn't want to reveal to Marcus what she really looked like beneath the façade. Sure, he got a glimpse, but she wouldn't forget the look of surprise on his face. He was mocking her in his mind, she was sure, and she could feel just how disgusted he would be just being near.

And when she had to take the cloak off, she couldn't help but want to cry. Her security, her comfort, was gone, and then she was exposed, this time for who knew how long.

She tried to run, tried to get away so she wouldn't have to deal with the shame of him making fun of her. But no, he had to pull her back. He just had to get a good look at what she tried to hide.

And when he lifted her chin, forcing her to look at him in the eyes and face her worst fear, she couldn't hold the tears back anymore. She knew what was coming, knew the jeering was going to start at any moment.

He was quiet for a long time as he looked at her, each second feeling like a lifetime as she waited for his response. Then, after waiting forever, he opened his mouth, but no words came out, and he soon closed it again. She then felt his hand leave her face, and he simply looked at her.

She quickly bent her head, not wanting to see his reaction. It would be terrible. He would laugh and mock and cringe and...

"Your Majesty, why won't you look at me?" he asked softly.

"What's the point?" she muttered with a sniffle, wanting to tear that cloak off the roof and cover herself back up again, rain or not. Why, *why* did he have to look at her? "I know what you're thinking, so just go ahead and say it."

"And what am I thinking?"

"Ew! Gross! Out of all the people I had to get lost in the forest with, it was the ugly girl!" She felt her lip quiver more, and she bit it, hoping to keep it still. It didn't work, and more tears fell. Never was she so embarrassed, never did she want to run and hide so much in her life. Mother warned her so many times what would happen if a man found out she was losing her hair. They'd never want her, never even want to look at her…

"That's not what I'm thinking," Marcus said, his voice somewhat stern. He almost sounded…angry. Just how disgusted was he to be angry at being stuck with her?

"I'm sorry, Marcus. It's a condition the doctors can't explain. Some of them say I'm losing my hair because of stress, others think it just happened without a cause." She paused, nearly choking down her sob. "I'm sorry. I know you don't want to see this and when the rains stop I can cover it back up and…"

He lifted her chin once more, the gentleness of his touch remaining as he held her gaze, a frown upon his face. "That was *not* what I was thinking, either," he said. "Instead, I was thinking about how wrong you have been to *ever* listen to any negative word about your appearance."

"Marcus, you can give me a speech about flowers and your dad's opinions, but this is real life," Bernie interrupted, pushing his hand away. "Real life looks at people in two ways: pretty and ugly. The pretty people get all the friends, all the happiness, and all the love. The ugly people either stay that way or have to pretend to be pretty just to be accepted, and even then, it doesn't always work." She paused, wiping her eyes with the sleeves of his tunic. "You'd never understand. You're one of *them*. You don't have a blemish on you. You're not fat and bald. What would you know about wanting to hide what you look like?"

He frowned further, and he shook his head. "What would I know?" he scoffed, crossing his arms. "I know a lot more than you think I do."

"Oh yeah? Prove it." She looked back up at him, eager to see him fail at accepting her challenge. And how could it be any different? No one – not even he – could deny his handsomeness. Thick hair, dark eyes, a lean yet muscular build that any woman would drool over.

"I have scars," he muttered.

"Oh, such a hideous thing!" she mocked. "Scars don't have to be hidden, Marcus. You know why? Because people aren't disgusted by scars. Scars show them you've been brave and have been protecting people in battle. They see it as a badge of courage and honor. But what about baldness? Sure, men can get away with it because it's so common, but a woman? Any time you see a balding woman, what's the first thing people think? Oh! She must have a disease. She must secretly be a man. She must have been struck by God for doing something terrible!"

He frowned further, and for a moment Bernie wondered if she offended him. It didn't matter. She hoped she offended him, because he offended her! As if a few measly scars were something people would mock him about. What did he take her for? A fool?

"My scars aren't physical. They're emotional." He scooted closer, facing her with a warmness that took away the cold. "You think you're the only one trying to hide, but you're not. I've been trying to hide since the day I was born."

What followed was a small tale similar to what she overheard the knights back at the camp speak about. He told her of how his father impregnated his mother when they weren't married, how such a scandal ensued that it forced his father out of the knighthood and every title, coin, and respect the family had was taken away. Bernie let him speak, saying nothing in return, but what he said after the things she knew made her heart pity him.

"You feel shame because your hair isn't like others," he continued, looking in her eyes. "Instead it's thin and falling out, and in your desperation to hide it, you wear wigs and pieces so no one will make you feel shame. I understand your wanting to hide too well, not for physical reasons, but because I, too, want to avoid the shame my parents' scandal brought me. The only difference between you and I is you *can* hide, but I can't. I can't cover a scandal and I can't give myself a fake past because someone somewhere will know the truth and spread it before I can stop them."

Bernie frowned, feeling terrible. She didn't mean to make Marcus remember his past or downplay what he went through. "I'm sorry. I didn't mean to lash out. I know what you went through was difficult and that you understand shame. It's just…it's still different. People don't hold your past against you, you know? But if you're ugly, you're avoided. You know how many suitors I've had in my life? None. You know why? Because no one wants to court a girl that looks like me." She paused, rubbing her brow. "I'm sorry. I'm not trying to dump my problems on you. I know I shouldn't let it bother me."

"You know," Marcus began, leaning close. "A scandalous past *does* affect how people treat me. I've already told you I have few friends and no family. And as for suitors, I've had none as well, either because the women didn't want to know me because of my past or because I didn't want to know them because they were shallow and arrogant. There's only been two people I've ever met who have known my past and treated me well: King Edward, because he went through a similar experience, and you."

"You just told me your past, Marcus. How would you know I'd be different?"

"I'm not ignorant," he muttered. "If the guards talked of you, then I know they talked of me. I'm sure you overheard plenty."

Bernie pressed her lips together, nodding. "I didn't want to say anything, but yeah...they said a few things."

"And yet even though you knew, you treated me well. Why?"

"Because you couldn't help what your parents did," Bernie replied. "It wasn't your fault. Why should you pay for that?"

"And yet you were still kind to me," he said, a smile coming across his face. "Our situations, though different, are also very similar. You didn't cause your hair loss. None of it was your fault. So why do you think I'd hold such a thing against you?"

She looked away, unsure. Why didn't he mock her? He was supposed to, just like everyone else. "It didn't stop the others," she said.

"No, just like it didn't stop them from mocking me," he replied. "But there are people in the world, Your Majesty, who are understanding and kind. You don't listen to the ones who mock you, because they're ignorant. Instead, listen to the ones who care about you regardless of your appearance."

"Or past."

"Or past," he repeated with a snicker. He then paused, his face suddenly blushing as he bowed his head. "Anyone who has mocked you and I acted out of foolishness. They are too blind to see the beauty you possess. You are the type of woman that exudes beauty on the outside and in, and those are the most beautiful of them all."

She smiled at the compliment. No one had ever said that to her before, and she wondered if anyone would again.

He bent down, picking up a small flower near his foot. Bernie noticed it was a small dandelion, freshly bloomed from the spring rains. He lifted it and gently put it behind her ear, his fingers brushing the strands of her remaining hair. His touch felt so gentle around her, and she felt her heart flutter when it neared her cheek. "No matter what anyone says, I hope you know that you need not feel any shame with me. With…or without…your hair, you are still a lovely woman in my eyes. I just hope you learn to see it, too."

He lowered his hand, meeting her gaze, and it was at that moment that maybe…just maybe…she realized she had been wrong about him, too. Ever since they first met, Bernie thought of Marcus Peterson as the snobbish knight who defended the king no matter what. But now, after getting to know him and seeing him during his best and worst moments, she realized that they weren't so different after all. Sure, they had different likes, tastes, personalities…but they had one thing in common: lessons in life.

They both learned compassion from being treated poorly by others. They both learned loyalty after so many abandonments. They both valued beauty of the heart because they saw that was where true beauty lied.

"Why are you so different?" Bernie asked.

"Probably the same reasons you are," Marcus answered with a smirk. "God and life."

"I guess so." She smiled. "But you know what? I'm glad you're different."

He snickered. "You'd be the first to admit that."

"Really?"

"There are a few people who don't appreciate true chivalry."

She blushed. "I hope you know, Marcus, that I do. If more were like you, this world wouldn't be so cruel."

"That's why we kind folks need to stick together," he said. "Your encouragement has been refreshing. I've never had it from a woman."

"I've never had it from a man."

"Then I suppose this trip has had a benefit." He gazed at her, his lips curling upward.

She matched his look, and she found him quite handsome in the firelight. "I guess it has," she said. "Thank you for comforting me, Marcus. I know it wasn't easy telling me about your family."

"It wasn't any easier for you telling me about your hair," he replied. "But that's what we are, aren't we? Two brave souls surviving the Kurzwood with nothing but our minds and strength. What's a little scandal and hair going to do to us that we haven't already handled?"

She chuckled, nodding. "I'll give you that one."

"I mean, we survived edelbears and boars."

"And you survived taking care of me," Bernie added. "That's saying something. But Marcus?"

He faced her, a smile never leaving his lips. "Yes?"

"I know you said that I'd never have to feel shame around you, but I hope you know that...you should never feel shame when you're with me."

His smile deepened. "I wouldn't have told you if I didn't think you'd understand."

"Thank you for telling me," she said. "And thank you for letting me vent. I'm sorry."

"Don't be sorry for that. But promise me something, alright?" His face then became serious, his voice lowering. "When you get back home and you look at yourself in the mirror, tell yourself the words I'm telling you now: *you're beautiful.*"

"Well of course you are, Marcus. Any girl would say that!" She meant it as a joke, but he only shook his head as his gaze softened.

"I mean tell *yourself* how beautiful *you* are," he reminded. "Because unless you believe it, no one else will, either."

She nodded slowly, letting the truth of his words sink in before a burning smell passed by and interrupted their conversation.

"What's that?" Bernie sniffed.

"Smells like..." Marcus paused, looking to the fire and widening his eyes. "BURNT FISH!"

He scrambled up, hurrying to the blazing fire as it burnt their dinner to a crisp. Marcus held up the skewers for a moment before they snapped and gave way, and he turned to Bernie with a sigh.

"Shall we hunt for more boar once the rains stop?"

"Only if you let me shoot."

Marcus cocked his brow, snickering. "I'll go back to the river, then."

When the rains stopped, she watched him from the shelter, her eyes never leaving his form. But it wasn't his body that she found herself liking the most (though she couldn't deny he *really* was a looker.) No, what drew her was simply who he was – his personality, his beliefs, his kindness. Mother always said if a woman wasn't beautiful, a man could never love her, but...Marcus was different. He was handsome enough that despite his background, he really could have any woman he wanted, but he didn't.

Instead, he complimented *her*. Called her beautiful, both inside and out. Listened to her rant and comforted her when she cried. Built her up instead of tear her down.

For a moment she wondered if she was becoming attracted to him...

She scoffed at the idea. He was the same man who annoyed her back in Reigal, the same man she tried to feed a bug-filled salad to at dinner. Heavens, she even tried to jump out of a window to avoid him because she found him so repulsive.

But as she watched him catch more fish for their dinner, she found her eyes never leaving his sight, and when he came back, she felt her heart flutter when he smiled at her, and she couldn't help but smile back.

# Chapter 22: Aftermath

Maria had been sleeping for hours when a pounding on the door awakened her.

"*YOUR MAJESTY!*" She had never heard such a racket, and she scrambled out of bed, barely having time to cover herself with a robe. She opened the door, almost perturbed at such an interruption, but one look on the guard's face told her whatever it was, the news was bad.

"Forgive the disturbance, my queen," the guard stammered, his voice shaking. "There's been an assassination attempt."

Maria froze, her mind suddenly going to her son. She prayed that Edward was alive, prayed that no harm came to him. "What happened?"

"An intruder attacked the king in his bed."

She felt her heart want to stop, but she remained strong. She was still a queen and couldn't falter no matter who wore her crown. "Is he well?"

"He's injured."

"How badly?"

"We're unsure. He's unconscious and hasn't woken."

She wasted no time in leaving her room, following the guard down the halls to where her son had been taken for treatment.    The palace was astir, servants and guards scrambling about doing their duty, but she paid them no heed. She had to get to her boy.  Grown man or not, Edward would always be her baby, and if he was hurt, she needed to be there to make him better.

"Was the intruder caught?" Maria asked, her spirit burning in anger.

"No, Your Majesty.  The guard is currently out in the city looking for him."

"Do we know who attacked him?"

"A Velori."

"Velori?" Maria paused, thinking back to where she heard the name before.  She remembered Edward speaking of them when he told her of his trip to Cathal.  They were a Verloris group, mysterious and unknown…but deadly.

"What of my son's wife?"

The guard pressed his lips in a frown.  "She was found unconscious and is resting."

"Did she know what happened?"

"Very little.    She's been asking more questions than answering them."

"Keep her under guard and comfortable lest the assassin returns," Maria said, her mind suddenly curious.    It was strange a Velori was in the palace, just so happening to attempt to kill Edward and not his wife.  She was suspicious, not feeling surprised if Malina tried such a thing for retaliation because of his undying love to Antoinette.

"Your son is in this room, Your Majesty, but the doctors are still working on him," the guard said, pointing to the king's bedroom. "He wasn't moved much. The bleeding was too strong."

"Your Majesty!" Sir Rikert called out, jogging to the queen mother.

"Samuel!" She looked at his uniform, covered in blood, and she suddenly felt very cold. Just how bad was Edward's injuries? "Is my son going to be alright?"

"We'll know more once the doctors finish working on him," Samuel replied. "For now, I will tell you what happened."

He led her to the parlor next door, and as she passed the room, she noticed Edward lying on the bed and surrounded by doctors.

He looked pale, his body red and bloating around the abdomen where a wound clearly lay. Maria stopped, watching as they worked on him, and she had a sudden desire to barge into the room and hold her little boy.

"Please, Your Majesty," Sir Rikert said, gently taking her by the arm and leading away. "To the parlor."

She reluctantly followed, saying a prayer for her baby to live.

---

Malina had been awake for a few minutes before it registered what had happened. Between the dizziness, anxiety, and confusion, she felt as if she'd gone mad for a moment during her fight with Edward. But after understanding the voices around her, realizing that she was no longer in her bedroom and facing a shadowed assailant before everything went dark, she knew what had happened.

Edward was near death, and everything was about to fall apart.

She knew it was Vacius who attacked them when one of the guards mentioned a Velori. She cursed his name, cursed every moment she had ever loved on the man and felt pleasure. Once, he was her helper in manipulating the board and playing the game. Now, he was the man swiping his hand across the pieces, destroying every carefully planned move with one stupid choice.

She knew what was coming next, knew that it didn't take a genius to connect her to Vacius and make her suspect in the king's attack. Even if she was knocked out unconscious, someone would make a connection, and all it took was a rally of Edward's friends and family to do her in for sure.

She needed a miracle, a clever plan to somehow keep her from execution or prison.

In truth, she needed Malum.

But how she was going to get to him was anyone's guess. She needed to escape, needed to flee to somehow get word to him of what happened...

"Your Majesty, I need you to tell us as much as you know about what happened before you were attacked."

Malina faced the guard's firm glare with her own. "I already told you. My husband and I were readying for bed. He was tired and so was I. He lied down to rest and I had gone to the door to check on our son before retiring for the night, and when I turned, I was grabbed by a man in the shadows. There was something on the cloth he put to my face that knocked me out, and the next thing I knew I was awaking in front of you all."

The guard nodded, the others keenly listening. "The witnesses say it was a Velori who attacked."

"And how do you know it was?"

"The attacker confessed himself to be one."

Malina wanted to curse him again for his stupidity. Never, *never*, should he have admitted who he was!

"Do you know anything about them, seeing as they are from your land?"

Malina shook her head, feigning shock as she weakened her voice to sound distressed. "Very little. They were simply villains in fairy stories told to children. I never thought they could be real."

"Well the truth was learned this day."

"As if I knew it ever could be!" Malina replied. "But enough of them. Tell me, what of my husband? Is he alright?"

"He is alive."

"And will he remain that way?"

The guard frowned, lowering his head. "We're unsure."

At least there was hope. If Edward died, then Malina had a chance to rally what nobles and friends she had to her cause, to put Calimus on the throne and rule in his stead until he grew up. And once that happened, she could overthrow him. Then she'd have the crown forever.

But she was curious over Vacius. Was he still out there? If he was, he would never stop until the job was finished. "Have you caught the Velori?"

"No, Your Majesty. We're still looking."

She nodded, unsure of whether to feel relief or anger. She would feign concern until she knew how to deal with it. "You will let me know if he is caught, of course. I don't like knowing my husband's attacker is still out there."

"We will find him, Your Majesty. You needn't worry."

But the truth was, she was already there. She lowered her head to her palm, a sick feeling in her stomach, and suddenly she began to panic. If she was pregnant, then Edward would know she was cheating on him. She never had a chance to sleep with him, never had a chance to hide her condition...

Her anger burned against Vacius, and more than ever she hoped her pregnancy was false, just like her undying love for the Velori had been.

---

Edward wasn't sure of the time when he started to rouse. Voices were muffled around him, a strange light hurting his eyes when he opened them. Everything was hazy, a giant blur he could barely make out, but once time had passed and his vision became clearer, he realized just what had happened.

He was in a bed, bandaged and sewn like a ripped curtain, surrounded by his mother and a few guards.

"What...happened?" His voice was slightly above a whisper, but everyone heard it like a yell as Maria put her hand to her lips and cried in delight.

"My sweet baby! You had us so worried!" She leaned forward, putting her hand on his cheek.

"I…" He paused, his mind suddenly becoming clearer. He was starting to remember what happened, how Vacius attacked him and told him everything he didn't want to hear.

*Malina.* There was no time to waste. If she wasn't arrested, she would escape to try and kill him again.

"Get…me…Samuel." Edward turned his head to one of the guards.

"I'm right here, Your Majesty," Sir Rikert replied, stepping forward. "What can I do?"

"I need…you to do…something."

"Anything, Your Majesty."

"I need you…to arrest my wife."

Sir Rikert widened his eyes and Maria gave a gasp. "Edward?" she asked. "What's going on?"

"Vacius…the Velori…" Edward had to force his words through the pain, and every syllable sounded like a grunt. "He was…her lover…he confessed…they wanted me…dead…to take the throne…"

"*What*?" Maria shook her head, shock overwhelming her.

"He…confessed to…killing Father…"

Shock soon turned to rage as Maria turned to Sir Rikert, standing to her feet. "Put that woman in jail *now*!"

"Right away, Your Majesties," Sir Rikert hurried out, taking another guard with him.

Maria sat back down beside her son, taking her hand in his. "Malina…she…she did all of this?"

None of it came as a surprise, though his father's death filled him with hurt. He hadn't told Mother of what really killed him inside. Calimus…the fact that he wasn't his son…

"Edward?" Maria looked at him with pity. "I'm so sorry…"

He only could close his eyes, the pain too much to bear. As he was nodding off again to go to sleep, he could hear Malina yelling through the hallways.

"Unhand me, you wretched beasts! What is the meaning of this?"

"For the assassination attempt on His Majesty, King Edward, the royal guard places you under arrest. You are to be held in prison until further notice." Sir Rikert's voice was firm, but Malina struggled for dominance.

"You can't do this! I am your queen!"

"And the king's word is above yours," Sir Rikert replied. "Now come along."

"You think a prison will hold me? The people will hear of this injustice and demand my release!"

"We have a confession and an attempted murder. The people will not care."

"What confession? From Edward? No word should ever be believed from him! He plots against me! He seeks to ruin me!"

"And yet your lover attempted to kill him."

"You have no proof! You are going by Edward's word alone!"

"And it is enough!"

"You fools! I have proof of his falsehood! I have proof that he has lied to you this entire time!"

Edward opened his eyes back up. Surely she wouldn't mention Stephen. Surely she wouldn't release his greatest secret...

"Edward is a liar, a thief, an adulterer..." But suddenly Malina's words were cut short as she sounded like she was being bound and gagged, and Sir Rikert's voice boomed in the hall.

"She has fed us enough poison!" Rikert said. "Lock her in the prison. The law will decide her fate once the king is recovered and the intruder found."

Malina was then dragged away, her muffled voice screaming as she undoubtedly struggled to be free.

Edward felt his heart racing, and suddenly he was afraid. He knew what was going to happen, knew what he was about to face in his near future.

Malina was going to tell his secret, and knowing her, she would somehow have proof.

He closed his eyes, his body aching for rest as the pain tried to overtake him. He would have to confess, have to admit his greatest sin and explain the truth before she could.

And if that happened, the future would be unknown. If the public found out, they'd demand he be overthrown.

"Edward? Sweetheart?" Maria's voice brought him out of his stupor, and the look on her face broke his heart.

No, he couldn't let her down anymore. He couldn't let his secret come out and take away the only family he had left.

He'd have to keep Malina locked up for the moment to protect himself and his son. And with an assassination attempt, the law would be on his side. But what else the law would decide was another worry...

Edward took in a deep breath, praying for guidance like he never had before. Then, after a sudden rush of pain in his belly, exhaustion overwhelmed him, and he was plunged back into sleep.

# Chapter 23: The Ambassador

It was early in the morning when Aldaric walked the king's halls on his way to the royal dining room.

He watched as the servants eyed him warily, a few of them gossiping behind his back. He ignored their stares, his hands holding tight to the stack of papers being carried, and he bowed his head.

The door to the dining area was opened, and after an announcement from the guards, Aldaric walked in, noticing neither the king nor his sons looked up from eating their breakfast. Aldaric approached the table, clearing his throat, and after an awkward moment of silence, Prince Ambrose finally looked up.

"I think we have a visitor, Father."

Prince Ulrich gave a snicker, bits of sausage falling from his lips. "What is it this time, Daric? Are you to annoy us with your rambles even earlier today?"

Aldaric barely acknowledged their sarcasm as he faced the king.

Erick lifted his head, sighing as if perturbed. "Come here." He gave a wave of his hand, allowing Aldaric to approach. "What is it?"

"I have letters to the ambassadors in Edeland," Aldaric replied, handing them to him. "With your permission, I'd like to arrange a meeting to discuss the incident that happened with my son and diffuse any harsh feelings or misunderstandings that have occurred."

Erick gave a laugh, shaking his head. "You must be truly desperate to be calling in favors, Aldaric." He read over the letters quickly, barely giving them a glance. "It won't work. I've made my decision and it is final. Emmerich's actions risked our trade agreements with Edeland, and such a blow would hurt our economy. I know you disagree with what I've done, but that is how it will be."

Aldaric pressed his lips together, silence becoming difficult. "Your Majesty, I understand that tensions between the nations are growing since Edward's...marriage...but please understand that I can help settle things down. I only ask for the chance and – "

Erick snapped his fingers, motioning for a servant to approach. The servant bowed, and the king pointed to the letters. "Add these to the fire. It's getting a bit drafty in here. Must be an extra wind."

The servant obeyed, taking Aldaric's letters and tossing them into the hearth behind them.

Aldaric tensed, but remained quiet as Ulrich and Ambrose's eyes were on him, waiting for an outburst to come forth. He knew Erick was pushing his buttons, just waiting for an excuse to be rid of him too, but he wouldn't give it. He wouldn't let the man win.

"Very well, Your Majesty. I will take my leave." Aldaric gave a quick bow, turning to hurry out the door lest his temper released, but Erick called him back.

"Wait."

Aldaric faced him, nodding. "Yes?"

"Are you still going to Audlin?"

"My wife and I plan to leave in the morning," Aldaric answered.

"Cancel it."

Aldaric blinked, his face showing concern. "What? Why?"

"I need you here. We are having a council meeting and the nobles wish to hear the report on your progress with the Braiden ore trade."

Aldaric watched as Ambrose gave a snicker behind his hand, Ulrich stuffing his mouth full of food before a laugh could be released. Seeing them take joy in being denied to see his son filled him with hurt, and he couldn't help but clench his fists in fury.

"Your Majesty, with respect, Anna promised Emery that we would bring his things to Reigal," Aldaric said, turning back to the king.

"I know," Erick replied. "But I need you here instead." He picked up a slice of bread from his plate, taking a bite. "Your first priority is your nation, Aldaric. As head ambassador, it is your duty to ensure the nations around us are happy."

"There are other ambassadors, Your Majesty," Aldaric replied, his jaw tightening.

"Yes, but they're not as eloquent as you," Erick said with a grin. "Besides, you've been gone long enough chasing your boy to Edeland and back. I need you here."

"But…"

"Either you remain here, or I will find another ambassador," Erick said, his voice firming. "I had no problem banishing Emmerich for his disobedience, Aldaric. Do not think I will hesitate with you."

Aldaric felt his heart pound in fury, but he remained quiet. Anna would be heartbroken at the news, and he almost wondered if she'd go on to Reigal without him because she wanted to be near their son.

"Now go. I'd like to finish my breakfast in peace," Erick said.

Aldaric nodded, hurrying out of the room as his anger nearly overwhelmed him. If his wife was there, she'd be livid, accusing the king of taking advantage of her husband's good nature and unwillingness to have conflict. Sure, it made Aldaric a pushover, but after a lifetime of family arguments and problems, keeping the peace seemed like the better option.

But when keeping others happy made him miserable, he almost started to wonder if everything he did was worth it. Erick was happy. Ulrich and Ambrose were, too. But they weren't having to part with their only child, nor did they have to sit back and watch their family be torn apart.

Aldaric grumbled to himself as he entered the hallway, but was soon interrupted as he was approached by a messenger.

"Chief Bohden received your letter," the man replied, handing Aldaric a small note. "He has arrived at the place you requested."

"Thank you," Aldaric replied. "Ready my horse. I'd like to leave immediately."

"Yes, sir."

Aldaric took the note in his hand, breaking the seal and opening it. Though the day had been full of hardships, at least one thing would go right.

Chief Bohden was there in Hugellia, and if anyone knew how to navigate the crisis, it would be him.

But as Aldaric read the contents of the paper in his hand, he suddenly felt the meeting would give him more questions than answers.

*You inquire about the hurricane, but rain is not your worry. The fire approaches, and if you remain, you will be burned.*

---

The scene of Emmerich's final moments before leaving Kettensburg replayed in Aldaric's mind as he trotted outside the city to a small camp in the northeast.

*"I don't want to go. I don't want to go." Emmerich repeated the words over and over as he stood, too shocked to move as Aldaric had to pack his things.*

*Anna's arms remained around her son's as she cried, but Aldaric knew he had to be fast. The guards only gave him so much time to leave, and if they were too slow, Emmerich would be forced out with nothing.*

*"We've weathered other storms before. We'll get through this one." He tried to be encouraging, but the look on Emery's face proved he didn't believe it.*

*"But…it's the hurricane, Dad. Bohden was right. I didn't want to believe it, but he was right…"*

*Aldaric had paused from the packing, looking at his son in confusion. He remembered hearing Emery mention entering a hurricane back in the carriage, but he thought it nothing but a figure of speech. Now that Bohden's name was mentioned, however, he started to wonder if the Recu chieftain gave him something other than a name.*

*"Emery, what did Bohden say?"*

*At first his son didn't want to reveal it, but after gentle prodding, he came clean. "Bohden had a vision," Emery replied. "Something about me being caught in a hurricane and nearly drowning. He thought there were some bad things ahead. I guess this is one of them."*

That was all Emery could say before the guards came in and forced him out. As soon as he left, Aldaric ran to the desk and produced a letter, wanting to know more. He knew little about Bohden, but what he did know was that the man was greatly revered for his prophecies, and they were always accurate. And if Emery was about to suffer, Aldaric was bound and determined to know not only what was ahead, but how he could protect his son.

He approached the small camp of Recu, the dogs wagging their tails happily at seeing Aldaric. Normally he'd stop and pet the creatures, but he was in no mood for a visit. He wanted answers, and there would be no time to waste.

He barely awaited acknowledgement before being sent in to see the chieftain.

Bohden was standing, facing the blankness of the tent wall, hands clasped behind his back and body still. Aldaric approached, about to speak a greeting, until Bohden interrupted.

"It's a boy."

Aldaric paused from his words, closing his mouth and looking at the man in confusion. For one, he never knew

Bohden to speak his language, and two, he had no idea what Bohden meant by saying, "It's a boy."

As if reading his mind, Bohden turned, producing a smile that exuded the confidence shown in his stance. "You must tell your son that when you see him. It will give him great comfort in the days to come."

Aldaric blinked, unsure of how to respond. "I don't understand."

"You're not supposed to," Bohden replied. "But it will all make sense in time." He held out his hand, motioning towards a chair beside him. "Sit. You wished to talk?"

Aldaric nodded as he took the seat, watching as Bohden sat across. "I did." He paused, shaking his head. "But I'm a little confused. How do you speak our language?"

Bohden smirked. "I learned."

"In a few weeks?"

"I've known for a long time, Aldaric, and I'm happy to finally reveal it to you." He rested against the chair back, relaxing his legs forward. "You are ready to rid yourself of this place and I no longer have to worry about you going to Erick." He paused, tilting his head. "At least...I hope. Your letter makes me think you're more curious about your son's banishment, though."

Aldaric nodded. "Emery didn't mention much because he had to leave so quickly. He did say, however, that you gave him more than just the name 'Recu-vera'."

"I did."

"And what did you tell him?"

"Only what he needed to hear," Bohden replied. "And it is up to him to deal with it. Where he is going, you can't follow."

"And why not?"

"Because your road is different." Bohden exhaled slowly. "I told Emmerich that he faces a hurricane, and it is true. What the hurricane is and how it will manifest itself, I cannot say, but it is clear that there are tough times ahead. But fear not – he will survive."

Aldaric swallowed hard. "You mentioned in your letter about the fire. Is this related to the vision you told me before?" He remembered back to when he first met Bohden, leaving with such confusion at the riddles he gave.

*It was the second time they met, nearly three years ago, and Aldaric thought it nothing but another discussion on setting up trade. But before he could say anything about economics, Bohden stopped and said he had a vision. Troubled times were ahead, and what he saw was anything but clear.*

*"Fires scorch from within. Family will betray you. If you remain in Kettensburg, you will be burned, but if you leave, only smoke will be seen from a distance. Make your choice soon, for the armies are coming."*

He remembered asking for an interpretation, but Bohden said little save that he spoke what he saw and nothing more. Now, as he stood before Bohden again, Aldaric wondered if an interpretation had come.

"The fire remains. It is about to spark," Bohden replied solemnly, his face stern. "The same vision I saw before has appeared to me again as a dream. I fear the time is drawing near, and Emmerich's banishment is a part of it."

"How so?"

"It will save him."

"Save him? From these fires, whatever they are?"

Bohden nodded.

"But I thought you said Emmerich would go through hard times."

"He will, but the fire will not burn him like it will you if you stay." He leaned forward, his dark eyes bearing into Aldaric's. "I met you here today not to talk about Emmerich, but to warn you. My dreams, my visions…they're becoming more frequent, and every time I see them, they become more real. I cannot give you an interpretation, as I am not one with such a gift for it. But I can tell you what I see. I see Kettensburg burning and an army surrounding its walls. I see the king weakened and old, his pride turned to shame and humility. I see buildings crumble and people running to the hills. I see the death of Hugellia, and all I can sense is that it is someone from within who will bring it to pass."

He backed up into the seat, a casual stance returning to his form. "Sometimes I see you there amidst the chaos, Aldaric. Sometimes I don't. But seeing Emmerich's banishment, and knowing your relations with the king must be strained because of it, I give you warning. You have your chance to leave before the fires burn. If you do not take it, I fear you will not get another."

Aldaric breathed slowly, folding his hands and resting his lips on his fingers. "So you're saying I should leave and go to my son?"

"I can't make the decision for you. I can only warn you of what's ahead," Bohden replied. "But even if you go back, Emmerich will be alone in his walk. I did not see you in his vision. Nothing you do will help him."

"So it doesn't matter if I stay or go?"

"It doesn't affect him. It only affects you."

Bohden was silent for a few seconds, waiting for Aldaric to respond. Aldaric sat there, trying to process everything Bohden was saying, but still not understanding. Fires, armies, King Erick being humbled...it almost sounded like Hugellia was going to be attacked.

"Is war coming?" He hated to be blunt, but he had to know. As terrible as it was, he wanted to protect his family, his people. Hugellia may have betrayed him, but he didn't want to leave them for punishment.

"War is already here, Aldaric," Bohden answered. "It has been fought unseen for a while. But now..." He paused, giving a sigh. "Now it is different. Something's happened to bring what was hidden to light."

"Which is...?"

"I don't know," Bohden replied. "But I have a feeling we'll find out soon."

"What can I do to prepare, then?" Aldaric asked. "If Hugellia needs to gather their forces, I should stay and warn the king and..."

"You don't understand, Aldaric. Hugellia isn't the only place I saw fire burning." He paused, closing his eyes as if remembering vivid nightmares. "Audlin, Edeland, Braiden, Verloris...the fires touched everything it could see. No matter where you go, war will exist until the king rises again. But that is not connected to you. All you must decide is whether you stay here or you go." He paused, frowning. "But know that if you stay here, you will be burned. And there is nothing you can do to prevent it except leave."

Aldaric felt his pulse speed in his chest, the heavy *thump, thump, thump* seeming like it was about to jump out of his throat. He took a deep breath, trying to calm himself as he stepped into the room. What he was about to do, he had never done before. It was folly, foolish, stupid. But he had to make a choice. Bohden's words of warning rang clear and his message was taken to heart. No matter what, he couldn't stop the war that was coming. No matter what, he had to keep his wife and son safe.

And that meant saying good-bye.

King Erick sat at the center of the table, Ulrich and Ambrose beside him, finishing lunch when they saw him walk in.

"What is it now, Aldaric?" Erick asked, rubbing his brow. "We already discussed the meeting with Braiden. I'm sorry, but your trip to Reigal will have to wait and..."

"I'm going to Reigal," Aldaric said, his voice quiet yet firm. "I'm staying with Maria and will take care of my son."

"Don't trifle with me now," Erick muttered in disapproval. "I already told you that you are needed for the meeting with Braiden. I don't recommend upsetting them and your king because you want to take another holiday!"

"This isn't a short stay, Your Majesty," Aldaric said, looking up and facing his stepfather. "This is permanent. I'm resigning my post as head ambassador of Hugellia."

Ulrich gave a laugh as Ambrose followed, but Erick said nothing as his eyes widened. "Your jokes are improving!" Ulrich laughed. "I daresay we've found our new court jester!"

"I'm being perfectly serious." Aldaric lowered his brow, and his brothers began to quiet. "I've just spoken to Anna. She approves of my decision and is already packing our things."

Ulrich and Ambrose looked at each other in confusion, but Erick shook his head.

"If you're wanting sympathy for Emmerich, know that you won't get it," Erick began, his voice firm. "I won't bend on my decision to banish him."

"I'm not asking you to change your mind," Aldaric replied. "I'm only changing mine." He paused, watching as Erick's eyes narrowed into fury. "I have left a letter of resignation to be delivered to your chambers. I have also left a list of suitable replacements. It will not be difficult to fill my position. As I have nothing further to say, I bid you all a pleasant day. Anna and I will be gone by nightfall." He then bowed, turning to exit the room.

But before he could take a step, the king rose to his feet, his voice booming. "Be still, boy! Do not turn your back on your king!"

Aldaric stopped, turning around and facing his stepfather. "What is it?"

"You're not permitted to leave! I forbid it!"

"Why?"

"Because you are in *my* service. You are *my* ambassador! How dare you throw away your duties to king and country for some pathetic child who thinks himself a man!"

"That child is *my* child, Your Majesty," Aldaric replied, his voice desperate to remain calm. "And with respect, my duty is to him and my wife. There is nothing more I can do for Hugellia."

"You would leave us to rot?"

"You and I both know that my influence is small in the grand scheme of things. I am a mere ambassador, spreading your message to other nations and giving you their reply. The nation is not in my hands, but yours."

"Yet you would abandon your family here?"

"My family is my wife and son," Aldaric said. "And their future is in Audlin, which is where I will be."

Erick leaned forward and clasped the table before him, his knuckles turning bright from his clenching fists. "I know your heart, Aldaric. You seek to supplant me through Edward, but I will not allow it! If you dare stand against me, I will defeat you!"

Aldaric shook his head, scoffing. How pathetic had his stepfather become, suspecting that his wife's son was nothing more than a usurper seeking riches and power? If Aldaric truly wished for the kingdom, he could have had it. He was a friend of kings and princes of faraway lands and knew the laws of Hugellia better than most. It wouldn't be complicated to overthrow Erick with the connections he had.

But he was no usurper, nor was he greedy. He was content with his choices in life, and he would abide by them.

"You think me always trying to take from you, when in reality all I've ever done is give," Aldaric began, his voice shaking as he remembered the hurt from his past. Growing up with a distant father-figure who hated him. Feeling like an outcast as he became the only child in the royal family without a title. "Not once have I ever disrespected you. Not once have I gone against your word. I have built you up when you've done nothing but tear me down, but no more. I will not let you use me again, and I refuse to be parted with the only family I have that's remained loyal.

"I will leave with my wife and we will go to Reigal. I will offer my services to Edward and him alone. You needn't worry about me anymore, as I doubt you will ever see me again after today. I have never wanted your throne, nor have I ever wanted your power. I have only wanted the love of a father, and I see that no matter how much I do for you, you will never give it to me." He paused, lowering his head. "I am ashamed to ever think you would have. But now I know, and I refuse to give a second thought to it anymore."

He raised his head, watching as Erick listened to him in silence, his face unreadable. "Before I leave, however, I will share with you one thing that Bohden of the Recu has shared with me."

"Bohden? I thought we were ignoring that madman!" Ambrose scoffed.

"He is nothing but a dreamer with an ill-tamed tongue. He has nothing good to say," Ulrich added.

"Bohden has foreseen war coming to the nations very soon," Aldaric continued. "How, he does not know, nor does he know when. All he could say was that it would be soon and that we should all prepare."

"If you think your words of doom will scare me into giving him trade, think again Aldaric!" Erick spat. "I have nothing to do with barbarians, especially those who live in the snow!"

"I only repeat what Bohden has told me. He said that you would not listen," Aldaric muttered. "If war does come, then I pray you all are wise and keep this country safe." He turned around again, heading towards the door.

He didn't bother with a farewell, didn't bother with a good-bye. He heard Erick shout his name repeatedly, even ordering him to come back in threat of banishment if he didn't listen. But Aldaric didn't look back, nor did he say a word. He was done with Erick, with Ambrose and Ulrich, and he was not going to give them any more of his time.

He could only pray that somehow the coming war would spare them, or that Bohden's vision was wrong.

# Chapter 24: The Repentant Heart

They had traveled for days, the unending roads and sleepless nights almost too much for Antoinette to handle. Bernie – she could only imagine her sister's fear and loneliness as she remained lost inside the Kurzwood maze. Though the girl was never one to go down without a fight, Antoinette knew that even the bravest of warriors could be defeated in time because of a death trap like that. Wild animals, hunger, thirst, the cold. Anything and everything could prove the end, and Antoinette could only imagine what her sister had already gone through if she still lived.

She shook her head, refusing to acknowledge such defeat. Bernie was strong, smart, capable. If anyone could survive in the Kurzwood, it was her.

"Did you know that only five men have ever been found alive out of the hundred that have been lost in the last year?" Arnold's words from earlier dug under her skin, and she wished more than ever that his mouth remained shut. She didn't want statistics or false sympathy. She wanted hope.

But would that be enough after what she'd done?

They had stopped to rest for a few hours in the night, returning to the road once the horses had their energy back. While the others slept, Antoinette slipped out quietly into the night, walking towards an area of bushes where she could find a moment's peace. Mother had been in hysterics the whole trip and Arnold had been nothing but a bother. Emery was nowhere to be found, either remaining in Staalberg for word or secretly following her like she hoped. Regardless, she needed the time to think, to pray. Nothing she could do would help Bernie stay alive in the forest. The only one who could help her would be God.

She bent down on her knees, hands trembling as she clutched her sister's cross necklace from when she was a child. A gift for her first communion, worn so long ago and treasured as a keepsake. Now it was a reminder of who she beseeched the Almighty for. Surely God in Heaven would spare such an innocent soul from a gruesome death…

She tried closing her eyes, searching for words that were eloquent enough, but as her heart opened up, she realized all poetry and prose had left. All that came from her lips were sobs, cries from within, and the mutterings of a woman in desperate need of help.

"Save my sister," she pleaded in the night. "Save her, Lord. Don't let her suffer." She kissed the cross clutched in her hands, tears covering the rosy beads of the necklace. "I need Bernie. Don't take her away."

"What are you doing? Your mother wants to see you."

Antoinette was startled from her prayers, and she turned to see Arnold approach with cocked brow. He stood above her, rolling his eyes as he saw the tear-streaked face of "his wife" and her kneeling form.

"I was praying," she answered.

"Why?"

"Because God can do miracles that no one else can."

"Really, Antoinette, you worry for nothing," Arnold said with a sigh. "Your sister is in a forest. It's not like people haven't camped before."

She lowered her brow. "This is different."

"How so?"

"She has no food, no water, no shelter," Antoinette said, her voice harsh. "She is alone and afraid with nothing to defend herself!  Were it one of your brothers, surely you would be worried!"

"Were it one of my brothers, I should be glad to be rid of one more nuisance," Arnold muttered. "They're quite dull, you know. Perhaps a better example can be thought of."

Antoinette scoffed. "Do you care for anything but yourself?"

Arnold chuckled. "Not really."

"Then no wonder you are so vile."

"Better to be vile than to be weak. Now come, my dove. Your mother is asking for you."

"I will be there in a moment. I'm talking to God." She then turned with a huff, folding her hands once more and closing her eyes.

"Why?"

She wanted to curse Arnold's interruptions. Even if he didn't care for Bernie, he didn't have to try and stop her from doing so. "Because God listens to the cries of His people."

"And you really think that?"

"I know that."

Arnold smirked. "And what makes you think He'd listen to you?"

Antoinette turned her head, eyes glaring. "Because I serve Him."

"Ah," Arnold said as he stepped closer. "A fine job you've done, I must say. All this lying and deceit."

Antoinette lowered her brow. "What do you mean?"

"Forgive me if I'm wrong, my darling, but I thought saints followed God, not sinners."

"But I have done nothing wrong."

"Haven't you? Or do you call lying to your family and nation about your marriage to Emmerich a righteous deed?"

Antoinette suddenly felt cold, as if winter covered her head and body. Surely the Almighty wouldn't punish Bernie for the deeds she had done, would He?

No. He wasn't like that. God would not harm the innocent to punish the guilty. If anyone would bear the consequences of sin, it would be the sinner herself. At least…she hoped.

"Maybe instead of praying for something you know you can't control, perhaps you should pray for penance," Arnold said. "I'd think God would be better apt to forgive you than to save a lost cause."

"I don't believe you," Antoinette said, forcing her faith to the surface. "God won't abandon my sister! She is in His hands even now, whether in the forest or in Heaven."

"Oh, really! Don't get so worked up about it." Arnold shook his head in frustration. "Regardless, you must see to your mother. I do believe she's about to strangle a guard just because she has no one to vent her worry on."

"Then comfort her until I'm done."

"Can't you?"

"I'm busy." She waited, her face firm, until Arnold gave a scoff.

He crossed his arms in a huff. "Very well. Though I must admit my charms feel awkward on your mother. She's so...old."

She lowered her brow. "Just go."

He shrugged, shuffling away and leaving her alone with her thoughts.

She faced forward, folding her hands in the proper position of prayer. As she opened her mouth to speak, however, her heart became heavy, and all she could do was lower her head in shame.

*Forgive me for lying about my marriage,* she whispered in her heart. *I didn't know what else to do. I still don't know. But Father in Heaven, I beg you...don't let anyone pay for my mistakes...*

Worry consumed her, thoughts of Bernie being frightened and alone nearly overwhelming her heart and mind. Her body felt heavy as if a burden weighed it down, and Antoinette couldn't help but lower herself to the ground, bowing her head and resting it on her arms.

She wept silently to herself, not noticing the light of the moon peek through the clouds and shine down upon her back.

# Chapter 25: The Search

When Antoinette first saw the camp, she became overwhelmed with worry.

Though the bodies were removed and being prepared for burial, the items in the camp itself were torn and shredded. Blood and remains were strewn about the carriage pieces, and when Antoinette found one of Bernie's books scratched and red near what seemed to be her bedding, she couldn't help but burst into tears. What if it was Bernie's blood on that book? What if she was hurt? What if she was dying? What if she was already dead?

Antoinette dropped the book to the ground, not wanting to think of it. Her mind was already overwhelmed with anxiety and she had to be strong, at least for Mother.

Because Mother was already on the brink of insanity when they arrived. She bickered with the guards to no end, not sleeping since the news was first broken to her and insisting everyone else do the same. Antoinette was tired, exhausted, but at the same time she understood. It was hard to sleep with the mind so anxious, and since Father and her brothers helped the guards on the other end of the trail, it was up to Antoinette and Arnold to be strong lest Susanna fall apart.

But even that was proving difficult as Antoinette walked through the camp, her mother in the distance yelling at the guards to find her daughter lest they wanted to be tried and hung for their incompetence.

"My, she's getting worked up for nothing," Arnold muttered, stifling a yawn.

"Nothing?" Antoinette clenched her fists, her jaw tensed in fury. "My sister is missing and three people are dead! How can you remain calm through this?"

"My little dove, you know nothing of her fate except that she's in a forest. If a squirrel can survive here, anything can."

"It's not that easy," Antoinette muttered. "The Kurzwood is so thick and wild that people typically avoid it. Even guides can get lost in its woods."

"And yet you pass it every trip and are fine."

"Because we stay on the road," Antoinette replied. "Go off the road, and you're guaranteed to be lost." She paused, swallowing hard. "Or killed."

"Well look on the bright side," Arnold chimed in with a smirk. "With your sister gone, it'll be much more peaceful around the house."

Antoinette's face reddened and she edged close to him. "*You heartless, shallow dog! Don't you DARE insult my sister!*"

"Oh, touchy subject?" Arnold replied. "If you're going to be dramatic, at least keep it civil. Wouldn't want to upset your dear mother, now, would you?"

Were it not for Mother's hysterics already, Antoinette would've made a scene that would make an edelbear attack look like playtime. But before she could unleash verbal fury, she felt a small pebble hit her arm.

She looked around, wondering where it came from, and after another gentle *pop*, she found the source behind her through the trees.

Her eyes widened. *Emery*.

She wondered if he would be there, wondered how he could show his support when he was supposed to be hiding from the queen. But despite the risk and possibility of being caught, she was glad to see him. His words would be comforting and his touch would be warm. And if anyone would be willing to find her sister, it was him. He wasn't heartless like Arnold, and never would be.

"Keep the guards distracted," Antoinette muttered to Arnold. "I'm going to see Emery really quick."

"He's here?" Arnold asked.

"Yes, and don't ruin it," she ordered. "After all, we don't want to upset Mother."

He only rolled his eyes as he went on ahead to speak with the guards and distract them as Antoinette tiptoed towards the trees.

She made sure she hid behind a great trunk as she embraced her husband. "You're here…"

"Of course. Why wouldn't I be?"

"I didn't think you'd risk it."

Emery touched her cheek. "She's my sister too. Of course I would be here."

She held him tight, the feel of his chest filling her with warmth and comfort. "The guards have found little. They've seen some marks up ahead where a scout found the trail, but otherwise, nothing. The marks stopped and there's no footprints."

"There wouldn't be," Emmerich said. "The rains have washed much away."

She nodded, her eyes becoming teary. "Oh Emery, do you think she's still out there?"

"I think so." He pulled away and held out his hand. "I found this in the woods."

She looked at the object in his palm. "It's a twig."

"A broken twig."

"And how does that help us?"

"Look at the way it was broken," he said, pointing to it. "It's jagged, rough…but it's a clean break."

"What does that mean?"

"It means something stepped on it."

Antoinette rubbed her brow. "It could be an animal."

"It's a thick twig, Antoinette. The animal would have to be heavy to break it."

"So what are you saying?"

"I'm saying I think I found where she ran." He grinned. "Either her trail or the edelbears'. The guards are wasting their time going up the road and looking for prints when they should be looking at the land."

Antoinette shook her head. "How do you know all of this?"

"They train us in Hugellia," Emmerich replied, "to spot signs of grass lions when traveling through the country. When rains wash prints away, we look at the land itself for clues. And see?" He held the twig up close, pointing to a jagged edge on its side. Antoinette squinted her eyes, looking closer. On it was a tiny piece of white string.

"It's a thread…"

"Exactly," Emmerich replied. "And unless these are strange bears, I doubt they'd be wearing sewn dresses."

Antoinette felt her heart race in excitement. Hugellians were always known for their knowledge of the land and survival. Harsh winters and a history of nomadic living until they built Kettensburg instilled an instinct in its people that survived even now. She never felt more thankful for it!

"Emery, you should help the guards."

His brows rose. "Are you serious? Your mother is here and she'll arrest me on sight!"

"Not if you help her find Bernie," Antoinette replied. "Emery, this is a chance to win her respect."

"I don't see how…"

"She's worried," Antoinette interrupted, her face showing concern. "I know she's a difficult person to deal with and she seems hateful, but she truly loves her children. She's barely slept for days and she's scared about what's happened. If Bernie's found…" She paused, unwilling to say it. "If…this doesn't end well, Emery, I'm not sure how Mother will take it. She's never lost anyone close to her. I…I'm really worried."

Emmerich wrapped his arms around her, kissing her cheek. "How much have the guards found again?"

"Not much," Antoinette replied. "We've sent for a few guides on the Kurzwood, but there aren't many readily available."

"We don't have much time, then." He took a deep breath. "Alright. I'll help the guards. I just hope and pray it doesn't hurt us."

"If you can find Bernie, I don't see how it will."

"I'll make myself known to them, then. Perhaps not now, but in a moment so it won't look suspicious. I'll pretend to accidentally run into them."

"What excuse will you give for being here?"

He shrugged. "I suppose I can pretend Edward sent me."

"And no one else?"

He looked away, scratching his brow. "I guess I went on my own, then?"

"Maybe to send a message or deliver something?'

"Like what? There's no quill or ink."

She thought for a moment, thinking back to Emery's first suggestion. "Maybe you just followed on your own accord?"

"Just for the fun of it?"

"Pretend you were worried about Bernie," Antoinette replied. "Maybe Mother will think since our elopement failed, you're now interested in her to get back to me."

Emmerich widened his eyes. "That's a bit harsh, isn't it?"

"It's an excuse she'll believe."

He lowered his brow. "I'll give you that. But still…"

She admitted it sounded devious. Perhaps her time with Arnold and living a deceptive life was starting to rub off on her. It was becoming easier to lie. But she hadn't the time to think of the moral implications of it as she heard the queen call her name. "I have to go," she muttered.

"I'll join you later, then?"

"Alright." She gave one final glance to her husband, smiling. "Thank you for this, Emery. I love you."

"I love you too, sweetheart. Don't worry; we'll find her."

"I hope so."

She then rushed back to the camp as Emmerich returned to the forest.

---

*I can't believe I'm doing this.*

Emmerich trudged through the woods, careful to mark his trail lest he lose himself in the Kurzwood maze as well. He grunted, already feeling peckish from a lack of breakfast and lunch, and he reached into his pocket, pulling out some non-poisonous berries to snack on. He paused for a moment, taking a second to rest, and thought of Antoinette's plan.

He had come to find his sister-in-law, to save her from certain death. That part he had no problem with; in fact, he embraced it. But he didn't like having to deal with Susanna, revealing himself to help with the search, especially when she was at her most volatile.

Would it earn him respect? Possibly. But that wouldn't change the fact that the woman *hated* him. No matter how she reacted, his marriage to Antoinette would still be secret, and he risked imprisonment if their theory was wrong and Susanna went mad with him being there.

*But you aren't doing this for Susanna. You're doing this for Bernie. You're doing this for Antoinette.* The reminder set his resolve, and after a quick swig of water, he hiked on, searching the ground for clues. A broken twig here, a bunch of bear fur there. He knew he was on the right track in finding them, but he first had to get the attention of the Edelandian guard.

Fortunately, they weren't completely incompetent. They managed to find a similar trail as he did, though it took them a while. He'd already scanned a mile while they were still searching the road and the other side of the forest that turned up empty. He shook his head, wondering how any Edelandian even bothered with the road near Kurzwood if they didn't know how to survive it.

He sighed. It was best to get on with meeting them lest he waste any more time. The sooner they gathered together, the quicker they'd be able to find Bernie.

He upped the noise he made, making sure to step on every twig and leaf that would make the biggest crunch. He even tried clearing his throat, coughing, and forcing a sneeze. At first the guard didn't hear him, being too dense to bother to listen apparently, but after a really loud cough, they finally turned, aiming their bows in his direction.

It didn't take long for them to track him down in the forest, hurrying and blocking his path.

"HALT! IN THE NAME OF THE QUEEN!"

Emmerich lifted his hands to his head, stopping with his back to them.

"Who is it?" He heard Susanna's demanding voice as she approached. "Is it the missing scout? Is my daughter with him?"

"I'm not a scout," Emmerich replied as he slowly turned, and when he met Susanna's shocked gaze, he kept his face firm and brave. He couldn't let her see any fear, no matter how much he felt it.

"What are you doing here?" Susanna demanded.

He watched as Antoinette approached, looking surprised. "Emery?" He couldn't help but be proud as she stood beside her mother. She was getting better at her acting.

"I'm thinking I'm here for the same reason as you," he replied.

"Which is?"

"Searching for Lady Bernette."

Susanna narrowed her eyes. "How do you know of this?"

"I left Reigal to follow her and make sure she made it home safely. Only one carriage was sent and I didn't think it enough protection. When I came upon the road, I found her carriage ransacked. I've been searching ever since."

Susanna scoffed. "You expect me to believe that?"

He looked away, sighing. "No," he muttered. "But you have little choice in the matter. I want to help find her."

"And have you found anything of interest?"

"I have," he replied, holding up the twigs from his pocket. "I've found her trail and was about to trace it. And you?"

Her face softened, and she glanced at the guards. "We have found very little."

"Then may I propose a truce?"

"No." Susanna's face was firm. "I will *not* let you get near *any* of my daughters, Emmerich. In fact, you are not even supposed to be here. I should have you arrested and jailed immediately!"

"Fine! Then do it. But only after I help find Lady Bernette." He hated to call her bluff, but it was the only way. Bernie needed to be found, and if it meant jail, then he would risk it to see his wife be happy. "You *need* me, Susanna. You know how Hugellians are in the wild. We are trackers and are better with the wilderness. Would you risk losing a chance in finding your daughter because of a simple grudge?"

He noticed Antoinette look at Arnold, giving him a hinting nudge towards the queen. Apparently the man was told of their plan, and he played his part perfectly. "I would typically protest, Mother, but I'm afraid my love for Antoinette will throw reason out the door. If this man can help us find Bernette, then I think we should allow him to help."

"But what if this is a trick?" Susanna asked.

"A trick for what, Mother? Revenge?" Antoinette asked. "Emmerich only wants to please me, and letting my sister die is not the way to do it." She paused, giving her mother a sympathetic look. "If it helps us find Bernie, then we need to trust him for now."

"I agree, Mother," Arnold replied. "Though I am ashamed of admitting it. But I'm willing to try anything if it finds my sister-in-law."

Susanna was quiet for a moment, unsure of whether to agree or not. Emmerich found himself praying that for once in her life, the woman would be reasonable, and he held his breath as he waited for her answer.

"You cannot leave my sight, Emmerich," Susanna said with lowered voice. "And I won't allow you near Antoinette." She exhaled slowly, suddenly looking very weak. "But if you find my Bernette, then I…I will be grateful. Do not disappoint me."

"I promise you, I'll find her," Emmerich replied.

"Good," Susanna replied. "Now tell me what you've found so far."

Emmerich approached, explaining the trail.

# Chapter 26: The Queen's Saudade

Susanna was already on edge when she first learned of her daughter's disappearance in the Kurzwood, but she was nearly sent over it when Emmerich van Ketten showed up during the search.

Because last she heard, the boy was supposed to be in Reigal, locked in some room pining his life away and being cared for by his aunt. Now, he was offering his expertise in finding Bernette, and what made it...worse...awkward... perhaps fortunate...was that he was *good* at it. Already he found a trail that the guards had been searching an entire week for, all from snaps on a twig and indents in the ground.

She didn't want Emmerich to be there, didn't want him tempting her daughter into running away again, but she couldn't deny his helpfulness. Not that she would ever tell him that, of course.

When evening came, the search turned difficult. Light was scarce, and the moon started to crescent. Rain that had passed through days before left scattered clouds behind, and after a long journey from Staalberg, most of the guard was too exhausted to work through the night. The queen herself was tired, too tired to admit, but she refused to stop. Her baby was out there, possibly alone and afraid, and she'd let death overtake her before stopping and resting while Bernette needed her.

But as much as she tried, not everyone could go on. Prince Arnold insisted that the guard would be more help if they were given rest (at least for a few hours), and Susanna had no choice but to comply. As a few guards remained on watch, searching the surrounding area, she forced Antoinette (who fought with having to go back) and Arnold to their camp so they could sleep and continue the search in the morning.

She didn't know what to say to Emmerich (as most of his conversation had been with guards), but as midnight arrived, she figured she might as well remind him where his place was at their camp.

"Antoinette is with her husband. I've sent her back to rest."

Emmerich didn't look up as his knees remained bent, his fingers treading carefully through the leaves as if searching for something. "I know."

"Are you going to rest?"

"If I say yes, you'd only remind me that I'm not allowed near your daughter. If I say no, then you'd say that I needed to be near a guard because you'd suspect me of sneaking to your daughter anyways."

She crossed her arms. He was a clever boy, just like his father, and she hated that.

"What are you going to do then?"

"Stay away from Antoinette," he muttered, looking up and facing her. "Happy?"

"I am," she sneered back. "Remember your place here, little Emery. I only allow your presence temporarily."

"I know."

"And once this is over, you must leave."

"And if I won't?"

"Then I'll have you arrested."

He nodded, going back to the ground. "Thank you for your *mercy*, Your Majesty. Your kindness is most generous."

She never appreciated a sarcastic tone, and it was something that had to have been learned from Anna. She felt the bile in her mouth rise as she watched him, and she turned away in disgust. He reeked of the peasants, his rebelliousness and manner too shameful for noble courts.

A moment of silence passed between them, and she was about to leave before she noticed him get up, taking the torch stuck in the ground beside him in his hand and walking forward.

"You are not allowed in our camp, Emmerich! I won't let you get near Antoinette!" She'd stop him in his tracks before he could get to her. She knew the poison in his mind and knew just how terrible he could be!

"I'm not going to your camp," he said, his eyes scanning the ground. "I'm looking at the tracks."

She blinked, confused, seeing nothing of interest on the ground save some leaves and brush. Surely he did not think her foolish enough to fall for that trick! He was going to turn around and sneak towards the camp and find Antoinette. It wasn't like she wasn't young once. She knew how boys thought.

"You're not going alone, you know." She stepped in front, determined to watch him all night if she had to. "I know what you're thinking."

"You do, huh?" He rolled his eyes, and it made her want to smack him.

"Your father was just as sneaky in his days, Emmerich. I know how you van Ketten boys are."

Emmerich scrunched his face. "And how are we?"

"Always using good women for your own gain and pleasure," Susanna replied. "You're not going into my daughter's tent. I won't let you!"

Emmerich shook his head, looking frustrated. "Think what you want, but I'm not that kind of man. Bernie is more important right now and I'm trying to find her."

Susanna pouted, thinking that she'd have him caught. Why, why didn't he take the bait?

They walked on quietly, Emmerich stopping every so often as he checked the tracks near his feet. They were getting further away from the guards, going deeper into the woods, but Susanna didn't care. Sure, it was a security risk, but she almost wanted Emmerich to attack. Here was the woman who took away his wife and home! If she could goad him into showing his true self, then there would be no fear of Antoinette ever pining for him.

But as they continued to walk, he did nothing of the sort. He remained silent, his attention on the ground and what it could tell him, and she could see that his mind was racing through all the knowledge he had stored up over the years. Botany, biology, weather patterns and wilderness survival. She remembered watching Aldaric in his early negotiations as ambassador to Edeland, and he would have a similar look: eyes focused and face hardened as if everything else in the outside world didn't matter except the task at hand.

She looked away, almost feeling a pain of seeing it on him. Though many of Emmerich's features were of Anna – his lighter hair, his narrowed nose, his bigger ears – Susanna found that Emmerich resembled his father more.

Every time she looked at him, all she could see was Aldaric. And that was a face she wanted to forget.

His mannerisms, his walk, the way he held his shoulders back every time he stood…all of it mirrored the man she fell in love with as a young woman. She couldn't deny that seeing him brought back past memories, memories she grasped hard to never lose but prayed to forget so the hurt would disappear.

She turned away as Emmerich helped her over a large fallen branch, taking her hand and holding it for a moment so she wouldn't fall. Even his touch was like his father's, so soft and gentle that it made her heart ache in remembrance. She quickly pulled away, putting a distance between them, and after she refused to thank Emmerich for his hospitality, the young man only muttered something underneath his breath as he walked on ahead to check the trail.

She didn't appreciate his mumbling and sought to call him out on it. "What did you say?"

"I said, 'you're welcome'," he muttered louder as he bent down on the trail again.

"I needed no help."

"Forgive me, Your Majesty," he replied in a mocking tone. "I'll make sure to let you care for yourself next time. Please, don't trip over the next log we come across."

"You rotten brat! How dare you make fun of me!" Whether it truly was his attitude or the fact that she was starting to think of Aldaric because of his son, she felt a rage rise up in her. She was *sick* of remembering the past. Sick of reminiscing the hurt. Sick of being reminded of the one thing she always wanted but couldn't have!

"I wasn't making fun of you. I was only giving a suggestion," Emmerich muttered as he faced her. "But seeing as you never listen to anyone but yourself, I don't think I should have bothered with speech."

"You wretch," Susanna seethed. "You're just like your father!"

"I'll take that as a compliment."

"It isn't one, you buffoon!" She clenched her fists like a child throwing a tantrum, ready to strike. Heavens, how she wanted nothing more than to feed the boy to the edelbears and be rid of him once and for all! Then she'd find her peace. Then she could forget Aldaric for good.

"May I ask you something?" Emmerich stood taller, holding the torch up for light. "Why is it you hate me so? What have I ever done to deserve your scorn?"

"You tried to force my daughter to marry you!"

Emmerich snickered sarcastically. "Even before that you refused to let her see me. Why? Why are you so afraid of Antoinette caring about me?"

"I'm not afraid."

"If you weren't, you wouldn't be doing everything you can to keep us away from each other."

"It's because I *know* she deserves better!" Susanna replied, her voice rising. "I refuse to let you do to her what Aldaric did to me!"

"And what did my father do to you?" Emmerich asked. "Leave because he knew you made him unhappy?"

"I...I never made him unhappy!" She felt her voice crack as she defended herself, but deep down inside, the accusation hurt worse than anything else Emmerich had ever said to her. Aldaric was happy with her. He always was. It wasn't until

Anna came along and tore them apart that everything became ruined!

"Your father betrayed his vows to me!" she continued, her face reddening. "He betrayed my trust! It was all his fault! All of it!"

"And yet even though I've remained faithful to Antoinette, you still let your bitterness spill into your daughter's life!" Emmerich spat. "Do you not understand that she is *not* you, that I am *not* my father? What reason have I ever given to show you I would be unfaithful? I gave up my home, my family, my entire *life* for her!"

"And you wasted it all," she seethed.

"I never wasted it," he replied, his brows lowering. "Were I guaranteed the same outcome, I would love her again and again. You can force her to marry Arnold. You can separate us with the greatest distance you find. But you can't make me stop loving her. You can't keep me from remaining faithful and proving you wrong."

"You fool! I won't let you!"

"And what are you going to do? Stop me? Arrest me? Kill me?" Emmerich asked. "No matter what you do to me, Susanna, you cannot force Antoinette to become you – alone and bitter and angry at the world because it didn't go your way. She's stronger than that."

"I'm not bitter and angry!"

"Of course you are. If you weren't, it wouldn't matter who Antoinette wanted to marry as long as it was to a good man," Emmerich said. "Yet out of everyone she chose, it was I who you tried to push away. Not Edward. Not Stephen. Not Arnold. Just me. All because of that bitterness and anger."

Her breath heaved in gusts. How *dare* he speak to her that way! Didn't he know who she was? "I'm not bitter!" she yelled. "It's *you*! You can't handle the fact that Antoinette loves Arnold more than you! You can't understand why she wanted to leave you so badly!"

"And you are letting pride and jealousy overwhelm your rationality," Emmerich replied. "Or do you deny that you are forcing your own unhappiness on your daughter because she was about to live the life you wanted?"

Susanna stopped, her eyes widening as she suddenly became unable to speak. Her face softened and she felt her heart sink into her stomach, making it sour. "I...I..." Her words came as stutters, and suddenly she didn't know what to say. Surely he wasn't right, was he?

"I may not be royal and I may not be popular," Emmerich began as he edged closer, "but I am smart and I can read people well. Take my advice or leave it, Your Majesty, but you should know that forcing Antoinette to live your life will not take away your pain, but it will add to hers."

There was a moment of silence where they simply stared at one another, saying nothing, until Emmerich turned to leave towards the trail.

Susanna felt her heart race. "Wait."

He stopped, turning around.

"I'm not jealous of Antoinette," she seethed.

"Then let her make her own choices," he replied.

She frowned, crossing her arms and giving a huff. But before she could say anything, a snap was heard from behind, and they both faced the intruder that approached.

Susanna's face paled as she saw Antoinette stop near a tree, her eyes teary and face fallen. Had she heard the conversation between them? Did she hear Emmerich's accusations? Surely she must have, for the look on her face showed the hurt in her eyes.

"Antoinette..." she began, but her daughter shook her head.

"It's not important," she muttered as she walked forward. "I only care about finding my sister." She turned away, facing Emmerich. "Have you found the trail?"

"I have," he answered.

"Then let's follow it." They walked on in silence, the feel of the air cold around them.

# Chapter 27: The First Move

Jacob Ichabod was tired. Exhausted, more like it. After being pulled out of bed and hearing that there was an assassination attempt on the king, he had to hurry back to the palace and make sure Prince Calimus was guarded well lest the attacker returned. It was a long night, turned into a long day, and though the killer had not been caught yet, the palace was sure he wouldn't strike any time soon because the person behind the attempt – the queen herself – was locked up in a solitary cell in the dungeons beneath the ground. Not to mention every guard in the city was called to duty in protecting the king.

Ichabod sighed as he rubbed his brow, taking off his boots and throwing them to the floor. It was the middle of the night and his wife and kids were already asleep. He wanted to join them for once, the promise of a bed and pillow more desirable than gold, but as he stepped further into the manor, he suddenly felt a chill come over him. He looked around the room, noticing the hearth was lit, and he had a feeling that he wasn't alone.

At first he thought it a servant to come and greet him, but after a voice spoke softly from the shadows, he realized whoever was in his house was not of his kin or hired help.

He pulled out his sword, brandishing it towards the night. "Who are you, phantom? Reveal yourself before I gut you!"

"Such *fire*. Such *tenacity*," the shadow said softly as he remained in the dark. "The rumors speak true of you. You are a knight not to be trifled with."

"There's a reason the Ichabod name is mighty in Audlin," Jacob spat, his sword remaining high. "Now tell me why you're in my house!"

"I'm here to recruit you."

"Recruit me? For what?" Ichabod scoffed. "I'm a member of the royal guard and a servant of the king. You can't get any higher position than that!"

"Can't you?"

"Of course not! Unless I become king myself, but you have to be born into that role."

"A lowly position, one you would not want even if it were given to you," the shadow spoke. "What I offer you is a chance at real power and authority. You can control prince or pauper, a city or a nation."

"And who does that?"

"The Velori."

Ichabod held the sword steady, his face showing concern. He remembered the other guards talking of how Malina hired a Velori to kill Edward. Whether that was true or not was up to debate, but Sir Rikert was adamant that it was a Velori in the room when the king was attacked.

"You're the man who tried to kill the king," Ichabod said.

"No," the shadow replied. "On the contrary. I killed the assassin."

If the man was dead, they would know. The royal guard had been searching the city high and low for him. "If he's really dead, where's the body?"

"In a specific location," the shadow replied. "And I will let you deliver it to your guard so that your searching for him will come to an end. But first you must agree to join me."

"Joining you is treason. You tried to overthrow the king and hurt the queen!"

"I think you'd find you've been in treason all along, knight," the shadow said, his voice lowering. "The proposal I give to you now will save Audlin."

"How?"

"By exposing the king for the fraud he really is."

"Fraud?" Ichabod murmured, shaking his head. "What fraud? What has he done?"

"For one, he has framed his wife."

Malina? Ichabod knew the king was up to no good! Surely a good woman like the queen would never hurt her husband. The way she was dragged away and silenced, the way she was rotting away in a cell fit for beggars and thieves…

"I see I have your attention."

Ichabod nodded, licking his lips from nervousness as he lowered his sword. "The queen is highly respected by me. She gave me an honorable position in the guard when others denied it."

"Of course," the shadow replied. "But if you serve me, I will give you an even higher position…one that doesn't involve babysitting."

"Like what?"

"Head of the royal guard," the shadow answered. "Once the queen is in power. Not to mention a place amongst the twenty-four. The Velori seem to have an opening for a new member."

"But…it's still treason…I'd be going against the king."

"And that is the beauty of it," the shadow replied with a snicker. "Edward is not the real king."

"I don't understand…" Ichabod edged closer to the darkness, beading his eyes to get a look at the shadow that stood before him.

"You will," the shadow replied as he stepped forward. "As long as you do what I say."

---

There were many things Sir Rikert enjoyed about being a soldier, but interrogation was not one of them.

He walked slowly down the steps towards the royal dungeons, a cold and stony place buried deep beneath the palace reflecting a time when Audlin was constantly at war and needed quick access to prisoners. It was a time long forgotten, yet stepping into the tunnels reminded the knight of lessons learned in childhood, and he couldn't help but shudder at the chill that seeped his bones despite the warmth the torches gave on the walls.

The prisons were empty – had been for over a century – but one cell was occupied at the very end of the hall. Fire was the only light, small holes in the ceiling the only ventilation, and already Samuel felt his lungs tighten from the stuffy air. How anyone could stand living there was beyond him, but he had heard some prisoners lasting a decade or more in their confinement. It made him wonder how long the queen would be there, herself...

He stopped at the cell, looking at the woman as she sat quietly on the floor with her head up and eyes staring forward. She didn't look frightened, nor did she look ill. Rather, he had never seen her more confident, and that concerned him.

"Ah, a visitor," she said cheerfully, though her smile never showed. "Tell me, Sir Rikert. What can I do for you?"

"I'm here to ask you some questions."

"I'm sure," she replied, smirking. "Yet you've done that already. What makes you think me changing rooms will change my answers?"

Samuel nodded, knowing she was too clever for a confession on her own accord. "I'm following orders, Your Majesty. Forgive me if protocol is too inconvenient."

"It is never inconvenient," she replied. "Though locking me up with no proof save the word of a king does seem a little unfair."

"The king had good reason," Samuel said with a frown. "He nearly died thanks to a servant of your nation. Not to mention the assassin himself confessed to being your lover."

"Is that what you heard, or is that what Edward told you?"

"Does it matter?"

"Everything matters when my life is at stake," she answered, lowering her head and putting her hand on her stomach. "Though there is another life I worry over."

"What are you saying?"

"I am pregnant."

"Awfully convenient at a time such as this."

She looked up, glaring. "Surely you would not execute the king's unborn child!"

"The execution, if there is to be one, would be stayed," Sir Rikert said. "That is…if you're telling the truth."

"Ha! Of course," she scoffed beneath her breath. "Always listening to Edward. He is no saint, you know."

"I did not come here to speak of His Majesty," Sir Rikert interrupted, changing the subject. "I came here for information. What can you tell me about the Velori who attacked? If you speak, the king may grant you mercy."

"A mercy, of course! Because every woman wants a swift death." She shook her head, her lip quivering, though Samuel knew her tears were fake. "Can you not see the injustice being done to me? I have been completely loyal to my husband and his reign, but because he is against me, he has thrown me in jail!"

"If you are going to do nothing but blame the king, then I will take my leave until you are ready to talk," Samuel said, perturbed. "But I promise the next guard who comes in here will not be as lenient as I. When the king recovers and the courts are ready to try you, you will have wished to consider my offer."

He turned to walk away, but before he could take a step, he heard the queen call.

"Wait!"

He turned back around to face her. "Ready to speak?"

"I will give you no confession, for I have done no crime!" Malina said, her voice caught in a plea. "But I do have knowledge that will expose Edward for his deception!"

"And what knowledge might that be? That he is seeking to replace you with a lover? That the entire assassination attempt was a cover to have you arrested?"

"Of course not, fool! That is only minor compared to what I know." She paused, her face brightening as she straightened her back. "I have proof that Edward is a usurper."

Samuel cocked his brow. What madness was she speaking?

"Prince Stephen's death was not an accident. He was *murdered* by his brother out of jealousy."

Samuel lowered his brow. "It is a mockery of the throne to accuse the king of such treachery! How desperate are you to save yourself that you would tell such a terrible lie?"

"Don't believe me? Ask Edward yourself," Malina replied. "Or better yet, read the proof. Edward's been lying so long that I doubt he'd be honest with you." She paused, her mouth widening into a small smile. "In the king's office is a sofa. Underneath the cushion is a compartment that holds a small wooden box. That is the king's personal business, something he hides from even his mother. When you open it, there should be a letter written to Edward from Stephen. The letter will explain it all."

"How do you know all this?" Samuel asked, his face firming. "And how do I know this isn't another trick? You could've forged the letter yourself! I've seen you in the king's office."

"For one, Edward revealed much to me when he was drunk in Cathal," she replied. "And secondly, there is a chance I've forged a letter, but there's also a chance I didn't. Tell me you don't find it a coincidence that Edward's opinion of Stephen has always been so poor, and out of all the things the heir of Arden could have died from, it was a simple training accident!"

"Prince Stephen was training in the fields. It could happen to anyone."

"Of course!" Malina gave a scoff, rolling her eyes. "But it just so happened to choose the king's heir." She paused, her smile fading as her face hardened. "Think of me what you will, but know that I speak the truth on this matter. If you find the letter, Edward will not deny it."

Samuel narrowed his eyes. "We'll see. Until then, Your Majesty."

He then turned and walked away, Malina's words troubling his spirit as he made his way back to his duties.

# Chapter 28: Archery and Frost

"A little to the left."

Bernie felt herself huff as she took aim with the bow once more, the bush only twenty feet away but still remaining untouched by her arrows. She pulled the string, released it, and watched as the arrow sputtered two feet before hitting the ground.

She heard a chuckle from behind, making her fume.

"I told you a little to the left."

She turned around, whining. "I checked my aim!"

"I wasn't talking of your aim," Marcus said with a smirk as he fetched the arrow from the ground, handing it to her. "I was talking of your stance."

Bernie snatched the arrow from him, muttering to herself. "Then you should've said it in the first place."

He snickered, walking around. "Alright. Pay up."

"That isn't fair."

"No, but it's a fun way to learn. How do you think I became an archer so quickly?"

"You know, your teaching methods could be considered sadistic."

He stopped in front of her, grinning. "A deal's a deal. You miss, you get to tell me a secret. You hit the bush, I get to tell you one."

"You already know everything about me!" she said, putting her hands on her hips. "I told you about the chickens in the kitchen, I told you about spying on Antoinette and Edward, I told you about my favorite food being spinach. I even told you about writing that fake letter to Emmerich from Antoinette! What else is there?"

"There's got to be something."

"Like what? You want to hear that I picked my nose as a kid? Because frankly everyone did that."

"Alright, fine." He crossed his arms, his face showing too much glee compared to her chagrin. "Since you've ran out of secrets, then I suppose we can change the rules. I get to ask you questions."

She rolled her eyes. "Are you serious?"

"Think of it this way - we're getting to know one another."

She scoffed. "Fine. What's your question?"

"Did you (or did you not) despise me when we first met?"

She put the arrow to the string. "Yes," she muttered. "And frankly, I'm starting to go back to the original opinion."

He chuckled, nodding. "That wasn't so hard, was it?"

Bernie grunted as she took aim again, bound and determined to hit that bush so she could force him to answer embarrassing questions, too.

"A little to the left."

She wanted to groan in frustration. "I already aimed left! What does that even mean?"

"You need to move your arm. Here." He stepped close to her, holding out his hands. "May I?"

She was about to hand him the bow and arrow, but he shook his head. "No, keep holding it. Let me show you what I mean."

She nodded, but her heart nearly skipped a beat when she found him standing directly behind, wrapping his arms around her and placing his hands atop of hers.

Grant it, he was only showing her how to properly hold the bow by nudging her arm to the left so her bow wouldn't be so straight and slide the arrow out of place, but still... having his hands touch hers, having his body so close that she could practically feel his heartbeat...

"You want to have the bow slightly more horizontal so the arrow doesn't fall away from your hand. Now your right arm holding the bow goes a little to the left, just like I said." His lips were so near her ear that she could feel his breath on her neck, making her hair stand up in excitement. She tried to remember if a guy had ever been this close, and as she searched her memory, she realized one hadn't.

Well, that wasn't *completely* true. She had been this close to a guy before (the same one, surprisingly). The only difference then was that she head-butted him at the time.

She chuckled at the memory as he drew the string back, his hand still gently upon hers. "Remember to take aim. Take your breath, watch your stance."

She repeated the steps he taught earlier, but she was so tempted to purposely mess them up just so he'd have to teach her again, especially since he was now using the hands-on approach.

"Now we release the arrow." She let go of the string and watched as the arrow finally hit the bush. She turned her head, finding his face just a breath away from hers, and he was smiling. "Nice shot."

At first she didn't know what to say, feeling a mixture of nerves and giddiness and wanting to melt into a puddle of goo because even with that growing stubble coming up on his face, he looked so, so *good*...

"I...uh..." She paused, almost afraid she was going to flub up her words like she typically did when around someone she liked. "I have a good teacher. Thanks for showing me."

His grin widened, and she felt like cheering knowing she *finally* said something that made sense! "Well, then," Marcus continued, and she noticed he still held her close. "I believe I get to tell you a secret. Or at least answer a question for you. Either way, you pick."

Her heart beat fast...pounded into her chest so hard that it made her feel like a drum. This was the moment she could find out anything about him, learn what it took to get him to like her and...dare she even think it...court her!

She gulped at the thought, her stomach suddenly filling with butterflies. This was the moment that could bring forth destiny!

He watched her intently, his look growing curious after a few moments of silence. As he started to pull away, she cleared her throat, blurting out her question.

"What's your favorite color?"

He chuckled as he moved away, going off to fetch the arrow from the bush. "That's an interesting question. Can't say I haven't heard it before, though."

She stood there, watching as he headed to the bush to wrench the arrow from its branches. She wanted to take the bow and throw it towards the arrow, too. Why, *why* did she ask such a simple question? Surely her nerves got the best of her. "Well? I'm…uh…curious. Favorite colors can tell a lot about a person."

"Really?"

"Uh…yeah."

"Like what?"

"Uhm…depending on what you say, it'll tell me what kind of personality you have and…stuff."

"And stuff?"

"Uhm…yeah."

He pulled the arrow from the bush, walking back to where she stood holding the bow. "Alright. It's blue."

She wanted to sigh. As if that answer wasn't already known. Every man's favorite color seemed to be blue.

"So what does that tell you about me?" he asked, smirking.

"Uh…you like the water?"

"Sure," he answered. "Circh is near a bay, after all."

*Wow. That actually worked?* She chuckled to herself. Maybe there was something to that color thing after all.

"And…uh…it says you like seafood?"

He nodded. "True again."

"And...you like summer days."

"Eh..." He shrugged, making a face. "Sort of. I actually prefer fall."

"Oh..." She pursed her lips. "Well, two out of three isn't bad."

"I'd say you did pretty well." He handed her the arrow. "Now, take aim again. Let's see if you can hit the bush without me."

She took the arrow, sighing and putting it to the string. She aimed, pulled, and shot the arrow. Of course, it landed away from the bush and hit a tree trunk.

"You've got to be kidding me..." she muttered with a growl, wanting to take his bow and snap it in half. "How...how am I missing a bush twenty feet away?"

"You've just got to practice more," Marcus answered. "Don't worry – you'll get it!"

"But I've shot that stupid arrow thirty times!"

"Actually, it's been eight," Marcus replied. "Now...next question. What's your most embarrassing moment?"

"Right now," she muttered, snatching the arrow he fetched and setting it to the string.

---

Marcus shivered as he put more sticks to the fire, hoping the small blaze would hold out through the night. Cold weather was moving in – he could feel it – and as the moon rose higher, the wind picked up, and already he could see crystals of frost forming atop the blades of grass in the distance.

He was thankful their shelter kept them covered from the wind, but a frozen evening could still bring them harm if they weren't careful. They'd been fortunate their entrapment had been during warmer days, but now...the real test for survival began.

"It's freezing..." Bernie said as she clutched the cloak around her chest, shaking.

Marcus continued to try and grow the fire as best he could. Hopefully it would be enough to keep them warm. "A cold front's moving in tonight."

"I'd say it's an ice front."

He nodded, frowning. "Frost is already settling on the grass."

Bernie got up and looked out of the shelter, squinting. "That doesn't look good," she mumbled. "Hope we don't get hypothermia."

"Hence why I'm trying to get this fire stable." He set a final twig atop it before following Bernie to sit near the shelter wall. "I'll keep an eye on it tonight. If it goes out, I'll grow it again."

"Aren't you going to sleep?"

"I'll rest in the morning."

Bernie nodded as she laid down beside the fire, snuggling up inside the cloak. She still shivered, and Marcus wished he had another blanket or coat on him to give her. "Since you're on the mend, are we going to go looking for the road?"

"I'd rather us not leave our sources," Marcus replied. "If we get lost again, we may never find our way back. Losing water and food would be detrimental. Besides, we must still conserve our energy as best we can. We don't have enough food to replace it with."

"I wonder how long we'll be here," she said.

"Not long, I'm sure," he said warmly. "As long as we stay put, whoever is looking will find us more easily. Hopefully the smoke from our fire will be seen by a search party."

"You really think someone's out looking for us?"

"I'm sure word has reached your family that our carriage never reached its destination. They should be searching now."

"I'm sure they are," Bernie said as she shivered more. "Knowing Antoinette..."

"Are you too cold?"

"A little..." He watched as she shook under his cloak, and though she tried to shrug the chill off, it still wasn't enough.

He nodded, knowing that a simple fire would not keep them warm. They needed more heat, more warmth to last them through the night. And there was only one way to get that.

He hated to ask her, hated to seem indecent...but survival was everything.

"There's...one way to stay warm, but..." He paused, his face blushing. "Well...it sounds improper, but I promise I have good intentions. Here." He moved down, laying in front of her and putting his arms out.

Bernie widened her eyes, stifling a laugh. "Uh...what are you doing?"

"We can share body heat."

"That's a little forward, don't you think?"

"If you have a better idea in preventing hypothermia, I'm open to suggestions."

She snickered to herself, scooting into his arms. He faced the fire as she turned her back to it, her cheek resting comfortably near the crook of his neck. His hands and arms went around her back and he held her close, feeling her heat warm him.

"Better?" He noticed she stopped shaking, and he could almost detect a giggle coming from her lips.

"Yeah," she answered. "You know what's funny, though?"

"What?"

"No one's going to believe me when I tell them I just slept with a knight." She paused, her eyes widening back up again as her cheeks flushed red. "I mean...not that way...I mean..."

He let out a laugh, giving her a gentle squeeze. "That's about as believable as me sleeping with a princess." Suddenly he realized the double meaning behind what they'd both said, and he cleared his throat, blushing. "I mean...uhm...you know what I mean."

"Uh...yeah."

"Of course."

There was an awkward moment of silence, and he hoped and prayed the girl didn't feel his heart pound as she rested in his arms. Why he felt so nervous holding her and keeping her warm was beyond him. He was only doing it to save their lives. It wasn't like he *wanted* to have her lie in his arms or anything like that.

But he couldn't deny that it felt right. As strange as it sounded, it almost seemed like she fit being there, like that's where she wanted to be.

And maybe he was the same way, too.

"Are you getting warmer?" he asked, his eyes glancing at her form. He couldn't deny she looked peaceful there, bathed in firelight.

"Yeah," she replied. "Thanks."

There was another pause, and for a moment he wondered if she was going to go to sleep, but suddenly her voice spoke. "Do you really think someone out there is looking for us?"

"I'd say so. Your sister is probably worried sick right now."

"Sounds like her. But I wonder..." She paused, her brows lowering. "Do you think she's beat up Arnold for leaving me stranded in Reigal?"

Marcus smirked. "I'm unsure."

"Is it wrong to say I hope she at least smacks him?"

"I suppose not. He does, in my opinion, deserve it."

"He does. He deserves it for a lot of things."

"Wait," he interrupted, and she looked at him curiously. "What do you mean 'deserves it for a lot of things'? Is he cruel to you?"

"Not really to me," Bernie replied quietly. "I just don't like him, that's all."

"Why not?"

She gave him a look that showed her frustration. "Seriously? The guy conned my family into leaving me behind. What more proof do I need?"

"Fair enough. But you make it sound like it's more than that."

She shrugged, looking away. "Well, he's not exactly the most *decent*. Not all men are like you, Marcus. Chivalry's been thrown out the window by most."

He nodded, knowing the truth in her words. His father often reminded him as a lad that men too often forgot the old ways in being respectful and honorable in deed. *"Don't be like them,"* he remembered his father saying. *"Honor God in your actions and heart. Be faithful and merciful and kind. If you do those things, you'll be a man who will change the world."*

"I wondered of it," Marcus replied carefully, not wanting to sound like a gossip but knowing he had to learn more for Edward's sake. "At the dinner, Prince Arnold seemed very friendly towards other women."

"You think his flirts with Malina were awkward," Bernie said with a scoff, "wait until you hear how he was in Edeland."

"What did he do?"

"Flirt with every woman he met. Even on his wedding day, Antoinette saw him stay in the bathroom too long with Lady Albrecht. I may be ignorant, but even I know a guy and a girl don't share a bathroom unless there's something going on."

Marcus frowned. "How terrible. Is he always this way?"

"Yeah."

"And your sister knows?"

"Sure does."

"What of your mother?"

"She'd be blind not to see it, but she doesn't care. As long as Antoinette didn't marry Emery, she was..." Bernie paused, giving a sigh. She knew she said too much, but Marcus wanted to let her know she could trust him. "I'm sorry. I shouldn't gossip."

It was a lie to be sure, and Marcus wondered if she was stopping to keep the secret Edward had sought to find out. Was there something going on between Lady Antoinette and Emmerich? Now, more than ever, Marcus wondered if there was.

"I know I may seem blunt in this," Marcus began carefully as he met Bernie's gaze, "but...your sister. Did she want to marry Arnold?"

Bernie shook her head.

"Then why did she?"

"Had to. Mother made the deal and...well...Antoinette said yes."

"So she married him out of duty."

"That's what she said," Bernie replied. "But if you ask me, she shouldn't have."

There. Marcus listened intently, taking the opportunity to learn more. "What should she have done?"

"Stayed with Emery like she wanted to. That's what I'd have done, anyways."

He smiled. "You sound like a romantic."

She lowered her brow, almost looking offended. "It's not romantic, buddy. It's loyalty. Antoinette married Emery first and it was Mother who forced the annulment and brought in Arnold. Duty shouldn't be an excuse to hurt the ones you love."

"You say that like it's a simple thing."

"Isn't it?"

"Duty is never easy, Your Majesty," Marcus said. "But sometimes, for the greater good, you have to sacrifice your own wants and needs."

"So you're saying Antoinette was right in marrying Arnold?" She looked offended by that, and Marcus couldn't help but feel warmed by her tenacity. She had a spark in her that he couldn't help but find…intriguing.

"I'm not saying she's right," he replied. "I'm like you. If she loved Emery, I would prefer she'd stay with him. What I am saying, though, is that I understand her decision. When a great responsibility is upon you, and it is your duty to obey, sometimes the choice is not always easy."

"But she loved Emery and Arnold is cruel. Why is that a hard choice?"

"Because maybe your sister thought marrying Prince Arnold would help Emmerich," Marcus replied. "Or maybe she thought it her duty to obey her mother as a princess and serve her people by preventing scandal. I don't pretend to know the situation. I could be very wrong in my assessment. But being a royal and a knight, in this aspect, has some similarities, I think. We have to look after our people. We have to do what is necessary for their good over our own. We have to give up our wants and needs to see others prosper."

"So if you were Antoinette, and you had to choose between love and duty, what would you choose?"

There was no hesitation in his answer. "Duty."

He saw her expression fade into a type of sadness he never saw before. Bernie looked...disappointed, in a way.

"I would've been different," she replied quietly. "I would have chosen neither."

He cocked his brow, suddenly curious. "How can you do that?"

"I don't know," she answered. "But I wouldn't give up. I'd find a way to do both. Why should you be miserable in making others happy and why should others have to be sacrificed just so you can love someone? Choosing duty leaves you dead and alone. Choosing love leaves you selfish and vain. Choosing both, though? You're loving others and yourself. You both win."

He smiled, though in his heart the intrigue of her words made him wonder. Was she right? Could you do both?

His father chose love over duty and it destroyed him. So far, Marcus had chosen duty over love, though there was never a woman who had intrigued him enough to tempt him in leaving. Even so, he couldn't deny that his work had consumed him. And as death neared when he was so ill, who did he have at his side? No one, save the princess who was fortunate to be stranded with him.

He didn't admit it, but he almost wished...maybe he did have someone to love. But even if he did, being a soldier was his identity, his purpose. Even if he wasn't alone, the greater good would still come first.

He just hoped he wouldn't have to choose between them.

"You're thinking a lot," Bernie interrupted with a chuckle.

He smirked. "How could you tell?"

"You got that look."

"I have a look?"

"Yeah, when you think really deep about something."

He snickered as he held her close, noticing they both no longer shook. Their body heat had kept them warmer than the fire ever did. He almost wondered if he should have lied with her sooner.

"You're getting to know me a little too well," he said.

"You're an easy book to read," she joked back. "But…if you don't mind me asking…what were you thinking about?"

"Truthfully?" He looked at her, her eyes gazing back in a playful nature. "I was thinking that maybe you're right."

"Well, duh."

He laughed as he fingered the cloak around her, resting his right hand across her shoulder. "A balanced life would be more desirable," he said. "But is it really doable? Can you really follow your duty and heart at the same time?"

"I don't see why you can't."

"And what about your sister?" he asked, more out of curiosity for himself than Edward. "Could she do both?"

"Well…" Bernie paused, seeming unsure if she wanted to answer or not. "I guess…in a way…she sort of did."

"How so?"

"I wish I could tell you," she answered, frowning. "But…she won't let me say anything." She paused, giving him a small glare. "And don't you go saying I told you this, either. If Mother found out…"

"You have my secrecy," he replied softly. "And I understand your loyalty. There is nothing wrong with that."

"I appreciate it."

"I hope you know, though, that you can trust me...that you can trust King Edward. I know that he betrayed your sister's trust, and that of Emmerich's, but there isn't anything he wouldn't do for her if she asked it." He paused, lowering his gaze in shyness. "And I offer my services to you, as well, Your Majesty. If ever you or your sister should need me...I would be there."

She remained quiet for a moment, looking at him as if finding his words hard to believe. He looked back up and met her estranged gaze. "Do you really mean that?" she asked quietly.

"On my honor, I do," he replied. "As does the king."

She nodded quietly, looking away as she snuggled closer to him, trying to stay warm as a cold breeze blew by. He tightened his hold around her, wondering if what he said was too bold and forced her silence.

He was about to apologize before she said his name. "Marcus?"

"Yes?" he answered.

"Thank you," she replied, before closing her eyes to sleep.

# Chapter 29: Lost and Found

"It's about time you joined us."

Arnold gave a yawn as he approached, stretching out his arms as if freshly wakened from a long night's rest. Emmerich beaded his eyes, resisting the urge to strike the man for putting himself above the search for Bernie, but that didn't mean his mouth would be restrained.

"Bite your tongue, Emmerich, lest it be cut out of you," Susanna seethed. "Prince Arnold went through a great ordeal in Reigal and is still recovering. He has not the stamina we have at the moment."

"It still shouldn't stop him," Emmerich muttered as he returned to the ground, following the trail he discovered during the night.

"I am ill, sir," Arnold said in defense as he went to Antoinette, putting his hand around her waist. "Yet I am here now, ready to support my wife. The pain aching through my bones cannot stop me entirely!"

Emmerich couldn't force himself to stop as he watched Arnold give Antoinette a kiss, his touch lingering too close to her hips and his tongue too visible near her own. Susanna was watching, too, a gleam developing in her eye as she glanced back at Emmerich; and he felt his heart burn in jealousy at the sight of it.

But Antoinette was not in the mood, and she leaned away from the prince in disgust. "Not now," she muttered with a frown. "My sister is still missing."

"Very well. At least allow me to say you look lovely, my dove," Arnold said after finally pulling away. "Tell me, how goes the search?"

Antoinette met Emery's gaze with a sadness in her eyes. "We've found a trail, but so far there's no sign of her."

"Well a trail is better than nothing!" Arnold replied cheerily, making Emmerich clench his fists. "I'm sure she's here waiting for us to find her!"

"You comfort me so much, Arnold!" Susanna said with a sigh. "What would I do without you? I am strengthened by your encouragements."

"If you don't mind, *Arnold*," Emmerich interrupted as he tossed a small marking rock to him. "I need you to write an X on the trees we pass. We need to keep the trails marked so we don't get lost ourselves."

"Well that isn't too difficult," he answered, writing an X on the nearest trunk. "I am glad I can be of such good use!"

"For once," Emery muttered, and Antoinette gave a smirk.

He went on ahead, following the trail deeper into the forest. After passing a dense grove, however, he stopped, noticing the twigs and dirt around him looking scuffed.

"Wait," Emmerich said, holding his hand out. "There's been a lot of activity here."

"What do you mean?" Antoinette asked, coming beside him and looking at the ground.

"I'm not sure," he answered. "Just...let me look ahead first."

"Why?"

He frowned at her, and he could tell she knew what he meant. They were expecting to find something big.

"I'm going with you," she said firmly, stepping forward.

"Antoinette, please..." He tried to catch up with her, but it was too late. After passing another set of trees, she suddenly stopped, giving a gasp.

The others followed and Emmerich could see what was ahead. He held his breath, almost afraid of what he might find, but after seeing the decaying carcasses of two edelbears, he breathed a sigh of relief. Bernie was nowhere to be found, and another set of tracks led away.

"Where is she? Was she eaten?" Susanna asked, her voice shaking.

"I don't think so," Emmerich replied, a smile coming upon his face. "I think she's alive. Look!" He bent down, pointing to a bear. "These are marks made from a sword or long knife. The animal was thrust through skillfully."

"But Bernie doesn't know how to fight," Antoinette replied.

"Then she isn't alone," Emmerich continued. "My guess is the scout found her and rescued her."

"Oh, thank Heavens!" Arnold shouted with a clap. "Finally, some good news!"

Emmerich narrowed his eyes, but said nothing after a look from Antoinette. He went back to his gazing at the bear, studying it for more clues as Susanna gave orders to the guards to search the perimeter.

As Emmerich looked around the site, Antoinette came up and whispered to him. "What happened here?"

Emmerich noticed bits of flesh and cloth on the bear's claws, and he suddenly quieted. His eyes looked around the ground, and he could see small stains of blood on the fallen leaves. He let out an exhale, suddenly feeling worried. Someone was injured from the bear – either Bernie or the knight with her – and they risked infection being away from medicine for so long.

"Emery?"

He met his wife's concerned face, and he gave her a smile. "I found another trail," he answered. "We'll follow it. I'm sure we'll find her soon."

She smiled back, looking comforted for the first time in days. When no one was looking, she gently grazed his hand with her fingers in thanks, and he touched her own, praying that they'd find Bernie soon and well.

But from the looks of the battleground, it would take a miracle for a princess and guard to last alone in the forest for so long. Injury, infection, the cold…each day would be its own war just to survive.

All he could do was pray that his sister-in-law would be safe. He couldn't handle another loss.

---

Antoinette struggled against the rugged terrain, wishing more than ever that the Kurzwood was a meadow instead of a dense maze of trees and brush. How Bernie could have survived in such an environment was beyond her, but that didn't mean she'd lose hope. Every step she took became a prayer, every sign of a trail a leap of hope. Though fear threatened to overtake her, she refused to give up. If Bernie was dead, she would know it. Such was the bond with her sister…

At least the search had been vigilant. Though Emery's arrival brought its own set of problems (the conversation she walked in on between him and Mother was just a taste of what could be), she was thankful he was there. Aside from support, he had been able to find trails the others had not, the natural expertise of a Hugellian more valuable than any guide.

"Ugh! This cold is going to make me ill. I know it!" Arnold gave a sniffle so dramatic that Antoinette knew it was fake. "What I would give for some chicken stew right now…"

"You've only been out here an hour," Antoinette muttered. "Bernie's been here over a week."

"But the weather was warmer then," Arnold continued. He turned to a guard behind. "Good sir! Do you have another cloak I can have?"

Antoinette shook her head. "You're pathetic." She walked on towards her *real* husband, watching as he dusted off his hands after sifting through dirt.

"Found anything?" she asked.

"Nothing but footprints that look like animals have trampled through."

"Are you sure she was here?"

"It's difficult to see, but it's clear enough. Yes, she was here."

"Why would they move around so much?"

"My guess is they didn't mark the trail back like they did near the road," Emmerich replied before pausing and lowering his head. "Either that, or they didn't have a chance to."

Antoinette frowned, seeing the concern in his eyes though he tried to hide it. But she knew what he was thinking. Surviving animals was one thing, but it wasn't just nature that could kill them. What about water? Food? Shelter? The weather was so bitter now that even a bear could freeze.

"Have we found anything yet?" Arnold's words sounded more like whines as he approached, making Antoinette scoff as she noticed him wearing one of the guard's cloaks. "My feet are aching so much! Emmerich, may I ride your horse?"

Emmerich lowered his brow as Waffles gave a neigh in defiance. "Why?"

"Because I'm still sore from Reigal."

Emmerich rolled his eyes. "Maybe you should be a man and give the ride to Antoinette."

"I already told you," she interrupted. "I'm not resting until I find Bernie."

"Does anyone care about my suffering? I am in agony!" Arnold's whines began to even annoy the guards, and as Antoinette was about to pull him aside and order him to behave, Emmerich stomped towards the prince, edging close to his face with a glare.

"If you are to be such a daisy in this search, *go home*," he seethed. "Do you care nothing for her sister?"

"Of course I do!" Arnold replied. "But you've no idea what it's like to have bunions."

Emmerich clenched his fists, ready to strike, but Antoinette gently put her hand on his arm, holding him back.

"Mother is watching. Don't," she whispered.

A shout from a distance was heard, and she looked up to find the queen approaching. "Is there a problem, *Emmerich*?"

Antoinette quickly let go of his arm, scooting closer to Arnold as Mother stood beside them, hands on her hips. "What's the matter?"

"It's nothing," Emmerich mumbled.

"I was only requesting the use of his horse, Mother," Arnold replied with a pout. "Forgive me. I am still sore from Reigal and the walking is giving me ache."

"How rude of you!" Susanna snapped as she faced Emmerich. "Denying the poor prince relief from his injuries!"

"I only suggest he offer the ride to his wife," Emmerich answered.

"But she has insisted she help with the search and walk," Susanna said. "Give him your horse, Emmerich. There's no sense in letting the animal run wild."

Emmerich sighed, giving a nod as he trudged towards Waffles, taking the reins. He patted the horse's nose as he leaned close in a whisper. "Sorry, boy," he said. "I regret you'll have to carry garbage on your back. Try not to let it bother you too much."

Waffles grunted with lowered brow, stamping his hoof in protest.

"I know, I know," Emmerich said. "I'll give you a good scrub after we get done here."

Waffles snorted as if he wasn't any happier.

"Step aside," Arnold said as he shoved Emmerich out of the way and took the reins. "Oh! My aching feet!" He put his foot in the stirrup and lifted himself up with the help of a few guards, sitting on the saddle and getting more comfortable.

Waffles gave a neigh as if perturbed, looking at Emmerich sadly. But after the man shrugged his shoulders, the horse gave a whinny and began to buck.

"What? Calm yourself, you animal!" Arnold bobbed up and down as Waffles continued to neigh and move around, this time in circles. Emmerich held his hands out to try and steady him, but the horse would have none of it, neighing some more.

"You monstrous beast! Will you behave yourself?" Arnold tried smacking the reins, pulling the reins, and even tightening them, all to no avail. Instead, he bobbed up and down again, each landing of the horse's bucks harder than the earlier ones.

"Waffles, steady!" Emmerich said as he tried to grab the reins, but instead of listening to his friend, the horse bucked again, this time throwing Arnold off and onto a pile of twigs and old, wet leaves.

"Arnold!" Susanna ran to the prince in a panic, and he moaned as he lied on the ground, clutching his back.

"THAT BEAST TRIED TO KILL ME!" he yelled. Arnold didn't take the time to dust himself off as he scrambled up and lifted his hand to strike Waffles. "You terrible monster! I should have you executed!"

Emmerich was about to fight the man, trouble or not, as he clenched his fists once more and stood between the prince and the horse. "It's not his fault! You were too insistent on riding him when he didn't want to be ridden!"

"You told that beast to throw me off! I know it!"

Emmerich scoffed. "How can I do that? I don't speak horse!"

"Either way, Prince Arnold is right!" Susanna jumped in. "I insist that *thing* be taken away! It is a danger to us all!"

"He's just a horse!" Emmerich shouted back, but as they argued, Antoinette noticed a feeling of being watched come over her.

"Wait..." she said, the feeling growing stronger to the point of making her panic. Her breathing increased and she felt terribly afraid. "There's...there's something wrong..."

The three continued to argue until Antoinette couldn't take it anymore. A feeling like they had to leave was pounding inside of her, and she ran to them, holding out her hands.

"Stop it! Something's wrong!"

Emmerich immediately calmed and looked to her in concern. "What is it?"

"Child, have you no decency by interrupting us?" Susanna interjected, but Emmerich waved his hand, shooing the queen away.

"What's wrong?" he asked again, but before Antoinette could answer, a great roar was heard.

They all turned around to see what was behind them, three large edelbears growling hungrily as they approached.

---

"So if you weren't a princess, what would you be?"

Bernie gave a chuckle as she gave another practice shot with his bow. Sure, she wasn't hitting her targets perfectly, but at least she could hit the bush...sort of. As long as it was progress, she would take it. "I don't know," she answered. "Probably a lot of things. Doctor, astronomer, teacher..."

"Maybe all three?" Marcus said with a smirk.

"Sounds like a plan to me," Bernie replied. "Although that sounds a little rebellious. Women are supposed to be in the home. Didn't you hear?"

He snickered, shaking his head. "Something tells me you'd ignore tradition."

She smiled as he handed her the arrow. "Something tells me you're right."

"Would you want to be a wife and mother one day, though, even if it is traditional?"

The question made her blush. It wasn't something that was typically asked between friends, and that made her wonder. Was he interested in her? Was he testing her out to see if she was a woman he'd like to court? Her heart fluttered at the thought, but she knew she had to answer honestly. She'd only want a man to love her for who she was, not who he wanted her to be.

"I would," she said. "But not a big family. Maybe a few kids, you know? Plus I'd like to do something else besides stay home. Like a trade...."

"You think you could do both?"

"I know I could do both," she replied. "I'd love being a mom, sure, but once the kids are grown, then what? I want to have my own purpose, too. Something I can do that they can be proud of."

He nodded quietly, crossing his arms. "Sounds ambitious."

"No sitting idly for me," she replied cheerily. "What about you? Do you want to get married and have kids one day?"

"I do," he replied, his face mellowing. "But…I'm not sure how feasible it would be."

She frowned at his answer. Was he trying to hint that he wasn't interested? She thought…

"It would be difficult," he clarified, facing her. "Being the head of the guard, I'm rarely home. I don't think a wife would appreciate me having to put work above my family. Even my own dog barely knows me."

"If you found a woman that was supportive of you, though," she said, lowering her bow, "would you consider it?"

He smiled, inching closer. "I might. I guess it would depend if she's my type or not."

"And what's your type?"

"Faithful, honorable, smart," he answered. "Loves God and others. Someone who is selfless and kind. And…" he paused, and she could've sworn he tried to wink at her. "I think a woman with a sense of humor would do me good. I've been told I'm a bit of a stick in the mud."

"Gee, I wonder who gave you that impression…" she said with a chuckle.

"Well, there was this one princess I had to escort to Edeland once…"

She laughed, shaking her head. "I don't believe it. You're actually attempting humor now! I think I've corrupted you."

"I doubt the king will recognize me when I return to Reigal," he replied, but then suddenly his smile faded, and a sadness came over his eyes.

She knew in an instant what had caused it. The thought of leaving, the thought of being separated, the thought of things going back to the way they once were. Not that they didn't expect it, of course, but it suddenly felt so soon, so…probable.

And that's what filled her with sadness. She finally met someone that was a good man, and if they were rescued…they'd be separated, never to see each other again.

The thought pained her to the point of never wanting to leave the forest.

"Come on," he replied, forcing his smile back. "Shall we go hunt for more fish for lunch?"

"As long as it's not frozen," she said. But as they were about to leave, they stopped at the sound of a piercing scream echoing through the trees.

"What was that?" Bernie asked, her eyes widening.

"Trouble." Marcus turned to Bernie, his face turning to what she liked to call "knight mode": firm, battle-ready, and serious. "Stay close. We'll investigate, but mark the trail as we pass it so we don't get lost. If there's combat, I want you to stay clear of it. Understood?"

She nodded, following him quickly through the trees.

# Chapter 30: The Husband

"Protect the queen and princess!"

Antoinette had barely enough time to breathe as the guard assembled as best they could, fighting against the three bears that attacked without warning. Waffles gave a neigh, bucking and kicking a bear in the face, and just as the bear was going to retaliate, a guard stabbed it with his sword, killing it with the help of two others. When one bear went down, the others fought harder, and pretty soon four of the ten guards with them were down, injured or gone.

"Run!" Susanna screamed, and she took off with a few other guards who led her back down the trail they had marked towards the road. Antoinette turned to Emmerich as he picked up a bow to help the guards fend off the attack, and she hesitated to leave without him.

"Emery!" she called out, but he didn't meet her gaze long as he shot his first arrow.

"Antoinette, go! Follow your mother back to the road – we'll hold them off!"

She shook her head, wanting to tell him that she wasn't about to leave him. She wasn't ready to be a widow so soon, and she refused to lose him to hungry bears who had probably hurt her sister.

"Please, run!" he called out again, but just as she was about to move, another bear – a fourth, now, if she counted correctly – had approached, and he had his eye on her.

A large, piercing scream sounded, and Antoinette felt her ears hurt as Arnold put his hands to her shoulders, shoving her forward towards the bear. "Take her! Don't eat me!" he stammered, and before she could do anything, she was pushed to the ground again, landing hard upon brush and leaves.

She picked herself up quickly, but as she turned, she watched Arnold run towards Mother and a guard, leaving her facing the bear alone.

The creature was only inches away from her face, growling and snarling with a breath that was fouler than fetid water. Antoinette froze, her bones shaking in fright, and she met the bear's gaze. He let out a mighty roar, so loud and thundering that it made her ears ring and her heart nearly stop. It shook the ground that she clutched, and she felt too terrified to move.

"Emery..." she whispered, her eyes trailing towards where he was at. Her breath came in spurts as the bear roared again, and she knew what would happen next. The bear would strike, killing her in one great blow, but before it could attack, she saw an arrow hit the animal in the belly.

The bear roared in pain, turning sharply to the left. Antoinette looked as well, and suddenly she felt fear leave her heart and go towards the man who had just saved her.

Emery put another arrow to string as he shot the bear again, this time barely grazing its shoulder.

"You! Get away from her!" he shouted. The bear suddenly began to move, his snarl great as he eyed his new prey. Emmerich reached for his quiver to get more arrows, but his hand met nothing but air. It didn't matter to him, though. He took the bow in his hand, using it as a weapon to swing with.

"Emery...what are you doing?" she called, but he gave her a nervous smirk as the bear started charging towards him.

"Trying to be noble and save the princess..." he said as he turned to run. "That's what the man always does, right?"

"Emery, don't!"

"I love you, Antoinette - now get out of here!" He then took off running, making the bear chase him through the forest.

Antoinette watched as he soon disappeared from her sight, and as the other guards took down the remaining bears, she scrambled up, running towards Emery and the last bear left.

"Child! Get back here! What are you doing?" Antoinette heard her mother's yell, but she ignored it, refusing to lose her husband like she lost her sister.

---

Emmerich's chest was burning as he sprinted through the forest, muttering a curse as each tree passing him by remained unmarked. He was guaranteed to get lost in the Kurzwood just like Bernie had undoubtedly been, but it didn't matter. Antoinette was safe and he had saved her. As long as she lived, there would be no regrets.

He sped on, his legs feeling stiff and tired as the bear edged closer. He couldn't outrun it for long – he knew that – and death was inevitable. Either he delayed it a few minutes or faced the creature like a man, taking a chance in defeating it with his bare hands. A marvelous feat, to be sure, but not an impossible one. And if Bohden's prophecies were correct, somehow he'd be able to survive it.

Unless the hurricane meant the afterlife...

Either way, he hadn't the time to decide as the bear swept his paw out, clawing Emmerich in the back and knocking him down. A surge of burning pain tore through him, and he gave a shout. The bear roared once more, and as he was about to strike again, Emmerich took the bow in his hand and swung it out, striking the bear in the face and breaking the weapon in half.

It barely nudged against the bear's strong hide, but it was a good attempt. Emmerich backed away as the bear growled, and as it was about to take another swing, this time towards his throat and face, he suddenly heard a whirl, and before he could blink, an arrow struck the bear in the heart, knocking it down dead.

Emmerich panted in shock as his eyes widened, looking around to see where the arrow came from.

"Emery!" He looked ahead to see Antoinette run towards him, and he couldn't stop her from plowing into him, wrapping her arms around his body and showering him with kisses and sobs. Pain radiated from his clawed back, but he ignored it, fearing the company that was hiding amongst them.

"Antoinette..." He tried to get a word in, but her lips barely left his.

"Don't...you ever, *ever* do that again!" she said as tears streamed down her face. "I can't lose you..." She kissed him again, and he had to pull her away, looking around to make sure the queen wasn't there. She was nowhere in sight.

"The others?" he asked. "Where are they? They could see us..."

"They're farther back behind," she said as she caressed his face. "They'll catch up and find the trail, I'm sure. But I don't care if they saw me. You just saved my life, Emery...I'm so grateful..." She bent down to kiss him again, but he kept her steady, thinking of the arrow. Who had shot it, and where had they come from?

"Antoinette...I don't think we're alone..." He didn't have the time to finish until another sound was heard, this time a clearing of the throat.

Antoinette and Emmerich both looked up as they saw a knight with a bow in his hand approach, looking rugged and worn as a young woman hurried up behind him.

Emmerich remembered the familiar face. One of Edward's knights, the head of the guard. "Sir...Peterson?" he asked.

The man could only nod as he looked at the Hugellian and his wife in shock, seeing them in a position that was rather...too close...

Antoinette hurried herself off of her husband, pursing her lips and blushing.

"Forgive me, Your Majesty," Sir Peterson replied. "I...didn't mean to walk in on your private affairs..."

Antoinette was about to make up an excuse, but at the sight of seeing her sister, she ignored the confusion and rushed to Bernie, giving a cry as she embraced the girl.

---

It was a case of being in the right place at the right time.

Marcus was ready for the edelbear. He could hear it, feel it, sense it. When he loosened the arrow and hit the target, he knew the animal would threaten no more. But when he saw the young Hugellian he was supposed to bring back to Reigal sit up, he knew Providence had to have been watching. It was a strange fate to find who he was looking for so quickly, but it was an even stranger fate to discover the secret that had been so keenly hidden from prying eyes.

Antoinette was supposed to be married to Arnold von Liegen, but the way she kissed and caressed the man in her arms, Marcus knew either that marriage was a lie or was a cover for where her heart truly laid.

He said nothing as Antoinette and Bernie embraced, both shedding so many tears that he felt terrible at not having a handkerchief with him. But after the sobs and hugs, a more pressing issue came forth, and as Emmerich was helped to his feet by the knight and quickly checked for any more wounds, Marcus was given an explanation.

There was no need to ask as Antoinette was quick to respond. "You must forgive me, Marcus. The moment overtook my emotions and I did some things I typically don't do."

"And...that involves a man who isn't your husband?" he asked carefully.

"It's not like that," Bernie intervened.

He turned to her, his brow raised in confusion. "Then how is it?"

She shrugged. "Complicated."

"Whatever the case, you must not say anything," Emmerich said, his voice firm as he approached the knight. "If you honor the king you serve, then you will honor my request and remain silent."

He could hear the guards approach in the distance as they followed Antoinette's footprints through the forest. It wouldn't be long until they arrived. "I promise, Mr. van Ketten, that my lips will stay sealed. King Edward has requested that I support you in this matter and I intend to do so."

"I don't need his support," Emmerich muttered as he narrowed his eyes.

"Forgive me, sir, but the king is insisting on it."

"I don't understand," Antoinette chimed in. "What does Edward want?"

"To offer you assistance," Marcus replied. "Though, I'm unsure what he will do knowing you are involved in intrigue..."

"It's not intrigue," Bernie said, smacking him in the arm.

"Then what is it? Because that's what it looks like," he muttered back to her.

Bernie sighed, turning to Antoinette. "We might have to tell him."

Emmerich snarled as if he was the bear. "*No.*"

"We can trust him, Emery!" Bernie pleaded.

"You're taking his side?"

"I'm taking your side and his. He can help us, I think."

"Help you with what?" Marcus asked.

Antoinette suddenly looked nervous, and she turned to Emmerich in concern. "Maybe we..."

"No. We don't need him." Emmerich crossed his arms in protest, but they were soon interrupted as the queen approached, giving a yell.

"My sweet Bernie!" The woman ran forward, embracing the young girl. "You're safe! Oh, thank the heavens!"

She held her for a long time, and Bernie seemed surprised at seeing her mother so distraught, but after an awkward moment of silence, the queen gave a scoff, yanking the hood on Bernie's cloak up and covering her head. "Child! What of your hair? You mustn't show it!" Her words were barely above a whisper, but Marcus heard it loud enough. Bernie lowered her head, looking perturbed and saying nothing as she met his glance.

"And you!" Susanna then turned to Antoinette, giving her a glare. "Don't you dare run off like that again!"

"I was so worried, my dove!" Arnold wailed as he approached, but Antoinette pushed him away.

"Worried? You tried to feed me to an edelbear! If it wasn't for Emery leading it away, I would've been eaten!" She smacked Arnold in the arm, making him give a yelp. "You left me!"

"I did no such thing!" Arnold argued back as even Susanna started to give him a look. "I was trying to lead it away myself! It's not my fault the thing didn't follow me!"

Emmerich scoffed, crossing his arms before cringing in pain and straightening them back up again.

"And what of you?" The queen soon eyed the knight, and he could feel Emmerich and Antoinette tense as Susanna approached. "Who are you? What is your name?"

"I am Marcus Peterson of Circh, Your Majesty," he replied with a bow. "I am head of the royal guard in Reigal and a servant of King Edward. Forgive me for my rustic appearance and for the lateness in bringing your daughter back. We had a meeting with edelbears and were fortunate to survive."

"And yet we managed to fend them off quite easily," Susanna said with a scoff. "It is a shame Edward could not send knights of more experience. You are fortunate my daughter is alive and well, for if she wasn't, be assured you would be on your way to the gallows."

"Mother, he saved my life!" Bernie stepped forward in front of him, and he felt a rush of pride seeing her so strong and opinionated. "Don't talk down to him at all! If it wasn't for him, I'd be bear food! He took down an edelbear with his own hands in the middle of the night and fog! And he's kept me alive in the wild for over a week, hunting and building a shelter and everything! If anything, he deserves a commendation for his heroism!"

"Calm down, child! I know!" Susanna softened her gaze as she looked to the knight. "You have my gratitude and thanks for bringing back my precious Bernette and keeping her safe. Fear not; you won't go to prison."

Bernie sighed in relief, making Marcus hide a snicker, as the queen gave a wave of her hand to the other guards. "Take my daughters, Sir Peterson, and Prince Arnold for treatment once we reach our camp."

"What about Emery?" Antoinette asked.

"He can take care of himself," Susanna replied.

"But he's hurt and…"

"Very well," Susanna said with a huff. "I suppose we can at least have the wounds bandaged." She turned around, her nose in the air. "Now come along! I want to be back on the road as soon as possible before more bears show up!"

"Here, Emery. I'll help you," Antoinette said as she touched his arm, steadying him.

Susanna gave a snarl. "Absolutely not! Your place is with your sister. Now help her to the road!"

"I don't need help!" Bernie muttered, but after a stamp of the queen's foot, they had no choice but to comply.

"I'll be alright," Emmerich whispered. "Bernie needs you more. Go."

Antoinette hesitated, but soon nodded, making her way to her sister.

Marcus watched as they began to walk towards the road, he and Emmerich bringing up the rear of the group. He noticed that Emmerich was slow in moving, his bloodied back paining him as he reached his hand to touch it. Marcus hurried along, coming up to the Hugellian's side and helping him walk.

"Don't touch the wound. We'll get it treated once we reach the camp."

Emmerich scoffed. "I've been hurt worse."

"I highly doubt it."

"I'm in no mood for a lecture," Emmerich replied. "And I don't need your meddling, either. You are sworn to silence from what you saw with the princess and I."

Marcus paused, remembering back to Antoinette's embrace. He had to tread carefully now that he knew the truth...or at least a part of it. "I won't involve myself in your affairs, sir, except what is required of the king."

Emmerich cocked his brow. "And what is required of the king?"

"We will discuss it once you are better." He lowered his voice, leaning close to his ear. "And when we are in less-suspicious company."

Emmerich nodded, his face softening as they made their way towards the camp.

# Chapter 31: Vengeance

Edward was too sore to move as he attempted to lift himself up on the bed. His muscles trembled and his body shook to the point of unbearable pain, and he barely nudged as he had to stop, his body too weak to do anything but stay alive. Exhaustion nearly overwhelmed him as his heart pounded within his chest, and he wanted nothing more than to take something and throw it at the wall in frustration...if he had the energy for it.

But no. Such was the fate of a man who cheated death and was bound to the bed for at least a month until he could recover from his wounds. Instead of working, he had to rest. Instead of keeping his mind occupied, he was forced to keep company with his thoughts.

And that was an even greater torture than not being able to move.

So many questions needed answering and so many worries plagued his mind. What of Vacius? Would he ever be found? And if he did, then what? Would he confess to his crimes? Would Verloris be pulled into a conflict with their princess being tried for attempted murder?

And what of Malina? Sure, she was trapped in jail, but that would never stop her. Would she confess about Edward's secret, how Stephen was killed? Would she use her popularity with the nobles to turn against him and stage a protest?

And then the thought came into his mind that pained him most of all. What of Calimus? The boy was his only chance at redemption, his only hope and joy after so much despair and loss. Now that he learned the truth...

Edward closed his eyes, not wanting to think of it. Wounds of the heart hurt worse than wounds of the flesh, and the thought of Calimus not being his son...

A knock on the door was heard, thankfully interrupting his thoughts. He turned, too weak to call out for the guest to come in, and he watched as it opened, revealing his mother peeking her head in.

"I see you're awake."

He gave her a small smile, though in truth he felt as if he could sleep some more. He would humor her, though. Visitors were always welcome, and if anything, he could use something of joy in his life.

"It's good to see you," he said, his voice weak and raspy.

"As it is you," Maria replied with a grin. "I brought a surprise. Someone to make you feel better." She opened the door more fully, and in her arms was the one thing Edward dreaded seeing.

His mother held baby Calimus in her arms, and he cooed and stuck out his hand as he saw Edward, seeming happy to see him.

Edward felt his heart sink at the sight, and it took every ounce of strength he had left to not look away. "Oh Mother," he whispered. "I...I don't think..." He paused, his voice catching in his throat. He had to turn his head. The sight of Calimus was too much to bear...

"Edward?" Maria looked at him in concern as she went to his bedside, the sounds of the baby grating against his ears. "What's wrong? I thought you'd want to see your son…"

He closed his eyes, hoping rest would take him, but the pain was too great to grant him such a mercy. He opened them back up, turning to Maria. "Calimus shouldn't be here."

"And where should he be?" Maria asked.

"In his crib or with his nurse."

"Edward, your son hasn't seen you in days! This isn't like you to not be near him."

"Mother…please…"

"What's the matter?" Maria turned him to face her, her features firm and searching. "I know when something is bothering you. Tell me."

"It's too painful."

"I can't help you if you don't tell me."

Edward sighed, exhaling slowly as he knew his mother wouldn't let go until he relented. The truth would have to come out eventually.

"It is something that Vacius said."

"Who? The assassin?" Maria asked.

Edward nodded. "He spoke to me during the attack…he told me things…"

"Like how he and Malina were having an affair?"

"Besides that," Edward said. "There was something I did not suspect or know."

"What?"

Edward paused, the words too terrible to speak as his eyes met the baby's. "He…he told me Calimus was not my son."

Maria's brows lowered, but she said nothing.

Edward looked away, his eyes meeting the ceiling as Calimus cooed softly near him, waving his hand and wanting attention. "Vacius said that Calimus was his, that the pregnancy was a ruse to trap me into marrying her."

"And do you believe that?"

Edward turned back to his mother. "I'm not sure what to believe," he answered. "Malina's treachery does not surprise me. She is one to lie and cheat with ease, and it is not like she hasn't deceived me before. But I thought…in my heart, at least…Calimus was mine and…" His lips trembled, and he pressed them together to keep them still.

"Oh, Edward…"

"Mother, there is no comforting me on this. Whatever hope I had has been taken from me. I have nothing left."

"That isn't true."

"How isn't it?"

Maria paused, lowering her head as she cradled the baby, taking his hand in hers. "Because a son knows his father and a father knows his son."

"But according to Vacius, I have no son."

"You said yourself that Malina is full of lies. How do we know she did not lie to this man as well?" she replied. "There will never be definitive proof that Calimus is yours. You can only go by what you can see and feel. And if that is not enough, you must go by faith."

"But Vacius said…"

"I don't care what Vacius said. Look at this child." She held Calimus towards him, and Edward met his dark, blue eyes with his own. "Does he not share your face? Does he not share your mannerisms? I knew you as a baby, Edward, and Calimus is nearly your twin. Despite what this monster has told you, I know in my heart that this child is *your* son. Why do you think he responds to you so well? Even he knows you are his father."

Edward watched as Calimus stuck his hand out to him, hoping to grasp. It was hard to lift his hand, even harder to reach, but he managed. Edward took his finger and let Calimus grab hold of it, and his touch brought the greatest comfort since before he was injured.

"I can never know for sure," Edward muttered. "My…my heart breaks at the thought of him not being mine."

"Whether he is or isn't, Edward…do you love him?"

Edward nodded. "With all my heart."

"And have you been raising him?"

"Since his birth."

"And will you be there for him for the rest of his days?"

"Always."

"And does he call you his father?"

"Well…he hasn't really learned to talk yet."

Maria chuckled. "But he will. And I can guarantee that you will be the one who holds that special title to him."

"I hope so."

"You will. You will be his father like you've always been, and he is your son."

Calimus cooed once more, pulling Edward's finger and stretching his other hand as if wanting to be held. When Maria kept him still, the baby soon began to whimper, and as Edward watched the child reach harder for him, he relented.

"I think he wants to be held by you," she said with a smile.

Edward looked to his shoulder. "You can set him with me."

Maria placed Calimus on his father's arm, and in an instant, the baby calmed. Edward reached his free hand and put it on Calimus' chest, the pain nearly overwhelming as he moved, but it didn't matter anymore. Looking into the baby's eyes, there was no doubt. Word or not, Calimus was his son. And when he recovered to get out of bed, he would get the proof he needed from Malina to confirm it.

Calimus cooed happily as he wiggled, and Edward tried his best to speak where the baby could hear him. "It's not very fun being bedridden all the time, is it?"

Calimus gurgled, a little bubble coming from his lips.

"Not very fun at all, but necessary at the moment," Maria added.

"At least you look cute," Edward said with a snicker as Calimus grinned. "I look like I've been put in a meat grinder."

They were about to converse more when another knock on the door was heard. "Come in," Maria said as she turned. The door opened and in walked Sir Rikert.

"Forgive me, Your Majesties, for the interruption," he replied. "We've caught the assassin."

Maria stood to her feet. "No one was hurt, I hope?"

"Two knights were killed in the pursuit," Sir Rikert said sadly. "But the bloodshed is ended. The assassin is dead after refusing arrest."

"That is good news!" Maria exclaimed.

Edward could only frown, matching Sir Rikert's look. He was hoping the man would be caught alive for questioning. "Who was it that ended this threat?"

"Sir Ichabod, the only survivor," Samuel replied. "He has just arrived with the body."

Edward pressed his lips together, a grave feeling coming over him as Rikert filled him in on what had happened.

---

Malina was cold, hungry, and angry. Angry at the fact that she had been given so little in her prison stay. Angry at the knowledge that she had told Sir Rikert about Edward's secret and he didn't believe her. Angry that her belly showed the bump that proved her pregnancy!

She had no alibi, no alternate plan, no claim that the child was Edward's because they hadn't had the time to sleep together. And once word reached her that Vacius was caught and killed, her only hope of escape had vanished. She could plead to her father back in Cathal, but she was too prideful for that. He would never help her, anyways. His respect always went to the strong and not the weak.

And so, in her frustration, she sat there alone in the darkness, waiting for anything to come forth and offer her hope.

It was days that passed before she heard anything. She had been sleeping when the torch light woke her. Whether it was night or day, she didn't know, but she suspected it to be late. There, with a torch in his hand, stood Sir Ichabod, and he approached her cell door with a confident gaze.

"My dear Jacob," she said, straightening herself up and facing him. "It is a pleasure to see you. Pray, tell me – have you word on Edward?"

"The king is of no consequence," Ichabod replied. "I'm only here for you."

"Here to interrogate me like Sir Rikert?" she asked, pouting. "I promise, my darling knight, that my story is the same. I am innocent and have done nothing wrong. It is Edward who is trying to frame me!"

"I know," Ichabod replied, and suddenly she felt confused. "I am here to help secure your release."

"You're breaking me out," she muttered in surprise.

"No," Ichabod said sadly. "It won't work like that, I'm afraid."

"Because there's been a change in plans." Malina turned to see Malum approach from behind, his face stern.

"Malum..." She gave a gasp, seeing him revealed along with the knight in Edward's guard. "I...I don't understand."

"Sir Ichabod works for me now," Malum replied, stepping forward. "He is part of our plans."

"Vacius was part of our plans until you killed him," Malina sneered. "At least that is what the guards say. What happened? Who killed him?"

"I did," Malum replied. "And I should remind you that your fate would be like his were you not useful for one last time."

"I don't need your help," Malina said, crossing her arms. Though the truth was she did, she wasn't about to beg. She was a queen, a daughter of Verloris! There wasn't anything she couldn't do.

"You are bound for execution, and at the state of your appearance, my guess is you have found proof that you're pregnant. I told you, you'd slip up."

"You beast! How dare you...!"

"*Silence*," Malum said, his voice firm. "You fret for nothing. Everything will work in our favor, but you must do as I say. No more mistakes."

Malina felt her breath heave in anger. It was Vacius who messed everything up, Vacius who nearly ruined their plans! How Malum would dare accuse her of failure was a mistake of his own accord. But alas...there was little she could do. Trapped behind bars, limited with who she could communicate with. There was no choice but to play along for now, but she would win the game in the end. Even Malum couldn't prevent that. "What must I do, then?"

"Keep quiet about Edward's secret until I give the word. You have told one man. That is enough for now."

Malina blinked, unsure of what she was hearing. "*What?*"

"Rumors take time to spread, and you must not rush it," Malum replied. "The truth will be revealed all in time. For now, you must let me work. Once the nobles hear the entirety of what happened, they will rally to your defense. This will put pressure on Edward, and he will cave when it becomes too great."

"The nobles are not enough. We'll need more support."

"And we will have it, but leave that up to me. Until then, remain in the prison. Do not change your story about being framed. You are the victim."

"Of course I am," she muttered.

"Now, I shall write your father. We must ask him for aid."

Malina shook her head, eyes fiery. "I will not allow that! I do not beg!"

"You will in this instance," Malum sneered back. "Fear not, though. I do not seek the comforts of Verloris. This will further our plans for domination."

"I don't understand how."

"You will."

She sighed, flinging her arms in frustration. "Anything else?"

"No."

"And what of you? Aside from this letter, will you stand there in the shadows and tell everyone what to do?" She meant it as an insult, but he only laughed.

"Me? I am going home."

"Home? You fool! How will you be able to do anything by going back to Cathal?"

Ichabod gave a smirk, and Malina burned at the sight of it. Did he know something she didn't? Was she kept out of the loop on purpose?

"You silly, silly girl," Malum said as he smiled at her. "I'm already home."

Malina lowered her brow. What riddles was he speaking?

She hadn't the time to ask as Malum turned to Sir Ichabod. "Go to the guard and start preparing for my arrival. I will let you know when it is time."

Ichabod nodded, giving a bow. "Yes, Your Majesty."

Malina turned to Malum in confusion. "Your Majesty? You are not a king!"

Malum snickered. "Did I not tell you, my dear 'queen'?" he asked. "Or did you not figure out who I really am?"

She shook her head, still unsure. "Who are you?"

"I am called Malum of the Velori," he replied. "But I was born Stephen Engel."

To be continued in

Book 5 of The Ripple Affair Series,

"Heir of Vengeance".


Turn the page for a preview of Chapter One...

# Chapter 1: The King of Verloris

Night had fallen on the lands of Cathal, the chill of winter's end echoing in the hallways of King Calimus. He sat on his chair, pondering in the silence, watching as his family finished the evening meal.

His wife swirled the soup in her bowl, commenting on the many bubbles it made every time her spoon was dipped. "What lovely little pops they make." She snickered underneath her breath, lifting the spoon and plopping it back down again. "Always so funny!"

The king said nothing, a quiet grunt the only reaction to his wife's silly fancies. He turned to his eldest daughter, her pensive and quiet nature more like his own. She met his gaze, an unspoken understanding between them, and nodded her agreement.

*A child behaves better than the queen.* He could hear his daughter's precise tone repeating his thoughts, but she had not his experience. Though frivolous and annoying, the queen had her uses, and he found himself unable to part from his lover despite the weakness it gave.

But that didn't stop Callida Serus from expressing her disapproval to him, by look or by word.

She took a sip of wine quietly, her eyes like daggers though her voice remained silent. The king sighed, feeling weary and unwilling to face his daughter's truth, and he returned to his meat, taking a knife and cutting off a piece to eat.

Before he could put the morsel to his lips, however, the door opened to the dining room, ushering a servant in with a sealed letter.

"What is it?" the king asked.

"A message from Audlin, Your Majesty," the boy stammered. "It is from Malum regarding Queen Malina."

Callida said nothing as she kept the cup to her lips, listening intently.

"I'll take it," the king replied, waving his hand and opening the seal. He quickly glanced at its contents, barely concerned with what it read. Malina was too much like her mother, caring only for fun and parties and men. He wondered what trouble the girl was in this time.

"I should like to hear what it says," the queen mumbled as she looked to her husband. "I rarely hear from my angel. Tell me, how does she fare?"

Calimus was about to toss the letter aside, thinking he'd be bored with pleasantries and gossip, but after reading the words upon the letter, he suddenly realized the stories about Malina were anything but their typical fluff.

*She is imprisoned. The king has accused her of betrayal and treachery after Vacius attempted to assassinate him, and there is little hope for a pardon. The nobility will rally to our cause, but I need you here for a task worthy of the Verloris.*

He stopped reading for a moment, Callida's eyes still upon him, and he met her stare.

"This letter is different," she said quietly, and the king could only nod.

She lowered her cup. "How?"

"She is imprisoned," he replied.

The queen gave out a gasp, but he silenced her with a glare before she could go on with any more dramatics.

"What has she done?" Callida asked.

"According to the letter, she is being blamed for trying to kill her husband, the king."

Callida's face remained unchanging as she returned to her drink, sipping it. "And failed."

The king nodded, embarrassment creeping up. The Verloris were always proud in their accomplishments, their ability to grasp whatever they wanted. But Malina...she was different. She was weak and always wanting. He was almost ashamed to even call her his own, constantly failing and puffing up any meager achievement.

"Will you go to her?" Callida interrupted his thoughts.

"I would not, but Malum has asked for my presence."

"You should go, then. Letting her die will ignore a rare opportunity."

He frowned, confused at his daughter's disagreeing with him. "You were never close to your sister. Why the change of heart?"

"I care not for her foolishness," Callida replied. "But you have a chance to show your strength to our enemies. Malina married into a weak family, Father. Would it not be wise to arrive and show them who we really are and how we should not be trifled with? Or do you think Malum only wants you there to pick up your precious little baby?"

Calimus lowered his brow. "I don't follow."

"A tiny mountain country is about to execute your youngest daughter. If this is allowed, then the surrounding lands will think they can bully us. We will look weak."

Calimus nodded, beginning to understand. "And we cannot allow that."

Callida's lips turned upward. "No, we cannot."

"Very well, then." Calimus motioned for the servant boy to come forward, handing the letter back. "Send a letter to King Edward, letting him know of our impending arrival. Be sure to state that my daughter is not to be touched until I am there. Understood?"

"Yes, Your Majesty," the boy replied, scurrying off to the nearest scribe.

Calimus exhaled slowly, turning back to Callida to see her reaction. Her face was firm, emotionless, but her eyes seemed pleased. He had met her approval, and he returned to his dinner in peace.

# About the Author

Erin is the author of *The Ripple Affair Series* and *The Adventures of Captain Patty*. When she isn't writing, she's learning new arts and crafts. Her house is now filled with knitted scarves and yarn. She currently resides in the United States of America with her family.

For the latest blog posts, news, and book releases, visit http://erincruey.com.

# Other Books by Erin Cruey

## The Ripple Affair Series

*The Ripple Affair*

*Reign of Change*

*When Dreams Break*

*Heart of Deceit*

## The Adventures of Captain Patty

*Captain Patty and the Nameless Navigator*